HOUSE

OF

ASH

HOPE COOK

HOUSE
OF
ASH

AMULET BOOKS
NEW YORK

I had four dreams in a row where you
were burned, about to burn, or still on fire.
—*Straw House, Straw Dog*, Richard Siken

Cataloging-in-Publication Data has been applied for and may be obtained from the Library of Congress.
ISBN 978-1-4197-2369-8

Text copyright © 2017 Hope Cook
Illustrations copyright © 2017 Sam Wolfe Connelly
Book design by Alyssa Nassner

Published in 2017 by Amulet Books, an imprint of ABRAMS.

Printed and bound in U.S.A.
10 9 8 7 6 5 4 3 2 1

Amulet Books are available at special discounts when purchased in quantity for premiums and promotions as well as fundraising or educational use. Special editions can also be created to specification. For details, contact specialsales@abramsbooks.com or the address below.

ABRAMS The Art of Books
195 Broadway, New York, NY 10007
abramsbooks.com

1

Mila, 1894

"I DON'T TRUST HIM, DIABLO."

Wynn's voice was soft, a whispered secret against the engine of the ship, the quiet nickering of the horses. Mila moved through the ocean liner's stable, the sawdust-strewn paths lit only by the flicker of low-turned gaslight. A bay mare stamped her hoof lazily, once, twice, her dark eyes large under feathery lashes as Mila passed.

"He has cold eyes."

Wynn's voice was closer now, and Mila heard Diablo's low whinny. He'd caught her scent.

"Wynn, Mother will kill you for this," Mila said as she rounded the corner.

Wynn bolted up from Diablo's glossy back, her small hands pushing off his withers. Mila was the only one who could ride Diablo, but Wynn was the only one who could fall asleep on him, her face tucked against his powerful neck, hands dangling down his ebony flanks. She'd sleep like a tired puppy and Diablo would wear her like a saddle, her black hair—just like their father's—almost invisible against the stallion, her white skin and red lips like a splash of stark paint against his hide.

Wynn's dark eyes stared at Mila a moment, then her face flashed with the look of haughty command she'd learned from their mother, shifting from a twelve-year-old child to a duchess in training. "She's asleep," she said, tossing her long hair back. She stroked Diablo's mane and he nickered softly. Mila sighed and gently scrubbed the horse's muzzle. His fine hairs were like velvet and her heart eased a little from the comfort of it.

"And we'd better return while that's still true," Mila said.

Wynn bit her lip. "I want to go back to Venice."

"And I want Father to return! I want to see him once more without the madness of opium in his eyes," Mila said, her voice flashing out amongst the sleepy stalls. Diablo's long ears trembled at her tone and a dappled grey kicked the boards of the neighboring stall. Wynn's eyes slid down, childlike once more.

Mila sighed again.

"I'm sorry," she said, touching her sister's arm.

"He scares me," Wynn said with a frown.

Mila knew she wasn't speaking of their supposedly deceased father.

"We have to adapt," Mila said. "Mother will marry him. We can't change that."

"That's easy for you to say." Wynn's fingers clenched in Diablo's mane. "You're seventeen. You can marry soon, escape him."

"I'm not going anywhere without you." Mila grasped Wynn's fingers tight.

Wynn's sharp jaw tightened. "You promise?"

"I promise," Mila whispered, leaning her forehead against Diablo's side. His breathing was slow and steady, and she wished she could leap astride him, Wynn's arms tight around her, press her heels into his flank, and ride for the ends of the earth. "We have to get back."

Wynn sighed and slid down from Diablo, landing with a little *whoof* in the wood shavings that lined the floor. Diablo shifted, restless.

"We'll be there soon," Mila crooned to him. "Tomorrow, you'll be free again. We'll ride for hours."

He nosed at her face gently, and her blonde hairs stuck to his nostrils. Mila smiled and pulled away as he snorted, his breath a warm puff of air against her cheek.

"Come on," she said to Wynn.

They made their way through the stables, the endless rocking of the sea almost undetectable beneath their feet. One of the stable hands smiled as they passed, his sandy hair escaping in messy tufts from beneath his striped cap. Mila smiled back at the boy. He was lean and tall with a strong face and stronger hands, and she knew she'd take a sweaty boy covered in dirt over a fine-suited gentleman with cold eyes any day.

They passed into the echoing crew passageway, up a narrow metal stair, and out into the plush carpet and walnut-paneled walls of the SS *Majestic*. It was after midnight and the grand halls and salons were quiet now, just the occasional scotch-swilling gentleman playing cards and trading cigar puffs with the other wealthy specimens of his kind.

Their gazes slid over her and she knew what they saw: a tall blonde with eyes too bold to be ladylike. She saw the way their brows darkened at the sight of two girls wandering the ship unescorted at this late hour. She stared back at them, one hand tight on Wynn's narrow shoulder.

I've as much right to be here as you.

She knew her mother would not agree.

They ascended the grand staircase, the leather soles of their shoes clacking on the polished marble, then passed through the long corridor that led to their staterooms. The red carpet was thick underfoot, and the gaslight gleamed against the dark wood paneling and golden sconces.

Mila put a finger to her lips and Wynn nodded. The black door eased open under her hand and they slipped into the sitting room. Only a single lamp was lit, and the gas flame cast moving shapes against the wall's elaborate wood inlay. Wynn ambled to the small bar in the corner and poured a glass of water from the heavy crystal pitcher. Mila moved to turn the gas down.

"Have you been *out*?"

Mila turned with a quick indrawn breath. Their mother stood in the doorway of her stateroom, long blonde hair loose against her shoulder, her sweeping satin nightgown dark red against her pale skin. Wynn stood frozen in the corner behind Ada Kenton, still unseen.

"I couldn't sleep," Mila said, her voice calm.

Ada's sharp eyes swept her daughter's unkempt state—the hasty upsweep of her blonde hair, the uneven knot of her sash, the sawdust clinging to the bottom inch of her blue satin gown.

"I went down to check on Diablo."

This moved her mother forward. Wynn gave Mila an anguished look and slipped behind their mother's distracted form, disappearing into the bedroom she and Mila shared.

Ada Kenton slapped her daughter.

"You're not even wearing a corset. My God, what must people think?"

Wynn was safe in their bedroom, and Mila felt the relief stronger than the blow to her left cheek.

I don't care what they think.

"I am about to marry the wealthiest man in all of Canada, and you will *not* bring shame to me," Ada hissed.

No, you do that all on your own.

"Your father tried to disgrace me with his *weakness* and filthy habits"—Ada's mouth twisted—"and it took all of your grandfather's connections to clean up that mess—"

"You had him declared *dead!*" Mila yelled, unable to stop herself, unable to stop the tears that formed in the corners of her eyes.

"He *is* dead," Ada said, stepping within an inch of Mila, her chest heaving, cheeks flaming with color. "Dead in every sense of what it means to be a man in good society. Now, if you bring so much as a hint of your father's bad character to reflect on this family, I will send you to a convent. And I'll have that horse sold for glue."

"Yes, Mother," Mila said, her voice under tight control once more.

Ada turned and swept back to her bedroom, slamming the door. Mila quickly smoothed the breath that shuddered up her throat, turning to the mirror beside the lamp. A red handprint flared against her pale skin, but she knew from experience it would be gone by morning. She stared at herself, wishing the messy softness of her insides were as sharp and steady as the face that gazed back at her.

She looked like someone who had learned the trick of turning pain to ice.

She took the pins from her hair and let the long blonde strands fall around her shoulders as she walked to the bedroom. The room was dark, but she could hear Wynn's breathing, fast and heated.

"I'm sorry," Wynn whispered.

"It's all right," Mila said, letting her gown fall in a heap on the floor. "I shouldn't have mentioned Father—that was stupid." She pulled on the nightgown she'd discarded earlier that night and slipped into the cool sheets.

There was silence, then: "Can I sleep with you?"

Mila opened her sheets in answer.

Wynn fidgeted for a few minutes, searching for just the right angle against her sister, then finally stilled with her head tucked tight against Mila's collarbone.

"Is Father really dead?" Wynn asked very quietly.

"I don't know," Mila said. "I guess it doesn't matter. He's gone, and now we are too."

2

Curtis, Present Day

LIFE NEVER DOES A DAMN THING YOU TELL IT TO, BUT A DIRT bike can be tamed.

You can slip inside the soul of 220 pounds of metal, plastic, and 91 octane and know what it's like to fly across the ground. You can match your heart to the speed of a masterpiece and leave life behind.

Curtis launched the bike through the air and cut the throttle.

For a moment, he lived only in the jump, in that sacred space between flying and falling where the air was just the whoosh flowing past him. Then the back tire touched ground and he and the bike were one creature, sucking up the impact, knees and suspension giving to the limit, then winning.

He cracked the throttle and peeled off into the woods, clenching his legs into the gas tank as the bike tried to bolt from under him. He blasted through the winding trail, ripping through pools of sunlight and shadow, his hands claw-curled and numb on the vibrating handlebars. The bike singing *brap brap braaap*—a gleeful top note over a grumbling baseline and the gunshot heartbeat of the exhaust—his heart pounding *thunk thunk thunk* as the humps and bumps sent him skipping over the dirt-packed and stone-strewn incline.

He should head home. But, no. Just a little longer. A little longer without responsibilities, without that house, without crazy.

His chest burned with anger, like a sharp-splintered hand had reached up to steal his joy. He wasn't ready to return—fists knotted and heart braced—to the everyday nightmare that was his life.

He retaliated by throwing the Beast to the right, crashing like hell on wheels through a dangerously overgrown trail he'd never taken before.

Trees sped past, curves coming up hard and fast. Branches whipped his arms, and a grim laugh built at the back of his throat as he almost lost control on a hairpin turn. He jammed into third and pinned the bike up the hill into a large open field. There was the final flight of speed down that long straight stretch, the air a growing *shhhhhhh* in his ears, the sting of it pulling water from his eyes.

For that moment, there was just the sharp thrill of skating on the drop-off edge of his skill and the bike's headlong rush to crash.

Take it to the brink—*and win.*

He dumped the clutch and let the back tire dig down, ripping a rut from solid ground. When he finally cut the engine, waves of heat radiated from the CR500's core, a mastered animal panting out its exertion.

He threw his leg off the bike and stretched, riding boots covered in dirt, his bare arms damp with sweat. The dust-covered Beast stood obediently in its rut, *tick tick tick*ing quietly into submission, the rhythm of metal and moving parts cooling, contracting.

His arms were rubbery and his core ached, but he smiled, satisfied, that dark ache in his chest ridden to exhaustion.

Almost.

It was an airless kind of fall day, a moment caught in the breath between seasons where the whole world turned sepia, unwilling to take that final gasp into the bleak grey of November. Almond-colored grasses rose knee-high from patches of rust-toned lichen, but today, their familiar rattling tones were silent, the usual nodding sway perfectly still.

No wind, no movement.

Straight ahead, a small copse of trees no different from any other. But those trees were *moving*. And a sound—as if a freight train were barreling past just out of sight.

The hairs at the back of his neck prickled. He looked around uneasily, but he was completely alone.

Curtis approached the circle of trees. Tangled willows and slim white poplar beckoned. The *sound* of the wind grew steadily, but his skin told him there was no breeze.

He shook his head, rebelling against the impossibility.

The edge of the copse was like standing at the brink of a rushing ocean tide. The leaves shivered and shook all around him, the branches tossing side to side. He stepped into the circle of trees and felt wind against his skin, whistling into his eardrums, coaxing him on.

He moved forward, his chest pounding *chuk-chuk-chuk*, a sudden desperation to reach the center of the copse, to find the *heart* of the thing. Dark need slipped past the reins of control and his pulse raced.

But all around was a howl, a shrieking voice that slid into his ears, slipping down into the darkness at the back of his eyes. The world was tipping, spinning on end all around him. He fell to his knees, grabbing his head—*no, no.*

Pain sliced his skull, whispering words he couldn't understand. His mouth parted in a scream that never came.

The pain stopped all at once.

He gasped for air, supporting himself on his knees and palms for long moments, dry fragments of leaves pressing into his skin. He tasted the scent of nature folding into decay, fought to keep the dread in place between his breaths. *One, two. One, two.*

He pushed unsteadily to his feet, pieces of his mind blunting together, fractured and smoking—something *not quite him* pressing at the seams.

The wind was still circling, stirring the leaves and branches.

I'm not like my father, he thought, the long-held fear finally breaking free in all its gruesome terror. *Please. I'm not sick like him.*

He turned his eyes on the woods.

Just get out of here. Get out.

He put one foot in front of the other, ignoring the screaming in his guts that ordered him to stay.

He reached the edge of the copse and fought the urge to look back—and the certainty that there were *words* on that wind.

His eyes were on his bike. One foot in front of the other.

Just get out of here.

There was no wind on his skin now, but he could still hear it calling.

Hands on the bike, leg hammering the kick-start. Gunshot roar of the engine.

He tore across the open field like death was right behind him. The void chased, and his bones wanted to crash down into the darkness like a jumper swaying at a cliff.

He made the tree line, felt the familiar cool of the forest settle around him.

He tried to feel like he hadn't shattered in the heart of that copse, like something inside him hadn't changed forever.

But that was a lie.

3

Mila

WYNN'S HANDS WERE TANGLED IN MILA'S HAIR, HER FINGERS wrapped around the blonde strands like she was seizing Diablo's mane. Mila lay with her eyes closed, listening to the sound of her sister's breathing, the way her breath hitched and her fingers tightened like a skipping pulse.

Mila gently disentangled Wynn's fingers without waking her, crawling from the bed in the barely there morning light.

Today they would meet their new home.

The sitting room seemed silent from this side of the door, so she went in cautiously, looking for a glass of water.

"Oh." Mila stopped abruptly, faced with Zahra Amahdi, the servant she'd been given by her future stepfather. Zahra straightened from the assortment of clothes she was leaning over and eyed Mila with the cool, evaluating look Mila hadn't yet learned to fully interpret. They were the same age, but the olive-skinned girl looked at her with eyes that were knowing and a little defiant. It was not the typical manner for a maidservant.

"Mr. Deemus has clothes for you," Zahra said. She spoke the name with a slight quirk of her full lips, as though the sound of it amused her.

Mila eyed the expensive clothes and nodded. She poured herself a glass of water and watched Zahra arrange the garments in order: chemise, corset, underskirt, the full linen skirt, a stiff white blouse, and finally, the smart grey jacket.

"Do you know much about the estate?" Mila asked.

"No."

"He's just inherited it."

"Yes."

"And the house has been closed up for a long while? Do you know why?"

Zahra straightened and speared Mila with a look. "I'm just a servant. The Master doesn't confide in me."

"Yes, you're a servant," Mila said, leaning her hip against the bar and crossing her arms. "Which means people order you around, or treat you like you're invisible. Either way, you hear things."

Zahra gave Mila a look of reevaluation. "Apparently the executor of the estate has been trying to find the Master for some years now."

"He hasn't been in contact with his family?" Mila said sharply.

"There was a falling-out." Zahra turned as the shadow of something crossed her face, then leveled cool eyes on Mila again. "Three weeks ago, he received a letter saying he'd inherited the entire Deemus fortune."

Mila's eyebrows rose infinitesimally. The surprise engagement had been announced three weeks past also.

Her mother had been making the most of the dwindling money by doing the society rounds in Venice, catching the eye of every wealthy man for a hundred miles. There was still too much gossip in London, so Ada had swept Wynn and Mila away from their country home and carted them off on a European tour.

The beautiful widow and her two lovely daughters.

They'd been introduced to Andrew Deemus in Florence and then met him again at the hotel in Venice. He'd been playing the fashionably bored admirer to Ada's refined grief, and even more refined flirtations, when suddenly he'd stepped up his attentions from novelty distraction to declaration. The abruptness was concerning.

"How long have you worked for him?" Mila asked. The man was still too much a mystery, and his choice in maids was not a comfort.

Zahra's eyes flickered and she turned away, busying herself with Wynn's new garments. "Not long."

You're hiding something, Mila thought.

The door from her mother's suite opened and Ada sauntered out, silk robe trailing from her slender arms.

"Amahdi," she said without bothering to look at Zahra, "I'll take breakfast in my room. Set out my peacock silk."

"Mr. Deemus asked me to see to Miss Kenton's wardrobe this morning," Zahra said, looking Ada straight in the eye. "But I expect that Winters will be back shortly to see to your needs."

Mila's chest tightened at the way her mother's jaw went still and her eyes narrowed. But Zahra turned away, unconcerned, and swept the bundle of clothes into her arms. Mila found herself being herded back to the bedroom by her own maid. She half expected her mother to follow, but a door opened and Ada turned angry words on Winters, the family maid.

Zahra closed the door and laid the clothes on Wynn's bed, motioning for Mila to sit at the dressing table. Mila sat and studied the maidservant in the mirror as she worked Mila's long hair into an elegant knot.

The girl was wearing a maid's standard grey and white, but the whole thing seemed a ridiculous costume on her. As though she should be draped in dark robes and glittering under a sultan's ransom in gold jewelry. Her cheekbones were sharp lines as she twisted and pinned Mila's hair, her fingers moving efficiently. A flash of white peeked out from beneath her smart cuff—a smooth cord knotted twice around her wrist. Mila frowned; it was a strange bracelet.

"Where are you from?" Mila asked her.

Zahra's large eyes met Mila's in the mirror.

"Do you mean what heathen country turned my skin this color?"

Mila blinked. *Definitely not just a servant.*

"It would be a mistake to take me for an ignorant provincial," Mila replied. "Or to take my questions for idle curiosity." She looked to Wynn, still asleep in the bed beside them. "We're traveling across the ocean, leaving behind everything and everyone we've ever known. A man we barely know will ask us to call him Father. A land we know nothing of will ask us to call it home." She looked back to Zahra. "I need to *know* what we're walking into."

Zahra's full lips twitched, her strong jaw relenting just a fraction. "All the knowing in the world won't change the life others have decided for you."

"Knowing changes everything," Mila said, her voice sharp, something sharper rising against her throat.

Some days, knowing the truth is all you have.

Zahra said nothing, but the slight twist of her lips told Mila she'd struck a weak spot. "What does the bracelet mean?" Mila asked, following her momentary advantage.

The girl's eyes flicked to the white cord at her wrist, then back to Mila's reflection. "Nothing of interest," she said, her voice a hard challenge. "Heathen nonsense."

The door opened, and Mila nearly hissed with frustration.

"Madam wants Wynn," Winters said, oblivious to the interruption she had caused. The woman was in her thirties, but she looked older. Strong, with plain features, her most remarkable talent was the wooden stoicism she displayed in the face of all ranges of treatment. Mila had the impression that Winters had long ago learned to disengage her facial features from any connection to her emotions or thoughts. Probably why she'd lasted this long in Ada's employ.

Mila slipped from the dressing table onto her knees next to the bed. "Wynn," she said softly, brushing the dark tangles of hair from her sister's face. Wynn's dark eyes flickered open. "Mother wants you." Wynn's lips tightened. "Just do everything she says," Mila said. "No trouble."

Wynn nodded and let herself be maneuvered sleepily to her feet by Winters.

Mila sighed as the door closed, then turned back to survey the enigma before her. "You were saying something very interesting about heathen nonsense?"

"It's an article of faith," Zahra replied, speaking the last word as if thrusting a knife.

"Which faith?"

"You wouldn't know it."

"I insist."

"Zoroastrian."

Mila shoved the nightgown from her shoulders and looked away, annoyed that the impossible girl was right. Zahra smirked and held the chemise for Mila to step into. "What is the bracelet for?" Mila asked, unwilling to admit defeat.

"Prayer," Zahra said, moving behind Mila to tie the laces swiftly. Mila thought of the women she'd seen in Venice fingering glittering rosaries of colored stone and ivory. This was no better or stranger.

And it got her no closer to figuring out her stepfather-to-be.

Zahra proffered the corset with a condescending flourish, and

Mila raised her arms, allowing the hateful device. "How did you come to work for Andrew Deemus?"

"My mother died," Zahra said, tugging the corset more roughly than necessary.

"So you've never been to the Deemus estate?" Mila pressed, unwilling to back down.

"I've never left Venice."

"Do you know what the falling-out was concerning?" Back to the previous subject; keep the girl off balance.

"I believe there's usually a romance involved," Zahra said without missing a beat. "But now his uncle is dead, and there's no one left to object to his taste in women."

Mila turned at that, but Zahra snapped on the corset laces, forcing Mila to grab the table edge. The comment was a clear insult to her mother, but Mila's feelings concerning Ada Kenton were complex at best—and at least her adversary had offered new information.

"His uncle died? What about his parents?"

"Dead."

"So he's completely alone in the world," Mila said.

Zahra gave a powerful jerk on the laces and Mila gasped.

"Everyone's alone in the world," Zahra said.

4

Curtis

HIS SISTER WAS WALKING UP THE TREE-SHADOWED LANE THAT idled past their house, her narrow shoulders hunched like she was braced for a storm.

She'd been waiting for him. That couldn't be good.

He slowed the bike and cut the engine, needing a moment before she reached him—a few more breaths to tuck the terror of the woods into the spaces between his bones.

Sage quickened her steps, her body stiff, like a toy soldier wound too tight. Her dark brown hair was pixie-short in back and artfully shaggy in front, and she usually had a scowl on her face that looked strangely at odds with her delicate features and large brown eyes. Right then, she just looked trapped.

Really not good.

"What happened?" he demanded, throwing his leg off the bike.

"Uncle Frank was here."

His chest turned a crank. "Shit."

"Yeah."

"How bad is it?"

"Halfway to Chernobyl."

"Shit. Are you okay?"

"Yeah, I got home just as he was leaving. I didn't go inside."

Curtis took a moment to think. "Take my bike to the shed. I'll deal with it."

Sage was fourteen and small for her age, and she looked so much like their mother it hurt. The bike was nearly as tall as Sage was, but she grasped the handlebars and set her back to it with a look of grim satisfaction.

Yeah, I'd rather manhandle a bike than deal with this too.

Curtis cut through the hedgerow of their lonely country road and headed up the long-overgrown lawn toward the house.

The house. The freaking house. Sometimes he wished he could burn the damn thing to the ground.

A three-story red-brick Victorian with sagging dormers and trim turning green with age. It had been beautiful once—the crowning achievement of the family in its day—but now it was just a reminder that the business was going to shit. The family always *had* been shit, and the house had become the blinking sign, the buzzing motel billboard that told the world there was something sick and festering at the heart of the Garrett clan.

He ascended the front steps of Garrett House, listening carefully. Yelling and pounding from the second floor.

Okay.

He opened the front door and called out: "Dad."

There was no response, just the continuing angry voice and loud scraping sounds from the floor above.

"Dad, it's Curtis. I'm coming up."

He took the stairs, eyes alert, the old steps groaning under his feet. He reached the landing and stepped into the little pool of muted rainbows cast by the stained-glass window that glowed in the base of the dark wood paneling.

He was seven when they'd moved into the old family legacy, and the rainbow was the only place he'd felt safe. He used to sit there on the plush carpet runner with its faded background of crimson and pale roses, moving his hands through that rainbow light. He imagined he could take those colors into himself and go through the world with the shades of light rippling over his skin, like a fantastic chameleon.

Sometimes his mother would sit there with him, and she'd pretend to catch the rainbows and pocket them.

But she was dead now.

Curtis glimpsed the study door down the long hall and took the next six steps more carefully, leaving the fallen colors behind. From the study came the sound of furniture being moved, a voice rising and falling.

"Dad, I'm coming in."

He eased the door open, careful not to get too close until he knew what he was dealing with.

His father was pushing an enormous walnut-carved bookcase across the wood-paneled room, the muscles in his broad back and thick arms roping with effort. Antique leather-bound books and gold-gleaming trinkets shuddered and toppled with each strenuous shove.

"Dirty, thieving, double-crossing, no-good, traitorous blood. Thinks I don't know. Thinks I don't *know*!"

With a final lurching effort, he shoved the bookcase against the back wall, blocking the large lead-paned window completely. A crystal paperweight shaped like a bull fell and shattered on the hardwood floor. He turned, and Curtis tensed, ready to dodge, but his father continued as if his eyes hadn't just slid over his own son. Crystal shards crunched under his steps as he put his hands to the massive cherry-wood desk, a thing that should have taken two strong men to budge.

"But I do know. I know. I'm no fool." He shoved and skidded the desk toward the bookcase.

"DAD." It was a risk to get loud with him, but the man couldn't be touched when he was in this state.

His father turned and seemed to notice him for the first time.

Tom Garrett was a handsome man: dark haired and strong jawed, with even features. He was Curtis, but magnified—six foot three inches where Curtis was six foot one, barrel-chested where Curtis was lean muscle.

He was the dark mirror Curtis hated to look into.

Tom's wide eyes took too long to clear with recognition, and Curtis swallowed hard.

"Oh, Son. Good. I need your help. I've got this room, you go start on the next."

Curtis was breathing very carefully, in through the nose, out through the mouth. As though mathematically precise control of his own body would balance the inequality between them, dissipate the hurricane of chaos that boiled at the other end of the room. "What are you doing, Dad?"

Tom took a sudden step forward, arms swinging, and Curtis's heart jolted.

"What does it look like I'm doing? I'm making sure that damn dirty thief can't worm his way in here in the night! That brother of mine, always plotting. Well, I've seen now, I know what we have to do."

"Dad, have you taken your pills today?"

"Didn't you hear me, Son? He's coming! He'll be back!"

"Okay, Dad, but first you've gotta take your pills."

"Pills aren't going to keep that son of a bitch from coming back here and taking what's mine!" Curtis's father bellowed, storming toward him. "They slow me down! And that's when he'll be back, that bastard—he's just *waiting* for his chance."

"I'll make sure he doesn't come back, Dad." Curtis could feel Sage in the hallway just out of sight, listening, trying to gauge how bad things might get. Her fear made Curtis stronger, left no room for error. "Take your pills, and I'll keep an eye out tonight. I'll make sure he doesn't get in." His father stared at him, eyes wild, chest heaving. "Please, Dad."

The man deflated all at once, slumping into a green damask chair, his hands going to his temples.

"My head," he moaned.

A movement caught Curtis's eye. Sage with a glass of water and a handful of pills. He took them from her and moved toward the giant slouched in the chair.

He stretched his hand out. For a moment, there was nothing, just his father's heavy breathing—then a large hand shot out and clamped around his wrist.

Don't react. Don't pull back.

His father stared at him through eyes too intense, then took the proffered pills and swallowed them in one gulp.

"You should get some rest, Dad."

His father nodded but didn't move. Curtis backed away, into the hall, into a full breath. Sage was standing at the top of the stairs, her face tense. She looked to him. He nodded his reassurance, even though he felt none.

They descended the stairs together.

There was no more noise from above.

5

Curtis

SPRAWLED ON HIS UNMADE BED, CURTIS STARED AT THE stained plaster ceiling and did *not* think about what happened in the copse. He did *not* think about how excruciating pain had split his head, how the wind had sounded like voices. He did *not* think—

He shoved himself up from the bed and threw open the window. The sky was dark navy blotted with black clouds, and the air tasted like rain. The wind was starting to pick up speed.

Sage's laugh sounded down the hall—on the phone with one of her five thousand friends. Curtis wasn't good at friends. He had one friend, and that was all he could handle.

He lay back and stared at the ceiling some more.

They'd made it through supper without any more disasters. That was good. *Routine*, Curtis reminded himself. *Just stick to the routine.*

Routine kept them all alive and together.

Routine kept his father manageable.

But it was getting harder to make him take the meds lately. Curtis balled up his fists. And Frank showing up—that was a disaster he'd been unprepared for. Frank always left his brother in a manic state of fury that Curtis had to somehow deal with, defuse, keep everything on the rails and—

Curtis's chest spasmed and he couldn't catch his breath. He forced air through his teeth and stared at that one particular brown stain in the right-hand corner of the ceiling. He'd named it Fred. He stared at the stain and forced his breath until he felt his chest unclench.

It's just you and me, Fred. Keeping watch over this shithole. Too bad you're fucking useless.

Fred said nothing. Curtis's Spartan room stared back at him, bland and impersonal in its emptiness. Just the way he liked it. He'd fed his childhood clutter to a bonfire when he was twelve, the day he realized it was all on him.

A gust of wind sent the thin white curtains flapping, and cool air washed over him.

A *whisper*.

Curtis jerked upright, muscles straining.

The curtain reached, trailing out like the veil on a bride, dipping and swirling, puffing out suddenly, then dropping still. Outside, leaves skittered like the clatter of tin pie plates, and the low rumble of thunder boiled far in the distance. A high note surged, the shriek riding the top gust of wind, like the keening of a wolf.

And he could hear a *voice* on that wind. A whispering cadence that nattered at the back of his mind, unintelligible but familiar.

The sound from the woods.

He slammed the window shut, shaking his head. No. He did not just hear that. *No.*

Sick people heard voices. People like his father.

He was *not* like his father.

He headed for the stairs, the kitchen. His mouth was dry, bile climbing the back of his throat. He needed water.

His feet pounded down the steps and across the vestibule.

His hand was shaking as he jerked the kitchen tap and grabbed a glass, cracking it loudly against the others. He shoved the glass underneath the stream of water and drank the whole thing before turning off the tap. He leaned against the counter in the darkened kitchen, the worn and chipped marble cool against his palms.

Get it together.

A moan came from the sitting room.

Curtis set the glass down and walked heavily down the dark hall, toward the dim reddish light of the single lamp, already knowing what he would see. His father sat on the antique couch, leaning forward, his head supported by the upturned barrel of a rifle resting on the floor. His one hand held the barrel steady—his other was on the trigger.

Curtis sighed.

His father moaned again. A low, sickly sound, like an animal trapped, injured.

"My heaaad."

"I know, Dad," Curtis said softly, invisible fingers of pity clenching the back of his throat.

The muzzle was still against Tom's forehead. There was a worn patch in the Turkish carpet where the rifle butt lodged almost every night.

Curtis reached out slowly, his fingers closing over the smooth metal of the barrel.

"Not tonight, Dad."

His father looked up at him. Nodded.

Curtis took the gun.

It was a familiar weight in his hands as he walked through the darkened kitchen, up the stairs to the third floor and his bedroom. He closed the door and slid the gun to its nightly resting place beneath his bed.

He turned the light out and lay back on the bed. Wedging a hand beneath his head, he stared up at the ceiling, at the brown stain he couldn't see in the dark, but he knew exactly where it was. He let out a shaky breath.

Just another night in the Garrett house.

6

Mila

THE CARRIAGE WAS STIFLING. IT WAS A HUMID AUGUST HEAT, and Mila could feel her chemise stuck damp against her skin. Above it, the boning of her corset dug into her ribs and stomach, pressing her insides in, and her shoulders back—making her nice to look at.

Her eyes rose to his face again.

Andrew Deemus.

Impeccable in his dark suit, tan vest, and white collar, he lounged against the seat cushions, his languid eyes roaming the Kingston newspaper he'd acquired upon landing. He had a high, pale forehead, dark, slicked hair, and fine, arched brows that gave him the appearance of being perpetually and quietly amused.

He looked up at her.

She shifted, trying to smooth the folds of her stiff underskirt to a more comfortable position. Beside her, Wynn was quiet, sitting rigid like a porcelain doll in her navy dress and lace collar. Their mother sat opposite, her embroidered skirts spilling over the seat and up against the carriage wall. The early afternoon sun caught the ivory fabric and set the tiny beads and metallic threads glowing with light—peacock blue, purple, green, and gold.

Andrew Deemus was still looking at Mila.

"The clothes suit you," he said. He set the newspaper aside, and Ada looked askance at the newsprint pages now scattered carelessly against her expensive skirts. Her jaw tightened, but she kept silent.

Deemus smiled, his full lips quirking as he let his eyes roam the smooth folds of Mila's linen skirt, the precise tucks of the grey jacket. "I ordered them from Paris," he said. "A little atelier known for its sophistication and elegant simplicity." Mila wished she were clad in the dust-covered trousers she used to wear in the stable training ring.

Ada shifted, and the glass beads and metallic threads on her gown made a tinkling sound as they brushed together. Her dress had come from the House of Worth and must have cost Andrew Deemus a small fortune. The look on her mother's face when she'd seen it had been transportive, a kind of rapturous and ravenous awe, as though *finally* someone had seen her value and bestowed upon her the treasures she so richly deserved.

Mila knew she needed to say something. She would not say thank you. She would not lie and say she loved the clothes. She settled for the truth.

"They're the finest clothes I've ever worn," she said with a jut of her chin.

His lip curved, as though he'd caught what she'd left unsaid. "Well, you won't be able to say that for much longer. I'll be filling the house with fine things. You shall all be dressed like queens." He looked pleasantly to Ada at these last words and her face changed like a lamp lit, displeasure instantly overtaken by the performance of queen-like graciousness.

"It's hot," Wynn said.

"Don't complain," Ada said, the fine planes of her face suddenly sharp with the irritation that boiled constantly beneath the surface.

"It's not a complaint; it's a statement of fact," Mila said.

"I beg your pardon?" Ada said, a dangerous undertone threading her voice.

Mila's eyes flicked to Deemus. He was leaning against the wall propped by one elegant elbow, his fingers curved carelessly. He tipped his head and let one finger half hide the amusement that tugged at his lips.

"Let me take Wynn for a ride, get some air," Mila said.

"And have you arrive at the house disheveled and stinking of horse?" Ada said.

"Oh, let the girl get some air," Deemus said with another wave of his hand.

"Andrew." Ada's voice was quiet, her jaw tight.

"It's hot as blazes, Ada," Deemus said, his voice rising just a fraction. "And besides, the girl has more skill on a horse than half the men under my employ."

All of them, actually, Mila thought.

"I like to see her ride," Deemus said. "Why else would I have shipped that wild devil of a horse all the way from Kent to Canada if not for her to ride it?"

Ada straightened her shoulders, her breasts dipping and swelling at the tight bustline. She nodded her head once, grudgingly.

"Bring the devil," Deemus called through the carriage window. A few moments later, a groom rode even with the carriage on a dark brown mare, Diablo's lead in hand. Diablo arched his neck and whinnied, eyes wide with the noise of the carriage, the jangle of the wheels. Mila rose, gripping Wynn by the hand.

"Wynn stays here," Ada said.

Mila looked to Deemus, but he was smiling again, that quiet, amused expression he wore so often.

"Wynn, you shall tell me what your favorite bedchamber in the whole world would look like," he said. "And I daresay when we arrive, you'll find the house will have at least two or three that fit the bill."

Mila let go of Wynn's hand, her stomach tightening with anger toward her mother. It was a move of spite. She'd been outplayed, and now she was taking it out on Wynn. But Diablo was right there and Mila's heart surged with the need to cast herself to his back. She looked at Wynn regretfully, then pushed the carriage door open.

"You're not actually going to—" Ada began.

"Enough," Deemus said sharply.

Mila clicked her tongue twice and Diablo shied closer. Mila leaned against his strong shoulder and twisted her hips, throwing herself onto his sun-warmed back. She kicked her leg free of the skirts and petticoats and hoisted herself up on his withers, settling her knees firm on his sides.

"Hyah," she whispered to his ear, and he pricked the great dark-furred things as she twisted her fingers in his mane, and they were off, shooting past the carriage and the line of coaches and wagons and horses. They pounded into the rolling field of green and Mila's lungs expanded. Her heart swelled with the pure wonder of it, and for a moment, she knew that she was more powerful than all the corsets, petticoats, and stays they had tied her into. She knew she was dangerous and wonderful and wild like Diablo.

They should fear me, she thought. *They should look in my eyes and know that I'm a devil too.*

7

Curtis

SAGE WAS ALREADY WAITING IN THE OLD CHEVY TRUCK WHEN Curtis opened the front door the next morning. She was slouched in the passenger seat, smartphone in hand, ear buds in place.

The cab door squeaked as Curtis pulled it open and folded his long frame behind the wheel. His backpack joined Sage's in the center of the scuffed leather bench seat.

Sage's ink-stained fingers paused over her phone and her eyes flicked to his, checking.

He nodded once. Status normal, no disasters on the horizon.

Yet.

The truck rumbled to life, and they left the house behind. Country dirt roads, clover-filled ditches, and tree-lined hedgerows for the next ten miles.

"Are you okay?"

He looked to Sage, startled. She was usually a silent texting fiend on the drive to school. The quiet suited him fine. The quiet didn't require anything except reciprocal reticence.

The concern in her large, dark eyes was unnerving. Not the status quo.

"Yeah," he said, unclenching his fingers from the cold steering wheel and stretching them quickly.

"You look tense."

He looked at her and raised a single eyebrow.

She raised both of hers in response. "More tense than usual."

"I am *not* usually tense," he replied. "I'm usually quiet. That's not tense. That's aloof."

She rolled her eyes. "Whatever, Curt. I think you've got a screwed-up definition of 'not tense,' but whatever. Be as weird and aloof as you want."

She tucked her petite, sneaker-clad feet up on the dash and went back to speed-texting.

Curtis studied her from the corner of his eye as she scowled at her phone, her fingers moving too fast to follow. She only called him Curt when she was annoyed.

She was probably just projecting her own worries on him. Because he had nothing to be worried about. He was *not* rattled from last night. Last night was just one more standard brick of crazy in the hundred-acre crazy courtyard that was Life with Dad. Nothing more.

And that thing with the trees? That feeling that the whole place had called to him? Had *wanted* him?

Weird crap happens in the woods, he told himself sternly. *Whatever. Let's not get dramatic about it.*

And the whispers he'd heard through the window?

Well . . .

"You take the gun away again last night?" Sage asked.

He looked back to her, frowning slightly. She was asking a lot of questions today. It wasn't like her. Sage's head was usually firmly in one of her invented worlds. That or holding court with her crowd of fashionably misfit friends. That was a good thing. A simple thing.

He approached the turnoff for the main road to town, and the windshield caught all the morning glare at once. For a moment, he wanted to keep going straight, just point the truck into that bright point of fire cresting the hill and never come back.

Curtis realized she was still waiting for an answer, her fingers hovering over her phone, fine dark brows raised.

"Yeah." His fingers clenched over the skinny knobs of the old steering wheel.

What's gotten into her today?

"Why do you even bother?" Sage asked, pressing her bottom lip between her teeth. Her finger dug at a crack in the door's buff vinyl upholstery, like a child prodding at a scab just to feel it throb. He could feel that she wanted something from him. Some combination of words or facial expressions. Something she could either lean into or assault. He came up empty and decided to stick with silence.

Sage stabbed at the upholstery, finger crooked into a tiny claw. "He never goes through with it anyway," she said, her voice just on the empty side of bitter. "I think he likes the feel of the barrel on his forehead. Just another one of his weird rituals."

"It's not his fault, you know," Curtis said before he remembered that he was going to stick with silence. Sage didn't remember what their dad used to be like. She didn't remember the father who bought Curtis a dirt bike when he was five years old, who taught him to ride, to be fearless, and never once laughed or yelled no matter how many times Curtis screwed up. She didn't know who Dad was before his illness took everything.

But she wasn't wrong about the gun. Last year, Curtis had gotten very drunk and thought about the matter from all angles. He'd concluded that his father needed this ritual. In the midst of manic episodes, paranoid delusions, and constant skull-splitting headaches that made migraines look like all-expenses-paid beach vacations, Tom Garrett needed to contemplate ending that perpetual agony—contemplate it, and every night choose *not* to end it. It was his only comfort in a world that had turned sideways on him.

And Tom didn't like it when that comfort was denied him.

"Maybe the doctor needs to up his meds," Sage suggested in a softer voice, like she was trying to make up for her earlier bluntness. Her fingers played with the almost-black hairs at the nape of her neck.

"Last time they did that, he slept for three days straight," Curtis replied, shaking his head.

Sage pressed her fingers down her neck and didn't answer.

"He's been fairly even on this cocktail. We shouldn't mess with it." He turned the truck onto Willowhaven Drive, the outskirts of the faded town. By all accounts, Willowhaven used to really be something, but now it was just dying by slow degrees. Half the shops on Main Street were closed and boarded up; the other half were going under. Houses stood for sale until they were given up for lost causes and left to rot. Curtis glanced to Sage. "You remember what happened last time they tested some shiny new combo on him, right?"

She grimaced.

The last time the doctors got experimental with their father's meds, he'd gone nuclear during a drive to Kingston. That was five years ago. He'd gotten it into his head that his heart would explode if a single car passed them. Two hundred kilometers in a hundred zone, three cop cars, and one stun gun later, Kingston's finest had hauled Tom Garrett into the fifth-floor ward of Kingston General and strapped him down while Curtis and Sage watched.

And that was what came of trusting doctors.

They'd spent the next week with Uncle Frank and Aunt Olivia while the "experts" evened Dad back out onto his previous course of meds.

He pulled into a parking space, and the crumbling red stone Victorian monstrosity that was Willowhaven High filled the wind-shield. He sighed, already done with the day. He could feel Sage's eyes on him, *wanting* something from him. He twisted the keys from the ignition with a sharp movement, feeling the cracks in his chest, the utter lack of whatever it was that she needed.

I'm not enough, he thought.

"See you later," he said, swiping at his close-cropped hair.

"Yeah," she said faintly.

He shoved open the truck door, seizing his backpack and pitching it over his shoulder. He slammed the door and strode toward the front entrance as people got the hell out of his way.

People always got the hell out of his way. Something about the leather jacket and the aggressive rhythm of his stride. That was fine with him. He had everything he needed.

He had everything he could handle.

A group of girls clustered around the entrance eyed him as he neared, their eyes flicking to him like he was something fascinating.

You wouldn't last a week, he thought as he strode past them. He yanked the door open and their voices resumed, nervous laughter skipping out against the walls. They thought he was dangerous and exciting.

But Curtis knew the truth—whatever it was they were looking for, it wasn't inside him.

Some days he wondered if there was anything inside him at all.

8

Curtis

THE PLAN WAS TO IGNORE THE PROBLEM.

What problem? *Exactly.* That thing in the woods yesterday—that was nothing. But chemistry class? That was a real problem. He might die of boredom before the class was over.

Curtis slouched in his chair, head lolling against the elaborate but cracked oak paneling. The town used to have money and all the public buildings were designed to show it off. But now the school was like most things in Willowhaven—formerly grand, currently dying.

Mary Vandenberg's profile caught his eye from the next row over. Her family owned the Willowhaven Grand Hotel, but Mary was the only thing remotely grand about the family these days. She was Paris-runway stunning with a great rack, and she knew it.

She and Curtis used to play together in elementary, but somewhere along the last five years, she'd turned into a pod person. Her specialty now was being noticed, tricking nerds into doing her homework, and crushing the souls of the less popular. Her slow slide into shallowness made Curtis feel vaguely disappointed with the world, as though Willowhaven's decline into decrepitude had taken her personality with it. Mary caught him looking at her and raised her perfectly sculpted eyebrows in a challenge. He gave her a bored smile, then looked away. They'd made out once, but it had felt empty and pointless.

Trying to connect with people always left Curtis feeling like shit. He could never maintain it.

Come back, a voice whispered.

Curtis jerked in his seat, hoping to see someone smirking at him, but there was just lumpy Al Mayhew, who wouldn't dare mess with Curtis on his best day. Curtis faced forward again, fingers scraping over the desk, trying to tell himself that he wasn't hearing a voice tripping and sliding and falling on the breeze from the open window.

But the evidence was contradicting him.

He stood abruptly and strode from the classroom, ignoring the protestations of Mr. Greenslate.

Through the hallway, to the bathroom, into a stall.

He slammed the door.

What. The. Hell.

This was not happening. *Not happening.*

He stood, bracing his back against one side of the stall, his hands wedged against the other. He waited. Forced himself to count down from twenty. Breathed in the smell of urinal cakes and bleach. The stained octagonal floor tiles stared back at him, the dark grout swimming in his vision. He realized he hadn't blinked in a while.

The lunch bell rang.

It sounded different . . . hollow and watery, like he was underground and—

Shit.

He wasn't in the bathroom. Blackness was all around him. The hot and clank of metal. Engines working.

Fuck, don't panic, don't panic. His hand grabbed for something solid.

He took a few steps forward and his brain interpreted the hulking shape of Victorian-age boilers like great beasts settled down for the night. He was jammed into a small niche in the school basement, the bitter smell of engine grease and desiccated brick pricking his nose.

How did I get here?

His finger was throbbing, and he didn't know why. He grabbed for his phone and fumbled with the flashlight app. His nail was bent back and bloodied, and there were scratch marks on the brick wall— they formed what looked like the word *below*.

For a moment, he wanted to cry. His father lost time like this, ended up in places he couldn't explain.

It doesn't matter. Fuck it. Just get out.

He made himself move forward and looked for the stairs. He had to act normal. No one could know what was happening to him.

Just be normal.

Curtis stood in the doorway to the cafeteria, ordering his heart to shut the fuck up.

In keeping with the spirit of the whole building, the cafeteria was more suited to a commencement address than the distribution of the grim food-like offerings peddled by the resentful lunch staff. Curtis selected the least disgusting item from the heat-lamp-addled gauntlet and paid the weary-looking cashier lady while scanning the space for Avi. He spotted his friend's unwieldy black curls with a surge of relief, and he headed for the back corner table, navigating through the chaos and distinct mingled aroma of chili fries and industrial cleaner.

Avi was slouched in the plastic cafeteria chair as though the dismal quality of his shepherd's pie had sapped him of the will to live, but the way he perked up when he saw Curtis implied he was ready with an Important Thing to Say.

"I'm seriously going to explode if Mr. Waters tells one more story about his disgusting diarrhea cats." Avi clapped a hand on the table with enough force to make everyone's trays jump a few inches. He leaned his lanky frame forward as Curtis took a seat across from him. A dark ringlet fell across Avi's eyes and he immediately head-bobbed it out of the way—a movement that Curtis could use to pick Avi out of the largest crowd. "I mean, how the hell does this guy keep his job?" Avi spread his always-expressive fingers wide and stabbed them dramatically in the air. "He's supposed to be teaching us AP calculus, and instead I'm being treated to the shit-filled adventures of Fluffy and Duffy. It's a freaking travesty."

"I warned you, man," Curtis replied, relieved his voice sounded almost normal. "Geezer is six months from retirement. He doesn't give a crap anymore."

"Then our brilliant faculty should rethink putting semi-senile cat fanatics in charge of the one class I have to ace to get into Cornell."

"You care too much, Avi."

"They don't let you be an architect if you flunk math."

"You've never flunked anything in your life."

"Except girls," Avi said with a grimace. "Well, and gym."

Curtis wanted to babble the truth—*I'm hearing voices and zombie walking to dark basements*—but he couldn't. His father heard voices. Now *he* was hearing voices. And having seizures in creepy forests.

The whole thing was very not good.

His fingers tapped out a rhythm on the side of his untouched food tray. He realized Avi was studying him. His fingers stilled.

His friend's large hazel eyes sharpened. He pointed a single finger at Curtis. "You okay, man?"

"Fantastic."

"I see that."

"Come baaa-aaack," the forest voices crooned.

Curtis bolted up from the table, dumping Avi's drink over in his panic.

"Dude, what the hell?" Avi moaned, pitching himself away from the spreading pool of soda like it was deadly acid.

Keys. He wanted his truck keys, and he wanted to get the hell out of there.

The hallway was too small, voices too loud, and he fought the urge to shove people. He turned the corner, and 180 pounds of Jared Arrondale blocked his path. The school's football and wrestling star. The guy was treated like Willowhaven royalty, and he definitely believed his own hype.

Curtis couldn't stand him.

The feeling was mutual.

"Out of my way," Curtis ordered, a sensation like drowning climbing his rib cage. He was at the bottom of a deep, black well and the sides were closing in on him.

"Pay the fag toll first, Garrett, for you and your boyfriend," Jared said, pursing his lips at Avi, who'd caught up to Curtis by now.

Curtis tried to control his breath, to push back the slick sides of that well. People were watching and their stares made it harder to keep the rage that fueled his chest from breaking free. "I'm not in the mood for this," he said, carving a step from the asshole's side of the standoff.

Jared smiled and made the space smaller. "Oh, are you in a hurry to get home and unstrap your crazy dad from the rubber room he's locked up in?"

Someone made a sound like *ohhh*, and Curtis grabbed Jared by the shirt and smashed him headfirst into the lockers. The sound of his skull connecting with metal was satisfying, and it made Curtis want to discover what other sounds he could make with Arrondale's body. His foot fit the curve of the asshole's stomach quite nicely, and Curtis was kicking him as hard as he could, the world a loud, distorted blur far above him. Hands were pulling Curtis back and he could vaguely hear Avi's panicked voice in his ear yelling for him to stop.

There was a hair's breadth of space where Curtis wanted to tear into the whole school. Just grab people and throw them. Flatten whatever got in his path. Because if you couldn't survive, you didn't deserve to. He could feel that dark pit of fury that bubbled deep inside him at all times, waiting for the cracks. It was waiting to surge up and take him, cover everything in black rage, and help him take down the world.

He shook off the hands grabbing him and stormed the few remaining feet to his locker. He grabbed his keys and headed for the nearest exit.

"What the hell, man? What was that?"

They were in his truck, speeding away from the school; Avi was staring at him like he was the family dog gone unexpectedly rabid, but Curtis was too busy walling the anger back in place to care.

"You've seen me get in a fight before."

"Yeah, you punched Andy Gibbons in the nose when he tried to take my wallet in fifth grade. You knocked out Lindy Freeman when he called Anya Taylors a slut. But I've never seen you almost kill a guy in front of a hundred witnesses!"

Curtis accelerated. How did he explain to his best friend that some days he just felt like killing people who were lucky enough to be born into a family where their dad *wasn't* crazy and their mom *didn't* die in a car crash? How did he tell Avi that some days he could almost kill *him* for having such a disgustingly easy life?

"Fine, fine, don't talk to me," Avi continued, throwing his hands up in another exaggerated gesture. "I'm only ditching school, blemishing my spotless attendance record to make sure that my best friend is not having a nervous breakdown."

Curtis hit the brakes, the truck skidding to a stop at the side of the dirt road. Avi swore in surprise.

"Get the hell out," Curtis ordered.

"DUDE!" Avi yelled. "What is your problem?"

They stared at each other, and Avi's face changed. His hands deflated, fingers curling inward. *Nervous breakdown.* "Sorry man, I didn't mean it like that," Avi said.

Curtis looked away, struggling to control his breath.

"Is crap going down with your dad?" Avi asked finally, his voice low.

"Something like that," Curtis muttered. He pulled the truck back up onto the road and they drove in silence.

Avi lasted about three minutes before his hands started playing with the radio dial, fumbling with the volume. He found something aggressively cheerful, then seemed to think better of it and fiddled until he found something with minor guitar chords, as if he hoped that some mid-nineties alternative grunge rock would be soothing to Curtis's tortured soul.

Curtis felt the inner equivalent of a laugh or a cry bubble inside him at the small gesture. It was the kind of funny little thoughtful thing that Avi did because he was Avi. Curtis thought bleakly that Avi's insides must look very different from his own. Then he wondered if Avi would ever get tired of his angry silence bullshit and find some normal friends. Friends who didn't live at the bottom of an anger well. Friends who didn't—

Curtis abruptly wrenched the wheel and turned onto a narrow dirt road made narrower by thick green woods.

Avoiding the problem had not had the desired effect.

It was time to try something else.

9

Curtis

"CURTIS, I KNOW YOU'RE HAVING A ROUGH DAY, BUT I'M NOT really big on hiking," Avi called from somewhere back in the bushes. Curtis sighed and waited for him to catch up. Avi pushed through a patch of overhanging willow branches and paused to wipe frantically at spider web strands caught on his face. He gave Curtis a pleading look. "What are we doing, man?"

"Nothing," Curtis said, turning back to the overgrown path. "Just some place I found when I was out riding yesterday."

"You rode your bike through here? Are you freaking suicidal?"

"I just need to make it another four months," Curtis said. The desperation in his own voice surprised him, like something inside had spilled open and now he couldn't take it back. He didn't talk about things like this, but all of a sudden it was pressing at his seams; it had to get out. He wanted Avi to understand. He wanted *someone* to understand.

"Four months? What, your birthday?"

Curtis felt a little throb of amazement. That was the kind of friend Avi was—he actually carried other people's important life events around in his head. It made Curtis feel like shit, because he never remembered things like that.

"Eighteen." Curtis pushed through another clump of overgrown willows. It must have rained in the night; the earth was damp and smelled like rotting leaves. "Stuff with Dad, it might be getting worse.

I don't know. If he had to go away . . ." Curtis paused, trying not to think of that fifth-floor ward in Kingston. "I can't let anything happen as long as I'm still seventeen. Sage, she'd get taken away. But if I'm eighteen . . ."

"You could get custody," Avi finished.

"Yeah, I think so."

"Man, I know you think you've got this all under control," Avi said, and Curtis could tell he was choosing his words very carefully, "but this is some heavy stuff. Don't you think there might be some people out there who could help you? No one expects you to be some sort of expert in bipolar schizoaffective with manic episodes, or whatever it is."

"But that's it, Avi," Curtis broke in, the words pouring out in a rush. "I am an expert. I'm an expert in Dad. I know his moods. I know his signs. All the hospitals do is dope him up and tie him down." The black well pushed at his sides and he resisted the urge to grab the nearest tree branch and break it in half. "They don't know him the way I do."

He stopped and turned away from Avi, struggling to find the right words. In the hospital, they turned Tom into something that wasn't his father anymore. They turned him into a broken, drugged-out zombie, because it was easier to switch him off than let the man keep a little bit of himself.

It made Curtis angry.

He wouldn't abandon his father to that living death. He didn't know how to explain that to Avi, with his doctor mother and doctor father and his very, very clear-cut, straightforward view of the world. He didn't know how to make Avi understand that what would send a normal person running for the hills was just another day for him.

"I know it all looks bad," he said, "but it's normal for us. It's never not been this way." This wasn't strictly true, but sometimes it felt like it was.

Curtis was six when a blinding headache turned his father into a different man. Tom had crawled like a wounded soldier to the steps of their little white house and lain there for no one knew how long. Curtis had found him covered in vomit, his eyes glazed with visions of the unspeakable.

Now Curtis had to stop and grip a willow branch tightly, the memory of finding his father in that condition burned forever into his brain, tied forever into that terrible feeling that the bottom of the world was falling out—that nothing was solid and you'd better always be ready.

Ready for whatever came next.

After that, his father disappeared into hospitals and test groups, taking their life with him. You wouldn't think that life was that fragile, that at any moment someone you loved could take everything your life was ever supposed to be and twist it into something unrecognizable. But they can.

And then you're left to pick up the pieces.

But there hadn't been much chance to pick up those pieces; a year later, they'd moved into Garrett House. And a year after that, his mother was dead.

Avi was watching Curtis with sad eyes, and Curtis turned away abruptly and pushed forward. He didn't need Avi to feel sad for him. It didn't fix a damn thing.

They'd reached the field.

His eyes zeroed in on the far-off copse of trees and his stomach lurched. One way or another, he was going to know if this was all in his head. He was going to find out if he was turning into his father.

He strode out toward the circle of trees, Avi beside him. The field was still, just like before. But he could hear that dull roar in the distance, the nattering rhythm that sounded almost like words; his heart was a wild animal leaping forward at the sound, and his hands itched to delve into the earth and find secret things.

He forced his breath to slow and glanced at Avi, but his friend had his head down, picking his steps carefully as they made their way through the tall grass.

He tried to keep talking, to feel normal. What were they talking about? Sage. Yeah. Sage. "The thing is, Sage could never handle foster care." They were halfway to the copse now. It was so loud. Curtis looked at Avi. Avi looked back at him, normal as could be. Curtis fought a wave of nausea. "I have to keep us together, no matter what." Avi nodded his understanding.

"I get it, man."

The cluster of trees was right in front of them. The wind was almost deafening, a shriek so loud and high it made him wince. Avi pulled out a stick of gum, nonchalant.

"You want?"

Curtis shook his head as something inside him howled in misery.

"Where are we?" Avi said, looking around. "We west of the creek?"

"Yeah," Curtis said weakly. "Melbourne Road is about ten miles that way." Normally he'd be impressed that Avi knew where they were at all. Avi had no sense of direction, as Curtis had discovered rather comically when they were ten. But right now, he was fighting the urge to sink to the ground.

Avi didn't hear it.

Avi didn't hear the sounds that were screaming at Curtis.

The crazy had caught up with him.

For a moment, he felt the bottom of the world tipping, felt himself swaying at the edge of everything. His hands were curled into claws and he could barely keep from throwing himself to the ground. He could not—*he must not*—let anyone know anything was wrong. They'd take Sage. He couldn't let them take her, let them break her. She was the one thing in his world that wasn't tainted—the bright spot in their broken family.

"You know, I think there used to be some old mansion around here, years ago," Avi commented.

Curtis was barely listening as he walked back toward the path.

"Apparently it was enormous—a castle practically. Burned to the ground with everyone inside."

Curtis had never been overly interested in history and now was really no exception.

"They say the place was cursed, or haunted, or something. And after it burned, no one would go near the site. Said it was pure evil."

Curtis turned so fast, Avi jumped backward to get away from him. Curtis felt hope flick within him, a long-dormant snake twitching to life. Hope was deadly and Curtis had little use for it, but today the snake uncoiled and Curtis felt his insides twist. His organs flinched and quivered and the snake tested the air with its tongue. Maybe there was an explanation for this nightmare. Maybe there was something that trumped the genetic sword of Damocles that hung by a single thread over his head at all times.

"Avi, does this place have a name?"

10

Mila

"GRAVENHEARST," DEEMUS SAID, STEPPING FROM THE CARRIAGE.
It was a dark shadow on the far-off hilltop, roofs and chimneys stretching like sword points toward the sky. Clouds raced overhead, and for a moment, sunlight flashed out and lit the hulking silhouette, and Mila had the impression of bone-grey stone and windows like a thousand staring eyes. She stared back, unaccountably frozen at the sight. Then a cloud overtook the sun and the house was a jagged blot against the sky again.

"It's enormous," Mila said, her breath tight, fingers knotted in Diablo's mane. He shifted restlessly beneath her, his ears pricking back and forth.

"Yes," Deemus said. He stood on a promontory of rock that rose from the rolling countryside, his back straight, gaze cast toward Gravenhearst. He was silent for a few long moments, then turned back toward the carriage. He looked up at Mila, his face pensive, and she shivered. He had the expression of someone who'd seen something momentous, a man about to step off the edge of the known.

Mila shrank under his eyes, unnerved by their impossible weight, and then he unpinned her and looked back to the carriage. Mila followed his gaze, saw the look of exultant hunger on her mother's features as she stared at the kingdom about to become hers. Deemus looked back to Mila and she had the disturbing sense that he'd made an important decision.

He smiled at her.

"Move on!" he called. The train of carriages and wagons rattled into movement once more. He stepped up into the carriage and closed the door, and the coachman slapped the reins.

Mila fought the overwhelming feeling that she should snatch Wynn from the coach, throw her atop Diablo, and race for the hills.

11

Curtis

THEY WERE IN A DIMLY LIT BACK CORNER OF THE WILLOWHAVEN Public Library, a place Curtis had never been before, because why the hell would he?

It was a small jewel box of a place, long and narrow with layers of red cast-iron railings rising up above them. An elaborate blood-toned wedding cake of pierced iron catwalks and scrolling balustrades lined the towering walls of books, rising up to a barrel-vaulted ceiling that loomed four stories high, like a dark, cupped hand.

It was a marvel of nineteenth-century industrial design—exactly the sort of past grandeur that showed just how far Willowhaven had since fallen—but Curtis didn't care, because for the last half hour, Avi had been scrolling through sepia news clippings on the microfilm reader, the oldness of which was matched only by their pointlessness. The images streamed by in a blur that made his head ache, and the whispers chattered and swelled in the background, impossible to ignore in the oppressive quiet of the place.

"Here," Avi said, pointing at the screen. Curtis gripped the edge of the table as the whispers surged, crashing against the interior of his skull.

A sprawling, smoking ruin of crooked timbers and mutilated stone filled the screen. Curtis leaned forward, trying to pick out some sense of the structure of the place, but the fire had left nothing but a pit of black ruination.

His fingers were on the microfilm knob, turning to the next page, but he was too aggressive, and the whole screen was suddenly a streak of flying newsprint.

"Wow, you are not built for libraries," Avi commented, swatting him away and retrieving the right page.

A headline filled the screen.

GRAVENHEARST BURNS

Curtis swallowed heavily and began to read.

Willowhaven, ON, October 22, 1894—A venerable chapter in Ontario history came to a tragic close last night when Gravenhearst burned to the foundations in an inferno that was seen for miles around. Despite the valiant efforts of the Willowhaven Fire Brigade, nothing could be done to abate the destruction of the Great House.

The famous Gravenhearst stables were narrowly saved and the priceless stock of horses spared from the blaze, but it is sadly presumed that the occupants of Gravenhearst were not so fortunate. Fire Marshall Evans concludes the blaze must have taken hold very quickly in the night while all were asleep in order for no survivors to be found.

The loss of Mr. Andrew Deemus, recent inheritor of Gravenhearst, cannot be overstated. Patron to the arts, generous benefactor to Willowhaven General Hospital, and admired figure of Willowhaven and neighboring Kingston society, the newly married Mr. Deemus will be greatly missed by all who knew him.

Perhaps most poignant of all is the loss of the two fine young ladies so recently come to Gravenhearst, Miss Mila Kenton, age seventeen, and Miss Wynn Kenton, age twelve. The elder Miss Kenton was greatly admired at the wedding of her mother, formerly Mrs. Ada Kenton, to Mr. Deemus on August 12th of this year.

Fire Marshall Evans relates, "The place was hot as the flames of hell when we got there. Nothing could be done. Breaks my heart to think of those two girls. So lovely they were."

The cause of the fire is yet unknown and the search is under way to retrieve the remains of the family and staff so that they may be given a Christian burial.

"There's nothing about a curse in here," Curtis said, turning on Avi.

"Chillax," Avi said, holding up his hands. "There's more, I've just gotta find it." He shook his head, rising to his feet. "Let me go talk to the librarian."

Curtis leaned back in his chair, swiping at his hair with tense fingers. There must be something there. Some kind of explanation for what was happening to him.

There had to be.

Avi returned. "She's going to grab some stuff from the archives."

Curtis nodded. He could feel Avi's eyes on him.

"Look man, not that I'm not thrilled to finally have you join me in a library for once, but what's going on?"

"What, I can't find evil, burned-down mansions intriguing?" Curtis said defensively.

Avi head-bobbed a curl out of his eyes and gave Curtis a don't-bullshit-me look.

Curtis sighed deeply. "Okay, fine. I have a theory about something, but I need a chance to figure it out first."

"You really won't just tell me?"

Curtis was silent—*I'm such an asshole*—but he couldn't give in.

"Wow," Avi muttered. "Um, okay. I'll leave you to it, I guess." He stood awkwardly, throwing his messenger bag over his shoulder. "I love walking home."

Curtis watched him leave, guilt eating his insides. But then the twenty-something librarian appeared and all he cared about was the long metal box she held.

"You'll have to wear these," she said with a smile, proffering a pair of thin white gloves. She sat on the edge of the table and tucked a strand of blonde hair behind her ear.

Curtis manufactured a flirtatious smile, brushing her hand with his fingers as he took the gloves.

"Thanks so much, I'll get this all back to you as soon as I'm done."

"Oh, okay," she said, backing away a few steps, her cheeks pink. She smiled again and narrowly missed walking into a chair as she turned back toward the reference desk.

Curtis tossed the gloves aside and surveyed the box.

His heart sank when he lifted the lid. There wasn't much inside. He lifted several newspaper clippings and a heavy envelope from the bottom and spread them out before him.

The first he skimmed quickly. An obituary for someone named Bartholomew Deemus. The man died without children, leaving Gravenhearst temporarily without an owner, causing it to be closed up in 1887.

Curtis glanced back at the microfilm screen. The fire had been in 1894, and Gravenhearst had been occupied by another Deemus, so apparently they had eventually found Bartholomew Deemus's closest relative—Andrew Deemus. The next article was about the sale of the horses. With the Deemus line now completely obliterated by the fire, the prize-winning horses were sold at auction and the proceeds went to various causes that Andrew Deemus had supported around Kingston and Willowhaven.

But then:

GRAVENHEARST CURSED

Willowhaven, ON, December 10, 1894—A series of strange and unnatural occurrences have revived old rumors about Gravenhearst.

Mr. Andrew Deemus's prize-winning horses, the only living creatures to survive the tragic blaze that brought down the Great House on October 21st of this year, were sold at auction for record-setting prices just a few short weeks ago.

Now it seems that each and every horse has met with a tragic and premature end.

Mr. Henry Rollins of Kingston reports that the two-year-old stallion he purchased took sick suddenly in the night, with no prior warning, and died without discernible cause while screaming "as if the very devil were upon him."

Mr. Edward Timmons of Lancashire in Great Britain reports that the three-year-old mare he purchased "went mad" while on the crossing to England and "threw herself overboard" into the sea without cause.

A groom from a well-respected local estate told this reporter that his master's newly acquired racehorse went into a "terrible frenzy" and strangled herself to death on her own lead rope.

Similar reports have come from every patron known to have purchased a Deemus horse from that final auction. More curious, every account has marked the date of the strange deaths as November 1, 1894—the date the Gravenhearst stables were dismantled.

One of the oldest residents of Willowhaven, a Miss Geraldine McKinsey, relates that her grandfather once worked for Mr. Kepler Theodore Deemus, founder and first owner of Gravenhearst. "Grandfather told me some very strange stories," she recounts. "He said that house was cursed. Something

happened in that place that he would never
speak of."

Curtis shivered, unnerved despite himself. The forest whispers were
shrieking with delight, and Curtis wished Avi were still beside him.

There was another small folder, this one containing a badly
water-damaged pamphlet called *Local Legends*.

And then we come to the strange account of
Kepler Theodore Deemus.

An inventor and alchemist, Deemus constructed a vast mansion called Gravenhearst
some   thirty   miles   from   Kingston.
Construction began in the mid-1700s and
continued for more than twenty years as
Deemus added more and more wings to the
Great House. Gravenhearst was said to be
a veritable labyrinth of curiosities and
strange devices of Deemus's own invention.
Rumors began to spread that Deemus was over
300 years old, some saying that he had con-
quered death and time, others speculating
that he engaged in sorcery in the depths of
Gravenhearst.

Deemus disappeared from the house one
night in 1800 during a terrific thunder-
storm, and his son, Jacob, returned from
studying abroad to manage the estate and
comfort his mother and sisters.

In 1802, history repeated itself as a terrifying storm shook Gravenhearst to its foundations, and Kepler Deemus's wife and five daughters disappeared without a trace. Only Jacob Deemus remained. There was some suspicion raised of foul play by a servant, but no charges were ever brought, due to a lack of evidence. Some commented that a large donation of gold and gunpowder to the Great Lakes British Naval Fleet seemed to smooth matters over considerably.

Rumors that the house was evil began in

Curtis tried to turn the page, but the rest of the booklet was stuck together.

He snatched up the final item, a stained and faded envelope of heavy paper. Three antique photographs in thick cardboard holders fell out. The first was labeled "Deemus Wedding, Gravenhearst, August 12, 1894." It was a panoramic shot of an elaborate garden party, Gravenhearst looming in the background. Torches, lanterns, and festoons of all description decorated the grounds; it looked like something the Rockefellers might have arranged if they were in a really extravagant mood.

The caption beneath read, "The social event of the season."

The next was a formal portrait of a bride and groom. She was tall and elegant with pale hair and skin, and she stood with all her angles turned just the right way. Pearls and jewels dripped from her wrists and neck, and her small mouth conveyed satisfaction, a kind of cat-that-ate-the-canary smirk that didn't quite materialize—because fine ladies don't smirk—but it was there, just in the background, lighting her eyes. The man was a few inches taller, with dark, slicked hair, a high aristocratic forehead, and strikingly full lips. It was the sort of face that might order twenty-five-thousand-dollar caviar, then have one spoonful and lose interest. A beautiful, privileged, bored sort of face. But his eyes were cold and soulless, and he gazed out of the photograph as if certain that the peasant handling his portrait was unworthy to look upon him.

The caption beneath read, "Mr. Andrew Deemus and his bride, Mrs. Ada Deemus."

Curtis reached for the third and final photograph. He flipped it over and the whispers shrieked like a mad flock of birds.

She was pale and tall like her mother—beautiful—but where the woman was sleek and satisfied, the girl was sharp and watchful. Cheekbones curved down toward perfect, unsmiling lips—wider than her mother's, and grave instead of satisfied. Her eyes were deep-set and strikingly shaped, almost feline.

She stood on a gentle slope of the garden, the house behind her, the fantastic party spread out before her. The photographer had caught her in a candid moment, just turning to look at him, the line of her back like the flick of an artist's pencil, her long, dark gown the curve of a mermaid's tail. She carried herself like strength was her unspoken birthright. But in her eyes, there was the slightest flash of—something. Not fear. Not quite that.

Unease.

As though she'd seen something not quite right, but couldn't put a name to the threat.

The caption beneath the image read, "Miss Mila Kenton."

Andrew Deemus's stepdaughter. The girl who perished in the fire. Curtis stared at her, feeling for all the world like she would step from the photograph and tell him something important if she could.

And he wished she would.

She stared back at him, silent.

12

Mila

THE CARRIAGE WHEELS CRUNCHED OVER THE GRAVEL DRIVE AS they made their winding progress up the hill. Mila rode Diablo at a walk beside the coach, and Wynn leaned out the window, her sharp chin propped against the crook of her arm, dark hair drifting in the breeze.

They turned a corner and Gravenhearst came into view, made small by distance, framed by the overhanging boughs of an ancient pine growing along the lane.

The house sprawled out like a city, the central structure a castle of

bone-hued stone and grey pinnacles. But this main core gave way to wings of newer additions, marked by abrupt changes in stone—little attention had been paid to balance or coherence of style. A tower rose up along one far side, a gaping hole slicing down its roof and rounded contours. On the opposite, great battlements, like one might command an army from, and a great bulbous dome whose metallic roof glinted dully in the waning light.

Mila had the sudden impression of falling, as if she looked up at the interior of that dark dome, and sank, down, down, into darkness—

Diablo shook his head with a nervous whinny and Mila gripped his reins. The house had twice unmoored her from herself, and she wanted to be annoyed, as if her mind were a wayward child she could scold into composure. But the lines of the house gripped her with dread she couldn't dispel.

Gravenhearst was momentarily obscured as they passed the massive pine tree, its limbs trembling with the changing air. Clouds were racing heavy and dark against the sky, only the topmost layers stark white and sharp. A slow rumble of thunder boiled in the distance, and the August heat cracked under a sudden gust of cold wind. Mila could smell ozone and pine needles, and she knew a storm was coming.

She steadied herself against the warmth of Diablo's withers, her fingers tense against his glossy hide.

Gravenhearst was directly before them, rising toward the sky. Green lawns and trimmed hedges spread out like an ocean, giving way to elaborate gardens and sculpted topiaries, and beyond—a sprawling structure that looked like stables.

Groomsmen and servants were lining the drive up ahead, a row of men in dark suits or worker's browns.

No women, she thought, her stomach twisting oddly.

Urging Diablo forward toward the looming face of Gravenhearst, Mila wrestled with the feeling that this line of somber-faced men was not right. There were always women on staff. *Where are all the women?* She glanced at Wynn, but her sister's eyes were large with the magnitude of the place.

The carriage stopped and Mila pulled Diablo up short beside. He stamped nervously as a groom came forward, and Mila raised a hand to warn the man off.

"Master Deemus."

Mila looked up.

The man who'd spoken was slowly descending the front steps of Gravenhearst, hands clasped at his back. Mila fought the unreasonable urge to recoil. He was middle-aged, with an unremarkable face, and he wore a dark suit and high white collar of good quality, but rumpled. His hair, too, had a messy quality, as though he'd taken off a hat worn for too long, the locks around his forehead kinked and fluttering in the wind.

Something about his eyes set Mila's skin crawling. They were empty, hungry things, and Mila felt bile rising in her stomach as her own eyes caught in the man's gaze for a long instant; he broke the moment and looked to Deemus.

Andrew Deemus descended the carriage and offered his hand to Ada, then to Wynn.

The rumpled man inclined his head once to Ada, then returned his attention to his new master. "I am Asher. I was your uncle's personal secretary and head of staff. It is my privilege to serve the house of Deemus once more." He bowed low. "Welcome to Gravenhearst."

Walking through the massive double doors was like walking into a forest of stone. Buff-toned columns of fluted granite rose to great heights like ancient oaks, resolving into intricate Corinthian entablature, and ribs of carved stone rose to arc into the upper stories high above.

Mila gripped Wynn's hand tight as they tread the chessboard foyer of charcoal and bone flagstones, and as the scale of the place spread out, seemingly endless around her, she tipped her head back and turned, trying to still the unnerving sensation that the place grew larger as she watched. The crumbling and age-stained figures of marble women stared down at her from sculptural niches, their nude forms lit by dusty grey light.

"Andrew, it's magnificent!"

Mila turned to see her mother staring rapturously about the cavernous foyer, her face lit with delight. Mila couldn't remember the last time she'd seen her mother look so happy. It made her stomach hollow, that look of pure joy transforming her mother's face to something she barely recognized.

You've never looked that happy about either of us, Mila thought, squeezing Wynn's hand. For a moment, her father's face flashed before her, his eyes lit with love and pride, his lips quirked in that soft half-smile he reserved just for her—

"Yes, magnificent," Deemus said quietly, his eyes distant. "Yes, well, I have things to attend to."

Asher stepped smoothly to his side. "Yes, Sir. Bennet is head porter. He will see that the ladies are settled and the belongings put away."

A middle-aged man stepped forward at these words. He wore a simple dark suit, and his square face was expressionless beneath heavy brows. He bowed once, and Deemus nodded his approval, then Deemus and Asher turned and strode from the foyer, their footsteps echoing across the flagstones.

"This way, my lady," Bennet said, gesturing. Mila thought her mother looked unnerved by Deemus's abrupt departure, but Ada recovered her poise, head tipping with a haughty nod.

"Come along, Winters, Amahdi!" she ordered.

Mila looked back to the front door. Winters was giving instructions to several men about the luggage, but Zahra . . .

She was standing stock-still.

Her head was tipped down and her hands floated at her sides, like someone trying to catch their balance on a rolling ship. Her lips were parted, like she'd just drawn a quick breath, and the lines of her cheekbones were stone. Then her whole body shuddered, and she clutched her wrist with a desperate instinctive motion. Mila recognized the frantic twisting of the girl's fingers working the knots of the prayer cord, over and over, her lips silently mimicking the gesture.

A chill swept Mila's spine.

Zahra's eyes lifted and met Mila's. The moment stretched thin between them, an unspoken horror radiating from Zahra's eyes that Mila felt right down to her bones.

"Mila!" Ada's voice cracked through the echoing foyer.

Mila turned, heart pounding. Her mother was already on the stairs, annoyance on her features. Mila swallowed hard and pulled Wynn close. She looked back to Zahra, but the girl wouldn't meet her eyes.

Her mother was waiting.

Wynn's hand tight in Mila's, they ascended the grand staircase of stone and wrought iron. Windows towered up at the landing before them, and then the staircase branched up and back on one side only, curving to the second-floor mezzanine. Mila glanced behind and saw that Winters and Zahra were following now, several porters trailing after them laden with luggage. Zahra still wouldn't look at her.

Wynn's eyes were huge as she stared at the ceiling. Stone ribs arched to sharp points like in a cathedral, and the intervening panels were painted a deep teal, like the sky just before dawn; golden stars were scattered across the blue depths. The walls beneath the painted sky were a brilliant red, and golden symbols were picked out in the same metallic foil.

Wynn reached out a finger to touch a single golden star.

"Wynn!" Ada's voice came sharp from the stairs above them.

Wynn shrank against Mila, her hand returning to her side. Bennet waited, his face expressionless. His manner was courteous, yet it struck Mila as strangely cold, as if their opinion of him were completely irrelevant. It was inexplicable behavior for a servant; Mila didn't like it.

He turned and Ada continued after him.

Mila and Wynn followed them to the second-floor mezzanine and through a pointed-arch doorway, leaving the brilliantly colored stairway behind.

A long passage stretched before them.

Mila's feet sank into thick carpet the color of eggplant; gaslight flickered intermittently against the wood-paneled walls. Portraits stared down, their ornate frames alternating with tall inset mirrors. Mila caught a glimpse of herself as she passed a glass.

I look like a ghost, she thought, her pale face and hair stark against the black of the hall. The thought echoed in her mind and she struggled not to stumble, as though Gravenhearst had plucked itself up from a long sleep and shifted lazily, then settled down again like a waiting beast.

"It's easy to become lost in Gravenhearst." Bennet's voice startled her, and she gripped Wynn's hand a little tighter. "So the family rooms are all situated here, just off the main stair."

He opened a polished ebony door and gestured to Ada.

The room was a sumptuous palace of red: elegant couches upholstered in scarlet velvet, the floor carpeted in a mottled pattern of mid- and deep-toned red. The walls, too, were upholstered in dark crimson, and drapes in a heavy purplish claret muddled the light from the tall windows. It was oppressive to Mila's mind, but she could tell her mother approved of the obvious expense evident in every surface: the gleaming mahogany furniture, golden trinkets scattered about, the queen-like scale of the place.

And mirrors. Everywhere, ornate mirrors.

Ada worked her gloves off with a satisfied twist of her lips, and held them out beside her without concern. Winters took them.

"I'll have tea now," Ada said, making a slow circuit of the room, her peacock skirts brushing across the carpet with a shushing sound.

"Certainly, Madam," Bennet said. He nodded at one of the porters. The man nodded in return and left. "This way," Bennet said.

Mila realized he was speaking to her. She glanced at Zahra; the girl's face was grave, distracted, but she followed them down the hall without being told. Mila couldn't shake the disconcerting sensation that Zahra was listening for something no one else could hear.

Bennet led them to the adjacent room and Mila felt an internal pulse of relief that it looked nothing like her mother's. The carpet was ivory and grey, and elaborate, bone-white moldings arched in curving panels around the room, rising up to a ceiling like a lavishly iced cake. The walls were papered in charcoal grey and decorated with a silvery metallic pattern that caught the dim light.

Mila walked slowly through the sitting room to the heavily can-opied bed. It was tucked in a curtained niche, and the bed itself was upholstered to match the drapes.

"Miss Wynn's chamber is next door," Bennet said.

"Wynn will stay with me," Mila said, still looking about, trying to reconcile herself to the thought of waking in this room.

"I'm sure that—"

"She will stay here," Mila cut him off, turning abruptly.

He hesitated, the light catching the greying peaks of his hair, and then nodded. "There's a bellpull just there"—he indicated a rope next to the bed—"should you need anything. Someone will escort you to dinner or the drawing room, so you don't become lost."

Mila stared at him, silent.

He nodded once and left.

Mila looked to Zahra. "What was that?" she demanded.

"What?" Zahra said, her face flashing quickly, something uncertain in her dark eyes.

"I saw the look on your face."

"You saw nothing," Zahra said.

"I saw—"

"You don't know what you speak of!" Zahra shouted.

Mila blinked. The sheer shock of being shouted at by a servant would have been odd enough, but the look in Zahra's eyes was unnerving her most of all.

Fear and pain and fury.

Zahra turned and stormed from the room.

What in the world just happened? Zahra's reaction was too strange, too *furious*. Servants didn't behave like that.

Who is this girl?

"Mother would throw her out for speaking to you like that,"

Wynn said, as though she couldn't decide whether that was the proper course of action to be taken.

"I don't care how she speaks to me as long as she tells me the truth," Mila said. "Don't tell Mother." She speared Wynn with a sharp look. Wynn nodded.

Mila went to the window, a tall mullioned thing, deeply inset in stone. She peered out through the lead joins at a black-and-navy sky. Beneath her window, gravel paths lined intricate formations of clipped hedges and sculpted topiaries, and beyond that, she could just make out the long, low form of the stables. Gravenhearst was large and silent around her.

It's just a house, Mila told herself, fighting to regain control. Her reactions to the place were not normal, were not *her*. *It's just new and strange*, she thought firmly. *Don't let the superstitions of a* servant *turn your head*.

Thunder cracked, and a moment later, fingers of light pierced the sky, so bright they burned afterimages into her vision. Rain poured from the sky as though a great hand had slit the clouds with a knife. Wind pressed against the glass panes, rattling the casements, and Mila thought of the hundreds of windows she'd seen staring out from the face of Gravenhearst—the chimneys, gables, and towers that rose up from the roof like the skyline of a city.

We're inside the belly of a beast.

For a moment, she felt pure panic—she was miniscule in the shadow of a monster.

It's just a house, she rebuked herself again. *It's a house, and you are a devil.*

She turned to Wynn, heart pounding in her chest.

"Let's go exploring."

13

Mila

THE LONG, DARK HALLWAY WAS SILENT.

A large oil portrait glared down at Mila, facing her door. The young man was blond, his face less refined than Andrew Deemus's—something almost petulant in the set of his chin—but the full lips and arched eyebrows were unmistakable.

Mila moved closer to read the engraved plate at the bottom of the portrait: "Jacob Deemus, 1799."

There was something cruel about his eyes, the cold gleam at once hungry and dismissive. Mila felt an intense wave of dislike for the man and moved on to join Wynn in examining the next portrait.

Just as big, but less showy, this one read: "Kepler Theodore Deemus, 1762."

It was a dark painting—moody brown background with no detail—but the face was magnetic: ageless brown eyes, high cheekbones, and a shock of messy dark hair. He seemed unlike his haughty Deemus descendants—something more of the poet than the aristocrat about him—but he had the same full lips and high cheekbones, and there was something powerful about his gaze. As though the man had gazed upon immensities and did not quite belong in this world anymore.

The effect was slightly unnerving, and Mila moved back. "This way," she said to Wynn, nodding in the opposite direction from their mother's room and the main stairwell.

They walked the passage together, passing more mirrors and portraits, till they turned a corner and traveled yet another hallway just like the others. Mila felt a fleeting sense of vertigo but pushed it down, scanning the hall. A passage branched off a little ways down, and when they reached it, she saw a rounded stairwell crafted from stone, the entrance seeming to call to her mind. She hesitated, but Wynn pulled her forward eagerly.

The descent fell in a tight spiral, curving around a central pillar, with only the narrowest of wall-slits cut for light. Mila kept one hand on the wall and Wynn did the same, but though the stone remained still under her fingertips, the dark pillar seemed to twist in the shadows of her vision. Mila fought the feeling that she might come upon a silent figure at the next blind turn.

"Stay close," she said to Wynn, and then felt irritated. The house had gotten the best of her again.

She sped up her steps. They should have passed the next floor by now—should be in the cellars for all the time they had spent traveling *down*. When they finally reached an exit, she fought a shaky breath and took in the large gallery that stretched forever.

The gas wasn't lit in this room, and the only light came from the windows periodically cut from the outside wall. They had clearly come down only a single level, and Mila strangled the impression that the stairs must have lengthened into some other *non-place* for them to have gone on so long.

This place is playing with us, she thought, then immediately rebuked herself for such nonsense.

The storm was worsening; rain slapped against the glass and a flash of lightning leapt across the polished parquet floor, throwing the edges of the gallery into stark relief. The barrel-vaulted ceiling was painted in elaborate panels, and the walls were lined with books and columns, punctuated by mirrors on one side and windows on the other.

"We'll have lots to read," Mila said quietly, slowing to study the spines of the many volumes.

"Look," Wynn said, pointing down the hall at a standing globe, its surface lit almost ghost-like by the opposite window. She ran to it and spun the sphere hard. A satisfied smile appeared on her face at the creaking sound it made.

Mila investigated a table full of glass cloches, the skeletons of birds and small creatures trapped beneath. Her own face flashed and hovered in the multiple mirrors that covered the wall, and she had trouble shaking the overwhelming sensation that someone was watching her.

She turned and looked about, but they were alone.

The next gallery was marked by two immense pillars decorated with the writhing figures of extruding stone skeletons. More dusty mirrors covered the walls, and carved statues of female figures enclosed in cloudy glass cases littered the cabinets and pedestals scattered across the length of the room.

The place felt unaccountably like a tomb.

"Lots to sketch," Mila said, glancing to Wynn. Her sister looked thoroughly fascinated by it all, and Mila felt a pang of relief that at least Wynn was not scared.

Another flash of lightning skirted the walls and Mila bit back a gasp at the sight of hands reaching down toward her. She grabbed at Wynn, but then her breath returned as she realized what she'd seen.

Two alabaster arms carved from stone.

They reached down from the stone moldings, one hand clutching the pillar, the other one strectching toward her, like whoever they belonged to was trapped just out of sight.

"Mother would *not* like that," Wynn said with authority.

"No," Mila said. "She wouldn't."

I don't like it, she thought.

She quickened her pace and left the gallery behind, entering an intersection of passageways. There was another spiral staircase here, this one of wood and much larger than the last. The stairs circled around a central column cut with notches—the source of the dim light—and Mila peered through one; the column itself was hollow and seemed to stretch upward forever. She could just make out the shape of a descending staircase through a notch on the opposite side of the column, and Mila realized that it was not one staircase circling the hollow column, but two, partners who would never meet in an endless dance.

How far do they go? she wondered, hesitating on the landing.

"Let's go to the top!" Wynn said, her voice strangely foreign in the close space. Mila tasted dead wood on her tongue, as though she were stuck in the husk of a giant tree, horribly alive as it decayed from the inside.

Wynn pelted ahead and Mila grabbed at her cumbersome skirts, propelled by a grim determination to keep her sister in sight. The dark stair seemed to turn around her, her footsteps and breath too loud, and then she burst out to the top and found Wynn standing openmouthed in awe.

They were at the top of a wide balcony, and stretching out below them was a derelict theatre stage, the likes of which Mila had never seen. A crumbling and peeling ceiling of burgundy and gold stretched above her, sweeping down to an enormous gold-framed proscenium that towered many stories high. It framed a shattered wreckage of beams, metal struts, and fallen stone where the backstage should have been. Equally ornate gilded theatre boxes of purple and gold slanted back from the proscenium, looking down over strewn and battered theatre seats scattered like broken teeth.

"I could hide in here and Mother would *never* find me," Wynn said, a savage smile lighting her face.

"Wynn, you must promise me never to come here alone," Mila said, grasping Wynn's shoulder. "It's wonderful, but it's falling apart. It's *dangerous*."

Wynn swept her cool gaze over Mila.

"I'm not stupid," she said.

The wave of panic swept Mila again, stronger this time.

"Wynn you must *promise* me!" She dropped to her knees, fingers digging into Wynn's skin. "After Father—" She shook her head. "I'd die if I lost you."

Wynn's eyes widened. Her lips parted, and she stood frozen for a moment, then she fell forward against Mila, clutching her fiercely.

"We have to take care of each other, Wynn," Mila whispered. "We're a team. They can't break us if we stay together."

"I promise," Wynn said.

Mila breathed in her sister, jamming the sick feeling back down in her gut.

What kind of house had Deemus brought them to? A palace that gave way to wreckage? Perhaps he wasn't as wealthy as he appeared. The petty reality of the thought was calming, and Mila rose to her feet, surveying the path at her side. "Let's go that way," she said, pointing toward a door at the far end of the balcony.

Beams creaked underfoot as they traversed the moldy purple carpet, the thin gaslight wavering in the golden sconces. The light flared as they passed, like a sudden breath, and the hairs on Mila's neck prickled as they passed into a rounded foyer. A large staircase curved down, encrusted in dust and grime and animal droppings. The walls, once white, were almost black with thick stains that bled across the paneling. The ceiling had the look of a half-healed scab, crusty and discolored.

Mila tested a stair; it was filthy, but sound.

They descended the stairs to the next landing, then the next, and farther until they came to another foyer whose red plaster walls were flaking away like great globs of dried blood. There was a black door near the single lit sconce, the light of which reflected off the gleaming trim. It creaked as Mila pushed it open.

A narrow corridor of black stretched before them: paneled walls with curious metal symbols set at intervals, and a stained red carpet at their feet. They reached the end and turned left at the only doorway. An iron staircase switchbacked down into what looked like a wall of books.

They hurried down the clanging stair and into the book-lined niche to find yet another passage, and then they were through it and standing in a lavish library of warm wood, a golden ceiling soaring above them. They were on the ground level of the immaculate space, the lower cabinets dust-free behind glass, the second level wrapped with a narrow catwalk and accessed by an iron ladder.

"Why would this be in the middle of a broken-down part of the house?" Wynn said, looking about her, dark eyes keen.

"That is an excellent question," Mila said, opening one of the glass cabinets. "Maybe because someone's trying to hide it." She scanned the titles, trying to get a sense of the subject matter. "I can't tell if these are scientific or religious texts," she said, frowning at the ancient spines: *A Chymicall Treatise of Arnoldus de Nova Villa*; *Apollogia Alchymiae*; *The Practise of Mary the Prophetess in the Alchymicall Art*; *Of the Division of Chaos*.

She seized *The Mirror of Alchimy*.

Alchimy is a Corporal Science simply composed of one and by one, natu-rally conjoining things more precious, by knowledge and effect, and con-verting them by a natural commixtion into a better kind.

She scanned the brief text. "It talks about minerals, metals, working the fire . . ." she trailed off, struggling to make sense of the strange text. She skipped ahead:

I will therefore now deliver unto you a great and hidden secret. One part is to be mixed with a thousand of the next body, and let all this be surely put into a fit vessel, and set it in a furnace of fixation, first with a lent fire, and afterward increasing the fire for three days, till they be inseparably joined together.

"I can't tell if this is philosophy, or chemistry, or madness," she said, picking another, very thin and labeled "Everburning Lights of Trithemius".

Two unquenchable eternall lights are founde and to be seen hearin . . . this famous Maus Trittemius . . . hath done much good with his artes, not mingled with divilish worcke, as some malicious men doe accuse his, butt he did knowe all what was done in the world of what he desireth by the starres of ministerie, he hath also tolde of things to come manie times.

Mila read on, her skin prickling at the mention of "devilish work."

The people of that castel tolde the Emperor that they had seene continually a lightning in that place, licke a lampe in a church. Wherefore this Emperor lefft the light years still burning wheare it shall burne still at this daye, which is a great secret in this worlde.

Wynn was pressed close against her, reading also. "They made a light that never went out?" she said.

"And had knowledge of whatever he wished," Mila said grimly, passing the tiny folio to her sister. She plucked another, no more than a page pressed between two thin covers, labeled "Verse on the Threefold Sophic Fire." She slid it into the waistband of her skirt, smoothing her jacket down over it.

"Can you see it?" she asked.

Wynn looked up from the book and shook her head after a moment's study.

"I don't like this," Mila said. She strode to another cabinet, scanning for anything that would either confirm or deny her suspicions.

Forty-Eight Angelic Keys caught her eye.

It was very old, and the pages released a musty odor as they creaked resentfully under her hands.

I am therefore to instruct and inform you, according to your Doctrine delivered, which is contained in 49 Tables. In 49 voices, or callings: which are the Natural Keyes to open those, not 49 but 48 (for One is not to be opened) Gates of Understanding, whereby you shall have knowledge to move every Gate.

Mila flipped ahead quickly, her unease growing, eyes passing over a series of squares and charts, strange symbols and words that looked like no language she'd ever seen.

"I think we should leave," Mila said, her skin crawling. "These are the sort of books people get in trouble for owning." She put the book back, her heart straining against the boning of her corset. She looked to Wynn. "We can't tell anyone we've seen this place."

Wynn nodded.

They made their way back to the staircase, then passed once more through the narrow black hallway.

"Maybe Mr. Deemus doesn't know the room is there," Wynn said.

"Maybe," Mila said, thinking. Deemus hadn't been in this country since he was a very young man. And she wasn't even sure if he'd ever lived at Gravenhearst. Zahra had said he'd had a falling-out with his uncle. Maybe the uncle had been the one with the dangerous hobby.

They began their ascent up the long putrefying stairs that led back to the theatre.

"A room like that . . ." Mila said. "It would take years to amass that kind of collection. Who knows *whom* the books belong to? Maybe they've just been forgotten."

But the words felt like a lie as she said them. It wasn't right that the gas was burning so far into the house, in places that had clearly been unused for years. It wasn't right that the gaping mouth of that derelict theatre was lit with thin dancing flames that made the proscenium glitter even as it fell into decay.

Mila suddenly wanted nothing more than to be back in that grey bedchamber with Wynn, to tuck themselves behind the bed curtains and wait for tomorrow, for the storm to cease. She wanted to wake and find this was all a terrible nightmare. She wanted to run to her father's stables and work the horses, break the new colt, hear her father laugh as she sprang from the rebellious creature's back as it tried to roll, then jump right back on again before it could buck away. She wanted the dust and manure of the training ring and the voices of the grooms who worked the stables and her father's proud eyes upon her.

She hurried through the doorway to the balcony and her heart dropped out.

The theatre was gone.

It was just a shadowed room, small and empty, and at its center sat a glass jar with a single disembodied flame.

14

Mila

MILA STARED AT THE IMPOSSIBLE FLAME, TRYING NOT TO panic, but Wynn made a small sound like a wounded animal, and Mila grabbed her hand, and they rushed from the room.

There was no doorway on the landing anymore. Nowhere to go.

Down the stairs.

They stumbled their way down, each landing leaving nothing: no options, nowhere to run. Only the last red foyer and the black hallway remained.

The black hallway.

The black door was still there, and Mila threw it open, her mind screaming that there was nowhere to go but back to the library, her body demanding that they get as far away from that unearthly light as possible.

The walls were taller, brushing Mila's shoulders as she dragged Wynn behind her. They reached the end, but the doorway no longer led to the left, but the right. Another long hall.

A door.

They rushed for it, and it wouldn't give for a moment, the handle petrified under Mila's throttling hands; then it burst open and they spilled out into a wide corridor, and Mila's heart beat again as she recognized the purple-black carpet of the main hall-way, the elegant paneled walls lined with portraits and mirrors. She looked down its length and saw the stone spiral staircase that had taken them to the first shadowed gallery of books and statues.

"This way," she said, forcing her voice to obey.

This monstrous house would *not* break her.

They turned away from the stairs and followed the passage, and when they rounded the corner, Mila's chest cracked with sharp relief.

It was their hallway.

She threw open the door to their room and pushed Wynn before her. She pressed her back against the door, eyes closing, the sound of the storm overwhelming the noisy clamor of her heart.

She opened her eyes.

Wynn was sitting on the pale blue couch, knees pulled up to her chest. Her dark eyes raced and she was biting her lower lip so hard Mila feared she'd draw blood.

"We're all right," Mila said. Wynn didn't respond.

Finally Wynn spoke. "That wasn't right."

"No," Mila said, pushing herself off the door, pulling the folio from under her jacket, and dropping it absentmindedly into the nearest drawer. She walked the room's length, then back again. Her reflection flashed in and out of the mirrors as she circuited the room, trying to find an answer, a scrap of logic that made some sense.

"That light was just like the book said." Wynn's fingers dug into her knees, scratching at the fabric of her dress. "An eternal light."

"We don't know that," Mila said quickly.

"It had no wick, no fuel! It wasn't right!"

No, it wasn't right. *Nothing* was right. It was as if the house knew what they had read in that room—knew and was taunting them.

"From now on, we don't make a move without each other," Mila said, her throat horribly dry. "We need to watch and listen. We need to understand what's going on here."

"We can't tell Mother," Wynn said, her voice breaking.

"No, we certainly can't," Mila said. "She'd think we were lying, or mad. Neither one helps us."

There was a knock at the door and Mila tensed. "Yes?"

The door opened. It was Asher.

"It is time for dinner," he said mildly. His hair and suit still had the strangely rumpled quality that seemed so at odds with his precise manner, and his voice felt thin, as though he were keeping its true tone concealed.

Mila realized he was waiting for her to acknowledge him.

"Yes," she said, pushing down the repulsion she felt toward the man. "Dinner." She looked to Wynn, who stood, and they followed him from the room.

He led them down the hall to the beautiful blue-and-red staircase, then across the grand foyer and its checkerboard floor. The house suddenly seemed almost ordinary in its ornateness—nothing strange or unnatural. They passed through an enormous sitting room, the low gaslight making great shapes of the carved mirrors and hulking paintings. Thunder rumbled low outside, and Mila heard the tinkle of crystal shivering as Asher led them into the dining room.

A long table filled the space, three great crystal chandeliers glinting overhead. Andrew Deemus sat at the head of the table, Ada seated to his left, her white neck stiff and straight. Asher pulled out the chair on Deemus's right and Mila sat, the feel of Deemus's eyes heavy on her skin. She met his gaze and his languid eyes gleamed with amusement.

Mila studied the room as Asher seated Wynn at her side. The long walls were mostly gilded, and ornate columns bedecked in pale champagne foil rose at intervals. The far wall behind Deemus was painted in an indistinct mural of sea green, the light from the chandeliers was pale, and the whole room had the quality of being underwater.

Four serving men moved forward with silver-domed plates.

"A feast for our first night," Deemus said as the covers were removed.

The scent of game hen and truffle-roasted potatoes filled the room and Mila's mouth watered despite her fear. She'd eaten almost nothing all day. A servant poured her a glass of dark wine, and as she picked up her knife and fork, she could almost believe that all of it—the theatre, the impossible flame, the shifting black hallway—had been just an awful nightmare.

"Did you enjoy the library?" Deemus asked.

Mila's fork froze halfway to her mouth. She looked at him, and he surveyed her with a quiet smile on his full lips. She lowered her fork. She could feel Wynn beside her, breath held.

"Wynn liked the globe," Mila said, letting her lips slip into a polite smile. "I've been meaning to improve her geography, so it will be very helpful indeed." She took a small sip of wine. "And the statues will be lovely for sketching. I do so need to give more care to my drawing— Wynn is already more skilled than I."

Deemus smiled. "I'm pleased there is so much to interest you."

"How did you know we were in the library?" Mila asked, keeping her tone light.

"Oh, one of the servants," Deemus said with an easy smile.

Mila nodded and took a bite of game hen.

"And the books?" Deemus said, leaning back casually in his chair. "They were to your satisfaction?"

"Books are always to my satisfaction," Mila said, her blood kicking up in her ears.

He knows, she thought. Even though it was impossible. *He knows we were in that secret room.*

He smiled again and nodded. "You will need to take care," he said, his elegant fingers toying with the gold-edged rim of his wineglass. "This place is a labyrinth. I'd hate for you to be frightened."

Ada's eyes were narrowed, and Mila could tell her mother was skating on the edge of rage with this subtle thing that Deemus had been doing all day—speaking to Mila and not to her. *This man is dangerous*, Mila thought.

"It takes a lot to frighten me," Mila said.

Deemus nodded, and Mila knew that he'd taken the words for a challenge.

You won't break me, she thought.

That evening, Mila knocked on her mother's door, heart frozen against her ribs. She was already bending the rule she'd set for Wynn, leaving her alone in their room like this, but she needed to speak with their mother—needed to *try*.

Ada was seated at her dressing table, removing the wealth of jewels Deemus had heaped on her. She stared at Mila's reflection in the mirror for a moment, then went back to unclipping her earrings.

Mila eyed the wedding dress, displayed like a ghostly apparition on a dress form in the corner of the room—the symbol of the life that was rushing toward them, unstoppable. She felt the moment rise up around her, futile, doomed. But she *couldn't* stay silent. Not when every inch of her was screaming that this place was wrong, Deemus was wrong, this life in front of them was *wrong*.

"Mother," she said hesitantly, "I'm afraid."

Ada sighed, exasperated. "Don't behave like a *child*, Mila."

"There's something not right about this house."

"Stop it."

"There's something not right with Andrew Deemus."

"That's *enough!*" Ada yelled, getting to her feet.

"He hardly speaks to you," Mila said, trying to lever into the weak spots in her mother's armor. "He dismisses you."

"I don't *need* him to speak to me," Ada said, her eyes flashing steel, jaw lifting. "I have secured us a *home*, money that won't run out. We don't *need* him to do a thing for us. He can do as he pleases as long as *we* are secure." She sat back down at the vanity, a little sneer curving her lips. "Men need to feel important, Mila. They need to feel like they have the upper hand. You give them that, you can get almost anything you need from them." Their eyes met in the mirror. "You would do well to remember that."

"I won't bend my neck to make him feel better," Mila snarled.

"You will do what I tell you!" Ada shouted, hurling a crystal bottle with an abrupt swing. It smashed into the wall beside Mila, little bits of glass embedding in her skirts. She stared down her mother, feeling her heart turn black within her.

"You deserve every bit of pain he heaps on you," Mila said. She turned and left, rage shaking her throat. The door pulled shut under her hand and she stood for a moment, trying to stow the anger before she returned to Wynn. The hallway was a vast corridor of darkness, the gas lamps like nearly extinguished fireflies in the black. She let the immensity of the house build up around her, the useless feelings slipping away into the night.

There was the sound of a door opening and she quickly pressed herself back against the wall, adrenaline spiking.

Deemus exited a room far down the hall. He turned and locked the door, pocketing the key. Standing before the door, his hand slid up over the paneling like a caress. Something about the expression on his face turned Mila's stomach.

He turned and headed farther down the passage.

Mila followed silently.

He passed the length, the passage opening up on one side to the stone hall far below. Finally he reached the end of the long hall and opened a door; Mila caught a glimpse of an opulent room of dark wood with a massive desk and, behind it, an ornately carved golden mirror.

Mila's breath caught at the sound of an angry female voice, a figure running from a corridor intersecting the hall.

Zahra.

Deemus turned, and Mila recognized fury in the set of his shoulders, his hands fisted at his sides. He grabbed Zahra by the elbow and hissed something at her that Mila couldn't make out. He forced her into the room and slammed the door behind them.

Mila streaked forward, crossing the passage silently. She pressed herself next to the door; heated voices were muffled within.

"*This place is wrong!*" she heard Zahra cry out. "You think I can't see? I am my mother's daughter. Or have you forgotten?" The next moment there was the familiar crack of a palm striking flesh. Deemus's voice was low, too low to hear, and a roll of thunder crested around the house.

The door opened and she was face-to-face with Zahra.

They stared at each other, and Zahra quickly pulled the door closed before Deemus could see them.

Zahra's large eyes were wide and her lip was split. Her breath hitched and she looked around quickly. She seemed on the verge of saying something, but then she hissed through her teeth and shoved past Mila without a word. Mila grabbed her arm, and Zahra turned, knocking Mila hard against the wall.

"Tell me what's going on here!" Mila demanded.

"*Do not speak!*" Zahra whispered, her face a mix of panic and rage. Her fingers dug into Mila's shoulders, and her eyes flicked to Deemus's room, then back to Mila. "*Be quiet,*" she breathed, her expression freezing Mila in place, puncturing her anger. Mila swallowed despair, caught in the urgency that vibrated through the strange girl. She released Zahra's arm, and Zahra drew her own hands back. She stared at Mila a moment, a terrible look on her face, then shook her head once and walked away.

Mila took a shuddering breath, collecting her wits.

She was on her own.

She retraced her steps back down the hall, pausing a moment before the door Deemus had locked. It was unremarkable—dark polished wood, just like the others. She bent to the keyhole for a moment but could see nothing.

She stood, the back of her neck prickling with the sensation that she was being watched. She stared into the darkness at either end of the hall, but she saw nothing.

She went back to her room.

Wynn's breath was soft against her in the darkness, her sister's fingers curled in Mila's long hair, deep in slumber. The storm screamed against the windows and Mila stared into the shadows of the canopy above her.

Her father had loved storms, even though they made the horses nervous. He'd said they made him feel small and unimportant. Mila had thought that sounded like a bad thing, but her father stared up at the stars and said he liked to feel the weight of his own insignificance. "The heavens are vast and we're so small. The storms make me feel that, Mila," he'd said. "They make me feel like maybe my sins don't matter so very much."

Mila swallowed tears and shifted her head closer to Wynn.

You left me, she thought. *And you didn't come back.*

That sin mattered very much.

It had all fallen apart so quickly. Sixteen years on a country estate with the sun and the sky and the horses—her mother's quiet disapproval in the house, but her father's jubilant pride in the stables. Those stables had been her whole world.

Until the night everything changed.

She'd been sent out to find him late one night by her mother. She'd run to the stables, expecting to find him fussing over the horse that had been favoring its front right hoof. But she'd heard a quick rough sound, like someone shoved against the boards of a stall, then a gasp like pain, but different. She'd turned the corner, her breath stuck.

And then she saw.

Her father, his back pressed to the stall, his hands tangled in another man's shirt. His mouth was open to the furious onslaught of the man's lips. A throaty sound fell between them and her father turned, swapping their places with a quick movement, and she saw the man's face—David, a stable groom who'd worked for them for years. His lips curved around a smile, and he leaned his head back with a little groan as John Kenton pressed his lips against the line of his neck.

David's hand grabbed at her father's thigh, and Mila backed away, her heart seizing at the sound that escaped her father's lips. Then John's eyes fluttered open and he saw her.

Passion and hunger slid from his features and he stepped back from David, his eyes lost, like he couldn't believe the moment was real, like her presence had tilted the world from its place in the heavens. David jerked around to look and his face went slack, his fingers instinctively reaching out toward Mila's father. His hand settled on

John Kenton's shirt, like someone grasping a lifeline, but then he seemed to catch himself and drew his hand back, his eyes wide and pale under blonde brows.

Mila stared, frozen.

A broken sound fell from her father's throat, and her heart twisted at the pain on his face, at the pain caught between the two men.

She took a step forward. Her father's chest shuddered and his hands lifted, clutching at his dark hair like the motion could keep him from going to pieces.

She took another step forward.

His face crumpled.

She took a final step.

"Please don't tell your mother," he said, his face wrung with quiet desperation.

"I won't," she said, and then she didn't know what to do. She looked at David, saw the tears sharp in his eyes, that easy smile she'd seen a hundred times obliterated beneath a grimace of pain. "I won't," she said again, and then she turned and walked away, feelings she didn't have words for clawing up her throat.

The next day, David was gone, and her father didn't leave his room. Soon after that, his trips to London started—first for a day, then longer. He'd return with bloodshot eyes and pallid skin, his high cheekbones clammy under sickly sweat, dark shadows carving his eyes deeper. He was falling apart, and she could do nothing.

David had gone to work at another farm, and when two weeks went by without word from her father, Mila sought David out. She knew she'd seen something real between them, something more powerful and alive than she'd ever seen between her father and mother.

But David had looked at her with eyes worn hollow and dead, and she'd known then that he didn't know where John was. She'd left and never gone back.

Her father had come back once more before the end.

His eyes had been wild and he'd laughed at Ada while she screamed at him in the foyer, calling him terrible names, threatening terrible things. Wynn had tried to run down to him, but Mila stopped her, seared by the ghastly look in John Kenton's eyes, like he wasn't their father anymore, like he'd lost the thing that made him theirs, made him *himself*. He'd stared up at them as Mila gripped Wynn tight, his eyes broken. *He's going to leave me*, Mila thought. *He's going to leave and never come back.*

And that's exactly what happened.

You left us and now I don't know what to do, Mila thought, the darkness of the room—of the whole monstrous house—pressing down on her. Lightning flashed at the window; for an instant, the foil pattern in the wallpaper lit up like a thousand staring eyes, then fell dark again.

Mila pushed up from the bed, anger shaking her limbs. Wynn mumbled something, but Mila felt a desperate need to be free, to not have the weight of the world pressing her down, not have her little sister attached to her hip. She wanted to be selfish and careless and heartless. She wanted to run through the halls screaming at the top of her lungs. She wanted to set the place on fire and not stop until the whole world was ablaze.

She wanted to be *herself*—horribly, wonderfully herself.

She pressed her fingers to the cold windowpane and stared out into the night.

Lightning flashed again, and she saw a figure dart across the gravel path toward the stables. Just a glimpse, but she was sure they'd been carrying something large. She stared into the black, her eyes straining to make shapes from nothing. No one would go out on a night like this unless something was very, *very* wrong. Thunder cracked, tugging at the space in Mila's chest, and then a sheet of lightning covered the gardens in light. Mila stood, her heart filling her throat, the roar of the downpour devouring all sound.

And then Mila heard it.

The shriek of a horse, the pounding rhythm of hooves flying against gravel. The sound neared, then passed.

A finger of lightning pierced the sky, but the rider was gone.

15

Mila

MILA AWOKE TO SHOUTING.

Wynn was curled against her, still asleep in the pale morning light, and Mila slipped from the bed without waking her. She went to her door and eased it open. The hallway was dark—just the flickering glow of the gas lamps lit the way—but it was easy to see where the commotion was coming from.

"I want it found, and I want her brought back here to me!" Deemus's voice carried clearly from the far end of the hall. Several police constables stood before him. Mila slipped down the hall, keeping to the shadows. She pressed herself into a sculptural niche just in time to hear one of the constables say something about procedure.

"I don't give a damn about your procedure!" Deemus said, stepping close to the man. "She stole my property and I want it back. She has family in Willowhaven. Start with them. Arrest them if you must!"

"On what charges, Sir?" the constable said.

"*Make some up!*" Deemus yelled. The constable stepped back quickly and Mila's heart raced, a sick feeling chasing down her spine. Who was Deemus that he could speak to officers of the law like this? They feared him—his influence clearly surpassed what she'd assumed.

And her family was in his power.

Deemus and the constables were standing before the room Zahra had rushed from the day before. Mila could just make out the massive desk, and behind it an empty place on the wall: a dark spot on the wallpaper where the golden mirror had hung. Was that what he was so desperate to get back? She thought of the figure she'd seen running across the grounds in the storm, the bundle she was sure she'd glimpsed in that one instant of illumination. Had Zahra run away and stolen a *mirror*?

Mila edged back toward her room, wanting to get to cover while Deemus was still distracted with the constables. She slipped through the door and found that Wynn was awake, her knees tucked against her chest, huddled in the center of the bed.

"You said we wouldn't go anywhere without each other," Wynn said, her voice unsteady.

"I'm sorry," Mila said absently, her mind racing. "I had to find out what was happening." She went back to the bed and sat on the edge. "I think Zahra ran away last night. I think she stole a mirror and ran."

"Why a mirror?" Wynn asked, raising her eyebrows.

"I don't know. It doesn't make sense. If she wanted to run, it would be smarter not to steal anything. Now she's committed a crime, given Deemus a reason to hunt her. The only reason to do that is if the mirror was important somehow. Important to him, important to her . . . I don't know." She stood and paced the room, rubbing her hands down her neck. Last night, Zahra had shouted something at Deemus about her mother, and now Deemus had told the police the Persian servant girl he'd brought back from Venice had family in *Willowhaven* of all places? It was a bizarre coincidence. Maybe Deemus had known Zahra's mother?

The door banged open and Mila turned, the pieces of the puzzle scattering in her mind.

Winters bustled in, her face unusually grim. "Well, this is a pretty situation," she said. "Foreign trash scarpered off in the night—leave me with three ladies to attend to on a day like today."

"What is today?" Mila said uneasily.

"Master Deemus has moved up the wedding."

"To when?" Mila asked, her heart seizing.

"To today, child!" Winters snapped. Mila stared at her, too shocked to be annoyed at the uncustomarily familiar tone Winters was employing.

"Today?" she echoed.

"Yes. There's an army of servants transforming the grounds as we speak. And tonight your mother will become Mrs. Ada Deemus. And there's not a single lady's maid in this whole grand house—only men! Everywhere I look, nothing but useless men!" Winters shoved Wynn down onto the vanity seat and began aggressively brushing her hair. "The Master is sending up your gowns, so for heaven's sake, put your dressing robe on, child!"

Mila grabbed for her robe, feeling as though the house had begun to spin around her. It was all too much, too fast. She couldn't catch her footing, couldn't see how the pieces fit together. Her mother was going to wed this man and there wasn't a thing she could do. She had nothing to her name save Diablo. She could throw Wynn on his back, ride hell for leather, and leave Gravenhearst in the dust . . . but where would they go?

They were in a foreign country with no friends, no refuge to seek.

Run with Wynn and she did nothing more than condemn them to death in the streets. No one would give a strange girl with no references a job—and certainly not a girl with a younger sister in tow. Mila had seen what happened to girls who fell from society: they were lucky if they could starve as a seamstress or washwoman. More likely, they ended up in the gutter, in the brothels—used by men, despised by a society that had given them no better recourse for survival.

There was a knock, and then the bustle of men bringing in packages, spreading them like Christmas morning over the settee and tea table. Winters quickly shooed the porters out and fell to unwrapping the boxes, unearthing shoes, petticoats, swaths of satin and silk, trimmings, and baubles.

"I've hardly touched such things in my life," she said, awe coloring her voice.

Mila walked woodenly to Wynn, who was still seated at the vanity, and grasped her hand. She couldn't meet her sister's eyes in the mirror—could only think of their father.

Why didn't you come back for us? Her throat clenched, but she refused to let tears spill from her eyes. *I won't cry over you, you selfish bastard. You've left us to the devil.*

That evening, Mila descended the staircase, passing beneath the gilded foil stars, a doomed prisoner being marched to the gallows. Wynn had been hustled away a half hour earlier under instructions from Deemus, and Mila wanted nothing more than to have her sister close once again—though proximity would do little to save them from the ominous fate of this cursed wedding.

The silk crepe gown swirled up around her hips and chest like a coiling snake, a sheath of shimmering black that folded like the trumpet of a flower at her collarbone, the champagne lining dropping back over her left shoulder like a smooth petal. The skirt held her form, tight and sinuous, then opened up in a twist of cleverly manipulated bias cut to drape around her feet, trailing softly on the polished steps behind her. It was the most modern, stunning thing she'd ever worn, and she knew she looked magnificent.

The thought angered her. *I'm like a fine horse on parade*, she thought bitterly. *Curried till she shines, mane brushed and oiled, then sent out to the ring for all to see.* She paused at one of the numerous gilded mirrors and stared at herself, her fine brows sharp and arching over her pale eyes. Her lip curled as she followed the line of her collarbone, her bare shoulders, the glint of diamonds at her ears.

I hate you, she thought, glaring at herself.

A woman's face replaced her own: the mouth open in terror, the eyes wide and desperate orbs of panic. Mila felt a silent scream gust up through her own throat, her blood surging, and then the face was gone, just her own in its place, white and ghostly, breath heaving from her. Not another living soul was in sight.

Am I going mad? she thought, reaching out to steady herself on the carved edge of the pink marble table. The silence of the house was ghastly—too large, too hushed, like many ears listening—and she trembled, her ribs pressing against the straightjacket of her fine gown, too many feelings threatening to rise up and seize her, turn her useless and jabbering.

She pushed off the table and walked to the door, the windows a wall of flame-bright light before her. The iron handle turned under her shaking fingers and she stepped out onto the grand steps of Gravenhearst. The long gravel drive was a mess of footmen and livery and coaches and stamping horses. The sight of so many people made her want to scream—surrounded by people, and not a one of them would believe her if she tried to tell them what she'd just seen.

I'm alone, she thought. *I must be enough.*

The sky was awash in pink and orange, the sun dipping low on the horizon. Black-hat silhouettes and silk-rustling skirts shifted and gleamed among the clipped green hedges and sun-bleached statues that curved away from the house. Torches flared and silver-armed candelabras flickered in the evening's breath, and the voices of the guests rose up over it all, like the murmur of an ocean's swell.

The train of Mila's gown whispered over the gravel path as she approached the towering archways of shaped hedges, a cathedral entry of emerald leaves that bordered the maze of topiaries, benches, and flowers. The eyes of men and women alike passed over her, curious, cautious. Mila didn't like how their eyes leapt away when she met their gaze, or the way they seemed to hover between an admiring fascination and grim pity.

"Miss Kenton!" someone called.

She turned, and the flash of a camera burned itself into her eyes.

"For the papers, Miss," the man said.

Dear God, I don't know what to do, Mila thought.

16

Curtis

CURTIS GRIPPED THE STEERING WHEEL, THE FRAGMENTS HE'D discovered in the library flipping through his mind like a deck of cards snapping slowly. Words and images played by, mixing with the forest whispers that hissed and seethed through the open gap of the truck window. He couldn't get the girl's face out of his mind, this feeling that he knew her or wanted to know her . . . or maybe *had* known her.

He was driving slower than usual, the decaying town slipping past like a scene from an old movie—moldy façades and rust-chalked brick, dead-eyed windows like pools of oil, some boarded up, others milky-blind with grime.

This place is dying around us, he thought. It seemed appropriate somehow, like his shit life had bled through the cracks and infected everything around him.

The peaked roofline of the historic Willowhaven hospital was lit up like fire against a backdrop of sun-white clouds, and Curtis found himself changing lanes, pulling into a side street that bordered the old Victorian property. The newspaper article had called Andrew Deemus a "generous benefactor" of the hospital, and as Curtis studied the old stone building, he thought the place could probably use another wealthy patron now. The side wings of the massive property had long been closed, and just the central portion remained open.

The Deemus family was important to this town. But he'd never heard of them before. There was something off about that.

The story had implied that a bribe had been enough to smooth over the disappearance of Jacob Deemus's mother and sisters.

His eyes strayed back to the photograph of Mila on the seat beside him.

She stared out at him like she knew what it meant to be trapped in a nightmare. Dead over a hundred years, but in this moment, her eyes made him feel more understood than he had since the whispers began. That girl knew what it was to feel the walls closing in, to have no options.

The whispers dipped and swelled and his hands shook on the steering wheel.

I'm not crazy, he thought. *I'm not. This is a real mystery.*

He ran his fingers over the stiff cardboard edges of the photo. It was proof—the haunted look in her eyes stood between him and an abyss of madness. It promised that something ghastly had happened at Gravenhearst. Something that reached for him now—had thrown him on his knees in those woods and tried to destroy him.

I'm not sick. I'm not *my father.*

His eyes fell on the time display of the truck console.

Dad.

Shit. He was late—he should have been home an hour ago.

And *Sage.*

He groaned, grabbing for his phone. He'd forgotten her at school. His heart sunk at the alerts flooding his screen. She'd tried him six times before finally texting that she'd gotten a ride and would be at Diamond Mae's.

Curtis maneuvered the truck out of the lane and sped through town. Breaking routine was *not* a smart thing to do in his world. It whipped Dad into a frenzy and left both him and Sage vulnerable.

What the fuck is wrong with me? he thought furiously. Chasing fairy tales and forgetting that he already lived in a nightmare.

Swearing under his breath, Curtis wrenched the truck up the driveway and killed the engine. He stared a long moment at Garrett House, as if he could determine what kind of state his father was in just from the exterior air, but there was nothing to put him out of his misery, and Sage was still waiting next door.

He jogged the quick distance between the properties. Sage had been spending more and more time with Diamond Mae, and Curtis didn't know exactly what to make of it. Sage had more friends than Curtis could count, but he supposed the older woman's eclectic background was a draw for his artistic sister. A former costume designer for the Toronto Dance and Theatre Company, Mae was a bit of a local legend.

To call her eccentric would be putting it mildly.

Curtis climbed the front-porch stairs of the pink Victorian and banged the brass ring—an enormous dragon-headed knocker. He shifted uncomfortably, waiting.

He was such an *ass* for forgetting Sage.

He clenched his fists. The whispers were teasing his brain, twisting the light breeze into vicious shrieks that scraped his skull.

The door jerked open. "Dahling," Mae said, one age-veined hand sliding up the doorframe, her long nails glossy rectangles of blood-red lacquer. Today she was draped in long golden robes, and turquoise earrings dripped from her papery earlobes like little clinking chandeliers. Her jet-black hair was cropped close and slicked back, its raven exaggeration mirrored by her dark, drawn-on eyebrows and Cleopatra eyeliner.

"Hey, Mae."

"The prodigal is here," Mae called back over her shoulder, the motion setting off the unwieldy earrings like ships bobbing at sea. She turned back to Curtis, her diamond rings flashing in the sunlight. "Everything all right?" she said, her eyes sharp, assessing his every detail.

"Yeah, just lost track of time."

"Sage brought you this." She extended a yellow slip of paper between two fingers.

Curtis recognized the school's suspension form and groaned as he unfolded the paper. Two weeks.

"Arrondale is a prick," Mae said. "You did God's work, if you ask me."

Curtis attempted an unsuccessful smile.

Sage appeared in the hallway, her paint-stained satchel thrown over one shoulder, her eyes refusing to meet his.

"Bye, Mae," she said as she stepped around the satiny pool that was the hem of Mae's robes.

"Thanks," Curtis said.

"Please, *dahling*," Mae said, with a flick of her flashing rings. "This one has spirit. She's always welcome here."

Curtis nodded.

"You too," Mae said, her voice more serious than usual.

Curtis turned and looked back at her. Her eyes were concerned, lips pursed like she was trying to tease out a riddle.

Curtis could smell something amazing wafting from her kitchen—fried onions and homemade pierogies, he thought—and he knew her house was a warm wonderland, a museum of curiosities and treasures as strange and interesting as Mae. Suddenly he knew exactly why Sage had gone there. The only question was why she was willing to leave.

Now he had to take her back to their cold and dying home, a decrepit shell of a life that just kept getting worse.

Curtis fought with the sudden distressing urge to tell Mae everything—to stumble into her house, slide to the floor, and whisper his awful secrets from behind the cover of clenched hands.

The whispers chattered and shrieked, and Curtis bit back a grimace, retreating. No one could help him. He turned away from Mae and met Sage's accusing glare.

The door clicked shut behind him with a sound that he felt deep in his bones.

"You got *suspended*!" Sage said, smacking his arm. "Are you freaking stupid? Dad's going to flip!"

Curtis started toward the house, his shoulders too heavy.

"I know," he said. "I'm *sorry*."

"And you forgot me," she snarled, tugging at the straps of her backpack.

The anger in her voice twisted his gut, and he reached out for her, his hand just grazing her arm. She jumped back, eyes flicking fear-wide for a moment. Curtis shoved down a pang of hurt and then a rush of frustration at himself. He was no good at this emotional bullshit. Never knew the right thing to say, never knew how to make her feel better. She was the only good thing left of his family and he couldn't even apologize without freaking her out. Every day he was losing her, and he didn't know how to fix it.

He turned away and stormed up the front steps, steeling himself for whatever hurricane waited inside.

"Curtis."

She said his name tentatively, and he looked back at her, his throat squeezing tight, suddenly so tired, so *done*. His life was collapsing and there was no one to help him, no one who would *believe*. There was just white knuckles and a steel-braced chest—*just make it another day.*

Just get Sage through unscathed. Don't fail her.

His sister studied him, her eyes flickering slightly. "Are you okay?" she asked finally. "What happened to you today?"

"I just . . ." He stared at her, wanting to say something so badly, wanting to feel connected to her—the only other person on the planet who knew how hard their life was. Who knew what it was like to wonder if today was the day when Dad would finally snap, when they'd lose him forever.

I used to hold you and sing you to sleep, he thought, the memory like a photograph stolen from someone else. *I don't know how to get back there.*

"I just needed to get away," he said.

Her face fell and he tried not to care.

How could he tell her the truth—that not only did her father hear things that weren't there, but now her brother did too? That he felt like his sanity was unraveling, and some days he felt so alone he thought being dead might be preferable to being alive? That if it weren't for her, he probably would have launched the Beast off a cliff long ago and let the sharp bite of metal and stone take everything he was carrying away from him—let him finally, *finally* stop.

He looked away from the sister who looked so much like his mother and opened the door, the emptiness swelling inside him.

Music.

It was such an unfamiliar sound for the house that he stopped stock-still on the threshold, Sage hovering next to him. His throat clenched as a million memories poured back all at once—Mozart leaving him defenseless, gutting him open when he least expected.

His mother used to play classical records on the old player, and Dad used to dance with her.

Curtis passed through the hall and stood in the shadows of the vestibule, watching the scene unfolding in the sun-soaked kitchen. It was as if the fridge and cabinets had disgorged their entire contents onto the oversized, marble-clad island, and dead-center of the whole sticky mess was his father, humming the ascending piano scale, elbows deep in an enormous mixing bowl of raw hamburger.

Sage pushed past Curtis and started up the stairs with her book bag. Tom looked up.

"Son!" A wide smile transformed Tom Garrett's face into an image from Curtis's childhood. "I'm making meatballs. Come help."

Meatballs. He's listening to music and making meatballs.

This is all I need, Curtis thought with despair. *A good spell.*

Good spells were poorly named because they were actually cruel as fuck—a brief window where your loved one acted like normal, acted like the person they used to be, before going back to the hellish imitation you actually had to live with for the rest of your life.

Curtis swallowed tears and forced himself forward. *Just play the game.*

"Where's Sage?" Tom asked, arranging fat meatballs in the long baking pan.

"Just putting her stuff away," Curtis said, trying to smooth the catch in his voice. "Should I get sauce heating?" he asked, surveying the pot of boiling water on the stove, the box of pasta spilled open on the marble counter.

"Oh no," his father said with a disapproving laugh. "No canned garbage for us today." He pointed a sticky finger at an old recipe card on the counter.

Curtis's breath caught.

His mother's handwriting, faded and stained.

He picked the card up.

The rest of the kitchen was muffled and still around him as he stared at those faded pen strokes. It had been a long time since he'd seen her writing. He didn't know Dad still kept her recipe box around.

Curtis cleared his throat and reached for the tomatoes. "I'll get started."

The water was cold on his hands as he rinsed tomatoes, and he tried to focus on the way the late afternoon light was dipping behind the trees in the yard, sending fingers of amber in streaks and flashes that made him squint, rather than think about the way it used to feel when his mother filled the kitchen with the sounds and scents of cooking. He reached into a drawer for a knife, but instead his fingers found the meat thermometer.

A muscle jumped in his jaw.

Two years ago, Curtis had tried to take the gun away for good. It had occurred to him that letting a mentally ill man hold a rifle to his head every night might not be an entirely *normal* sort of thing. Someone might get the wrong idea. So Curtis stashed the gun in the attic rafters, where only he could find it.

Tom had gone absolutely, terrifyingly past-the-pale *psychotic*. He'd turned the house inside out, screaming at the top of his lungs, spit flying from his lips. Finally he resorted to a very colorful demonstration of just how many ordinary household instruments could, in fact, be used to end a person's life if they so chose to employ them that way. As Sage bawled in terror, Curtis watched his father hold the meat thermometer to his own throat and declare, "Anything can kill you if you point it the right way."

Curtis had given him back the gun. He'd let the man have his routine.

Now, as he listened to the sound of his father humming Mozart, Curtis wondered if the man even remembered that night, if he remembered the way Sage's face had crumpled up into this terrified, silent scream, or the way Curtis had thrown himself on his knees and begged him not to do it, begged him not to leave them all alone in the world.

Supper ended exactly as Curtis feared: one of Dad's stories descended into a rant about Frank, the business, how Frank kept secrets and was probably cheating them of the lumber mill's true profits. Sage retreated from the table and Curtis hurriedly grabbed the assortment of evening pills.

Once his father was settled on the couch, infomercials blaring, Curtis returned to the kitchen to deal with the dregs of their supper, forcibly shoving down the memories the night had revived. There was no Mother to help him. No Mother to whisper his secrets to.

Fuck it. He had no secrets. Everything was fine. Business as freaking usual.

He cleared plates and did *not* hear whispered voices coming through the kitchen window.

He spooned sauce over the meatballs and covered the tray in plastic wrap.

He did not hear voices.

He rinsed plates and put them in the dishwasher.

He did not hear voices.

He wiped the kitchen counters and rinsed out the cloth.

He did not—

Curtis strode from the kitchen and headed for the stairs. Up two flights, down to the very end of the hall.

Opened the door they never opened.

It was dark and smelled of dust and, just faintly, a perfume like decaying rose petals. The scent made something painful and vicious climb the back of his throat, and he struggled to beat it down.

He closed the door and stood in darkness, letting his eyes adjust. He took a few steps and sat on the edge of the bed. Through the windows, the horizon was stamped with the silhouettes of trees and a white sliver of moon. The trinkets on the dresser were furred with grey dust, his image in the long dresser mirror grimy and indistinct. Curtis picked up a framed picture, wiping the glass with a gentle motion.

His mother and father on their wedding day. Tom was carrying her down the steps of the little stone church as she screamed with laughter.

"Why'd you have to die?" He allowed himself this one whispered question. But there was no answer and he felt stupid and small for letting the words out of his mouth. He couldn't afford moments like this.

He set the frame down and turned away. He sat on the bed, and now he couldn't deny that even through the closed window, he heard a silvery jumble of skipping voices, darting and dipping, whirling and falling on the wind that hurdled the eaves outside.

He stared ahead into the antique mirror that hung alone on the opposite wall, its elaborate gold frame styled like an explosion of curling vines or tendrils. His own image stared back at him, hard and tired. The darkness of the night and the deadness of the room pressed in around him, sinking down into his skin, into that deep well at the center of his soul. He pulled the Mila photo from his back pocket and gazed at her.

I don't want to do this alone anymore.

The surface of the mirror glinted, as if a sudden shift of bright light had caught it, and then he was looking at her face in the glass.

Miss Mila Kenton.

17

Mila

THEIR MOTHER DISAPPEARED THREE DAYS AFTER THE WEDDING.

Searches were orchestrated, parties of men sent out into the woods with torches and dogs in case she'd been injured, in case she'd gotten lost while going for a walk. But her jewelry was missing and her clothes were gone. The constables looked at the room with shoulders curved in apology, their eyes sliding over things, over people, as though they already knew what they'd find and what they were supposed to say.

Mila screamed that their mother wouldn't leave them, would *not* have done this; Deemus apologized to the men in uniform, his hands slipping over her shoulders, the words *hysterical* and *delicate constitution* uttered in a syrup-toned voice. The constables' eyes flickered in discomfort; they looked at their shiny shoes, nodded at nothing.

They left.

Lawyers came. Mila overheard the word *annulment.*

Deemus looked at Mila hungrily.

Winters had disappeared, too, and this was deemed further proof that Ada was gone for good. Either Winters had murdered her and stolen her jewels, or she'd assisted her mistress in fleeing her marital responsibilities. Either way, Mila and Wynn were now legal wards of Deemus, their mother being dead or unfit.

Wynn cried great heaving sobs while Mila pressed her against her skirts, watching as Deemus dealt with the men of the law, playing the shell-shocked husband. Mila knew her mother hadn't run away. Not because of any great love for her daughters, but for the true prize that she'd fought so hard to win—the house, the title, the position. And Winters lacked the creativity for murder.

No. Deemus had done something. Deemus had wanted Ada out of the way.

Mila stood—her sister shaking against her, two figures lost in the darkness of the hall—watching as Deemus ushered the men from his study, as Bennet stepped forth to see the men out, as Deemus bowed his head with the stoic grief of a man so deceived in the character of his wife. She watched him await the men till they were out of sight, then pass the length of the hall to the locked-room door. He gazed at her and Wynn for a long moment, then unlocked the door and went inside, shutting it behind him. Mila heard the scrape and turn of the key.

Mila pushed Wynn into their bedchamber.

"When is Mother coming back?" Wynn wailed.

"She's not," Mila snapped. "She's dead, or as good as dead, just like Father. She can't help us."

Wynn dissolved into hiccupping gasps, her whole face red, eyes and nose running like a river. She reached out for Mila, and Mila brushed her off, panic gusting at the sheer terror—she was all that stood between them and Deemus now. She gripped the wall and struggled not to scream, grappled with the feeling that she should grasp Wynn under the arms, tear down that hallway, and fly to the stables. Throw her sister on Diablo's back, ride, and never stop.

But to where? Two young girls, unescorted, on a horse of Diablo's quality—even if their pictures had not already been splashed around the society pages—that sort of thing would attract immediate attention. They were Deemus's wards. His property.

No one would help them.

Mila had seen the way the constables looked at Deemus—not one of them would go against this man.

No, if they were to escape Deemus, she would have to do it herself. They needed money, and they needed to disappear, quickly. Maybe slip into the woods, work their way toward a farm, try to steal some common clothes—dress as boys perhaps. Buy a third-class ticket out of Kingston, get back to London. Their grandfather was a hard man, but surely he'd listen when Mila told him his fierce daughter had been obliterated by this quietly smiling man.

He'd *have* to listen to her.

Wouldn't he?

"Wynn, be quiet, I'm trying to think," Mila shouted, the hysterical sounds coming from her sister threatening to turn her insensible, to remind her that she was just seventeen, that she missed her home, her bedroom, the way the sun had come up over the eastern pasture and turned the whole field to gold, the way her father's voice had sounded in the soft heat of the stables, the scent of sawdust and horses and—

Mila screamed and threw a crystal vase across the room, watched it send spider-web fractures across the surface of the tall mirror and split her own reflection.

Blood rushed in her ears, and Wynn's silence was immediate.

They needed money.

Mila turned to the window, thinking. Mother's room had been stripped of all valuables. And if she were dressed as a stable boy and trying to sell fine trinkets, they'd be hauled up before the nearest constable. Nothing would do but cash.

Deemus's study. She'd seen the elaborately carved desk. It was the most likely place.

What if he keeps the cash in a safe? her mind pointed out helpfully.

Then we're damned, Mila thought.

No—the housekeeper. There's always money about for market.

But apart from Asher and Bennet, Mila had hardly any clue of who the staff were. She'd not seen the kitchens, the working part of the house. She'd feared turning a corner and finding herself in a room without doors again, haunted by lights that couldn't be.

Wynn was getting more hysterical. Mila sat beside her abruptly and pulled her sister onto her lap, letting Wynn grasp at her like a wet octopus, many-limbed and clinging. Mila ran her hand down Wynn's back in what she hoped was a comforting way as she continued to process the plan.

She couldn't leave Wynn alone, and she couldn't be caught—their best chance at success was that Deemus didn't suspect they'd try to escape. *Did* he? Surely he thought her too weak for that. *Men don't think women are capable of any courage that could exceed their own*, Mila thought grimly. *He'll think us too afraid.*

But Zahra had done it, her mind noted uneasily. Deemus might be on guard for such a thing now.

Wynn was suffocating her. Mila struggled free and checked the door, easing it open. She could just see the dark line of the study door ajar, far at the end of the long hall. Mila looked back to Wynn, who was still shuddering noisily on the floor. She couldn't sneak anywhere with that noise.

"Wynn, get in bed, and stay there. I'll be right back. You don't leave the bed for anything, and if anyone comes into the room, you scream as loud as you can and you don't stop screaming until you see me. Wynn, do you understand me?" she demanded, ripping at her laces, wrenching the high-heeled leather boots from her feet. Wynn nodded through tears and hiccupped her way over to the bed.

Mila slipped from the room, dashing down the hall on the balls of her feet. She paused at the locked-room door, breath shuddering in her ears, listening for a moment. She heard a movement and quickly leapt back, then pelted down the carpeted passage toward the study. She slipped into the darkened room, the only narrow slits of light seeping through the tall velvet-curtained windows. Mila looked further into the shadows of the enormous room and realized this wasn't just Deemus's study, but his bedchamber. A tall, black-curtained bed rose up against the far wall, like an openmouthed creature, waiting.

Mila turned her attention to the elaborate desk, inlaid with intricate patterns of wood, covered with the typical accoutrements of a gentleman—blotter, inkwell, papers. She tried a drawer and it opened, but there was nothing but ledgers, a letter opener, sealing wax, a small penknife. She seized the knife and tucked it into her corset, then tried the next drawer. Nothing of use. The next drawer. More nothing.

Her heart was a storm the entire house would hear. Her breath was the clatter of a hailstorm.

Think, she ordered herself desperately. *Think.*

The clutter was arranged to one side of the desk, irregularly spaced. Mila looked closer. The lacquer was worn dull in one spot on the desk front, a square inlay of dark rosewood. Mila passed a finger over it, felt the slightest gap between the woods. She pressed down on the inlay and a hidden shelf popped up from the desk surface. Inside it were a little red notebook and a stack of money. Mila seized the cash and quickly shuffled through it.

Better not to take all—enough to get them passage to London, not so much that it would be obviously missed if Deemus checked the compartment.

She shoved the money down next to the knife in her corset and closed the compartment. Her eyes returned to the notebook. She shouldn't waste time . . .

She flipped it open. "Debtors," it read in scarlet ink. A list of names and dates filled the pages. Each name was written in a different hand.

The signatures looked a lot like they were signed in blood.

She thrust the book back and returned the compartment to normal. Sliding herself against the doorway, she eyed the passage, listening for any sounds.

Nothing.

She ran down the hall, blood roaring in her ears, and burst back through the door to their bedchamber. Wynn was still on the bed, her eyes large and wet, face red. Mila pressed herself against the wall, watching through the narrowest gap she could leave in the doorway. She needed to think about how to get them out of the house, where best to find clothes, when to try, but another question had been building in her mind since the very first day at Gravenhearst, and now it seemed more important than ever.

What was in that locked room?

What if Deemus had her mother in there?

But why would he do that, she thought, her mind straining with frustration. What could he possibly need from Ada that he hadn't already had perfect access to by bringing them here? They'd already been completely under his power, isolated from a town that clearly feared him. Unless he was truly a monster who gained pleasure from physically restraining and tormenting a woman, there was nothing to be gained by pretending Ada was dead but actually keeping her alive somewhere in the house.

Was there?

She thought of the books, the strange texts that had seemed part science, part witchcraft.

If there's even a chance . . .

No. Mila severed the thought. She'd warned her mother. *Wynn* was her responsibility now. She had to get Wynn out of here. If she split her focus, started running around this changing maze of a house again looking in vain for a mother who was most likely dead—

Her knees wobbled and she caught herself, sliding down the wall with a little sound of terror, her vision going grey at the edges.

I'm alone I'm alone I'm alone

She felt hands on her and realized Wynn had run to her side, was grasping at her, saying her name. She pulled her sister to her and buried her face in her hair, swallowing hard on the sobs that wanted to break her.

"I'm sorry, Wynn," she said. "I'm sorry I couldn't stop this."

There was a knock at the door and Mila jumped, wanting to scream at whoever it was to go away. But she couldn't afford that. Couldn't show these men how close she was to breaking.

She pushed herself up, pulling Wynn next to her. She blinked her eyes furiously, trying to clear them.

"Come in," she called.

The door opened and she found herself face-to-face with Asher.

She blinked again. He was different. His hair smoother, his lines less slovenly. But it was more than that—more than just a smarter grooming than before. He seemed *fuller* somehow, like there was more of him. The thought pulled a wave of nausea over her.

"Master Deemus asked that I bring you some luncheon." His tone was mild, but his voice had greater resonance than usual. He turned and retrieved a tray from the stand in the hall. Mila stepped back as he carried the tray of covered dishes to the tea table, setting them down with the perfect grace of a man trained to service. He straightened and looked at her. "Do you require anything else, Miss?"

"No," Mila said faintly.

He nodded and left.

"You must eat," Mila said to Wynn. "We need our strength."

Mila waited until the windows turned black, only the pinpricks of stars giving evidence to the world beyond Gravenhearst. She'd instructed Wynn before bedtime to keep her clothes on, to be ready to follow and not make a sound. They'd head for the stables, look quickly for work clothes of any size, then ride Diablo out into the woods. Once they'd gained enough distance, they'd change and Mila would cut their hair with the penknife she'd stolen. Then they'd make their way to Kingston and be at the docks come morning. She'd purchase a ticket and hope to God it was for a boat leaving that day. Going anywhere. Once they were far enough from Kingston, they would head for London.

Mila prayed she'd taken enough money. If she had to sell Diablo—

She squeezed her eyes shut at the thought.

There was no storm this night. No noise to cover their escape. She shook Wynn, and her sister nodded, complying wordlessly.

They crept to the door.

The corridor beyond was silent and black. The gas had been turned off for the night, and Mila could see almost nothing without the moonlight from the window. She stood for a long moment, Wynn's hand in hers, waiting for her eyes to adjust, trying to find the edges of things. She kept one hand on the wall and moved forward slowly, listening. They finally reached the center of the corridor, and the slightest ghosting of moonlight filtered through the pointed-arch doorways that led to the staircase and the wall of windows.

The soles of Mila's shoes clacked softly against the first stone step and she cringed. She stopped and pulled Wynn down, quickly stripping the laces on Wynn's shoes and then hers, pulling the boots free.

She clasped hers to her chest and motioned for Wynn to do the same. They slipped down the staircase quietly, the faintest outlines of the white-and-grey checkerboard floor visible. Mila could just make out the pattern of stars through the massive wall of windows that towered up around the front door.

They were almost there.

"Like mother, like daughter," a voice spoke.

Mila gasped and turned, gripping Wynn against her. A match was struck and a flame sprung to life. Deemus was seated, fully dressed, in a chair against the wall, midway between them and the door.

He rose slowly, a look of weary regret on his features. "So you wish to leave me also."

Mila backed away, edging toward the door.

"Please," she whispered. "Just let us go."

"Go?" Deemus said with a smile. "Go where? To Kingston? To catch a ship? To travel so many miles by yourself? To cut your lovely hair and pass yourself off as a man? And for what?" He took a step toward them and Mila stepped back again, her breath shaking in her throat, fingers digging into Wynn's skin. "For a mother who left you? Who took the gifts I offered her and slunk from the house like a thief in the night?"

"She didn't leave!" Mila shouted, the words spilling from her before she could stop them. "You've done something with her!"

"You wound me, Mila. I am bereft at the loss of your mother—did I not give her everything? My heart breaks at what she has done to our family."

"You were more upset when you lost your precious mirror!" Mila spat, her voice echoing in the cavernous entry.

Deemus's eyes sharpened, the corners of his lips flicking ever so slightly.

Mila rushed for the door, and Asher stepped out of the shadows, Bennet close behind.

"This is your grief speaking, Mila," Deemus said calmly. "And I am very understanding. But you must be careful. It's not wise to give such feelings too much rein—your mind could become unbalanced."

He stepped closer, and Mila felt tears leaking down her cheeks. Even if they ran, even if she bit and clawed and they somehow made the door, they'd never outrun them to the stables, not Wynn, and they'd never get Diablo free in time.

She'd failed.

"I'm very fond of you, Mila." Deemus said, reaching out a hand to her. His finger trailed her jawline. "You needn't worry for a thing. We're still going to be a family." He gazed at her a moment longer, then drew back his hand and turned away. "I think it's time you went back to bed now," he said. "You need rest."

It's me, Mila thought with despair as she turned and led Wynn across the foyer, her heart turning to ice. *I'm the thing he had to gain by getting rid of Mother.*

He wants to marry me.

They climbed the stairs and walked back down the corridor. Mila pushed open the door to their room and let the boots she still clutched fall to the ground with a dull thud.

She led Wynn back to the bed and they climbed into the middle. Wynn wrapped her arms around Mila, her cheek pressed to Mila's chest.

The house breathed around them, enormous, listening.

I don't know what to do, Mila thought as she stared up into the shadows of the canopy. *What am I supposed to do?*

18

Mila

SHE WOKE, HER NECK CRAMPED FROM FALLING ASLEEP upright. The sun poured in bright through the windows and Mila squinted, feeling like death. The shock of last night, the pure horror of it—she felt sick and empty, like she never wanted to move again.

She looked beside her.

Wynn was gone.

She jumped from the bed, eyes raking the room. "Wynn," she said. She moved through the room, toward the lavatory. "Wynn!" she called, her voice catching. The lavatory was empty. "Wynn!" she screamed, running for the door. The hall was empty. She threw open the door to her mother's room. Tore open wardrobes, checked the bed, searched every place Wynn could be.

She wouldn't, she thought. *She wouldn't wander off without me. Not now.*

The edges of the room blurred. Her heart thrashed, breath rising in her ears. *Not Wynn. Not her too.* She couldn't breathe.

She screamed and cast herself toward the door, something building inside her: rage and terror and something else she barely recognized. It boiled beneath her skin, gripped her lips in a death grin, and sent her barreling down the hall to that locked door.

She hurled herself at it, shoulder first. *Thud.* Her shoulder flared with pain. *Thud.* She cried out as her bone jarred, deep and sharp. *Again.* This time she heard a crack.

AGAIN.

Her shoulder was on fire, her whole body screaming, singing with rage and desperation.

Thud, CRACK.

She fell through open space as the jamb splintered, the door whipping back to bang against the wall. She scrambled to her feet, shoulder throbbing, Wynn's name on her lips.

She stopped.

The room was full of portraits. Women. One after another. She walked the room's length, staring at mournful faces. Young; old; fine ladies; small girls. Their faces rendered in detail, a backdrop of fathomless black behind them.

Her heart froze.

Her mother's face.

Ada Kenton looked back at her, a sadness and defeat that Mila had never seen on her mother's features. But the portrait was different from the others. Faded.

No, that wasn't quite the right word.

Pale—like a flower just beginning to bloom, that hadn't deepened to its true hue yet.

Mila cried out a sound she didn't know her body could make, for she'd just seen what hung beside her mother's pale portrait.

Wynn's face, translucent and ghostly. If her mother's image was a new bloom, this one was an apparition, a whiff of smoke barely collected out of the black.

Mila screamed again, her knees giving. She pressed her forehead to the paneling, screamed till her throat felt like bloody shredded meat. She gripped the wall and smashed her head against it, welcoming the pain: a thing in black with open arms ready to receive her.

She heard voices.

She rose to her feet and left the room, her head singing with fire, and the feel of blood on her skin.

Andrew Deemus stood at the end of the hall, waiting for her.

"Give her back to me," Mila ordered, her voice so low she barely recognized it. She walked toward him.

"I'm afraid that's not possible," he said quietly. "The process has already begun. I regret that this pains you, but in time, I believe you'll find comfort in other things." He smiled. "You will make an excellent mother, Mila."

Mila laughed, because now she recognized the strange feeling that had overtaken her—it was the realization that she had nothing left to lose. Wynn was gone, and now there was nothing.

All her fear was gone.

"You know," Mila said, looking down at the carpet for a moment, rolling the thought around in her head, getting used to the largeness of it, the absolute earth-shaking *profundity* of the reality filling her veins. "I used to think I was like my father." She looked up at him, wild and unhinged, a great beast in her chest. "But I'm not. I am my mother's daughter, Andrew Deemus. I am a heartless, *vicious* bitch, and I will tear you apart!"

She launched herself, saw him take a step back in surprise, hands up, ready to restrain her from clawing at him. His eyes widened at the very last second as he realized how poorly he'd misjudged her intent. She threw herself against him, locking her arms and heaving upward. She tipped him back, sending them both reeling toward the stone railing.

The horizon revolved and Deemus screamed and Mila felt nothing.

19

Mila

MILA WOKE TO PAIN.

The realization that she was still alive was unwelcome. She opened her eyes with difficulty and saw dark rafters arching above her, grainy light cutting a swath through the gloom to her right. She turned her head and cried out at the burst of pain that shot through her body. The light came from a barred window, and by the slant of the roof, she guessed she was in an attic.

A voice spoke from the shadows. "You bitch."

Mila tried to sit up but found she didn't have the strength. She couldn't fight the waves of pain that made the room revolve and her vision haze.

Asher stepped toward her, his eyes narrowed, lips drawn back in a snarl. "You think you can defy the Master, that you could *do* that to him!" he yelled.

"Asher," another voice said quietly, a hint of pain straining the edges of the normally smooth tone.

Mila bit down a wave of panic as Deemus stepped into view, his arm in a sling, face cut and bruised, a definite limp to his gait.

But still alive.

Tears leaked from her eyes.

"You must understand, Mila," Deemus said, his voice very gentle, "this is not an ordinary house. And I am not an ordinary man." He came to the edge of her bed. "I will forgive this act of desperation since I know that women are prone to hysterical fits when caught in the throes of grief. As well, I understand that a fine horse may panic when the master first fits the rope. I've seen horses choke themselves to death in their own terror—their own ignorance."

"I'm not your horse," Mila hissed.

He reached out and stroked a single finger across her cheekbone, and she bared her teeth. He seized her chin firmly, but his fingers were still careful. "Do not let dumb fear choke you, Mila." He gazed at her for long moments, then released her and moved a few paces. "You've already benefited from the remarkably skilled ministrations of my manservant," he said, indicating Asher with a nod of his head. "He has *special skills*, you might say—but it would be wise not to push his abilities any further than you already have. I would be truly grieved if you should come to more *permanent* harm than this." He smiled gently. "I chose you, Mila. Your mother was a means to an end. I'd inherited and needed a wife. But quickly I saw that you . . . *you* were the prize."

He smiled again and walked to the door, motioning for Asher to go ahead of him.

Deemus paused on the threshold, then looked back to her. "You will be mistress of Gravenhearst, Mila. You are a creature worthy of her. You are truly magnificent." He left the room, and Mila heard a key turn in the lock, the scrape of something heavy.

She closed her eyes and lay silent, but she couldn't stop the tears that leaked from her eyes.

Mila slept for a long time, and when she woke, she didn't know how many days had passed. She dreamed of Wynn and her mother, dreamed they were skeletons straining to get free of the house, their limbs reaching from walls and pillars and ceilings. Sometimes she dreamed of her father, that he rode to Gravenhearst on Diablo, yelling her name; he fought his way through the house, bursting through the door to scoop her into his arms and take her away from all this. She woke with her pillow soaked with tears, her body still aching and weak.

She wished she were dead.

Asher came and went, bringing food, medicine, changing her bandages, refreshing the chamber pot. She could have forced herself from the bed, perhaps tried to surprise him when he came through the door. But what was the point? This house was a monster, and it had her in its jaws. She should have followed Zahra's example and fled when she'd had the chance.

Now Wynn's death was on her hands.

It was only right that she die here too.

Weeks passed, and one night, as the wind howled around the eaves, Mila stared into the shadows of the empty room trying to remember the way Wynn's fingers had felt when they curled in her hair at night. She used to get annoyed by it—the feel of her sister's breath on her cheek, when all she wanted was to stretch out and drift into sleep alone and unencumbered.

She let her eyes fall on the tall, dust-encrusted mirror opposite, large as a doorway and ghostly in the moonlight. She'd come to think of it as Deemus's torture device, her own wretched face staring out—perfectly, *miserably*, alone.

"I'm sorry," she whispered.

Mila . . .

She jerked upright and looked around. The voice had been so faint, like a muffled gasp, but she was sure—so *sure*—she'd heard it.

Wind whipped the eaves and Mila gripped the bedstead till her finger joints cracked. "Wynn?" she cried.

A flash of something white streaked across the mirror—a scream, like Wynn but not—her voice mangled up with screeching metal and then—

Silence. Mila stared at the mirror, willing Wynn to return.

But nothing—just her own cursed face.

Then everything inside her froze.

Her reflection no longer looked back at her.

There was a young man, and he was staring at her from within the pane.

20

Curtis

SHE WAS VERY PALE, AND THERE WERE DEEP CIRCLES UNDER her extraordinary steel-sharp eyes. Her wheat-blonde hair was loose and limp and fell around her shoulders as she sat on a narrow bed, arms braced like they were the only things keeping her upright. He recognized his own posture in her defeated stance. She was a worn reflection of her stunning image in the photograph, but no question—it was her.

His heart kicked staccato against his ribs and his breath stalled out in the back of his throat. The whispers shrieked excitement, and he felt like the whole world might fold inward.

She stared back at him, lips parted in surprise, her eyes wide. But then she seemed to collect herself, to really *look* at him. Her eyes read the contours of his face and he had the sense that she'd taken the measure of his character, and he'd passed some sort of test. She rose and came closer. He could just make out the room behind her, dark with a low, sloping roofline and a single metal-frame bed. She walked slowly, like she could barely manage it, and the sight made his chest do something painful and unexpected. What on earth had been *done* to her?

He pushed to his feet with a quick shove.

"Are you trapped too?" she asked in a low-voiced English accent, and he *heard* her. As if her voice emitted, just slightly muffled, from the silver-bright glass.

He could only stare at her, dumbfounded.

Doubt crept across her face, and her brows swept together. "Can you hear me?" she said, her voice close to breaking.

"Yes," he gasped quickly, his hands going to the opulent golden frame, as if he could make sense of what was going on if he got a good enough grip on the thing.

"Are you trapped too?" she said again.

"Yes," he whispered, because it felt like truth. But then his brain engaged.

"Don't go to Gravenhearst!" he yelled, the realization bursting from him. This was why the nightmare was happening to him. He could save her. He could un-write the past. "Don't go there, you'll die!"

"It's too late," she said, with a desperate laugh.

Fuck.

"Do you know what happened there?" he demanded. "Why's it cursed? Why's it in my head?"

"Andrew Deemus," she said. "He's a monster. He took my sister and he took my mother. The house is taking us, and I can't get out."

The surface of the mirror warped, a screech like grated metal searing his ears. Then the mirror flashed, and she was gone.

"No!" Curtis gripped the gilt frame and shook it. He pulled it from the wall and turned it around. Nothing but the old paper backing. He stared at it for a long moment until the futility of the gesture became solidly apparent, and he returned the mirror to its hook. He stood for a while, staring into the empty glass, then backed up until his legs hit the mattress edge.

Sinking to the bed, he fumbled for the photograph. Mila gazed back at him.

"The house is taking us, and I can't get out."

Something terrible happened at Gravenhearst—something worse

than a fire. And it was coming for him. Voices and whispers, echoes of the past. He was part of it now.

Yes, Curtis, you are part of something . . .

Yes, he agreed with the creepy forest whisper, *and I'm going to stop you.*

A scream split reality, and he threw himself toward the stairs, Sage's fear curdling his blood.

There was banging, his father's angry voice.

Shit shit shit.

He plowed into the second-floor hallway in time to see Sage dodge their father, running for her bedroom.

"Thief spirit!" Tom bellowed, banging a fist against the wall, a dark book clutched in his other hand. "Thieving Jezebel!"

"It's for school!" Sage screamed from behind the closed door, her voice somewhere between fury and agony.

"Dad!" Curtis yelled in a tone he never used—*authoritative.* It was a thing you didn't use on Tom. It was a spark that lit gasoline.

Tonight Curtis *was* the gasoline. Something unearthly burned in his veins, reckless and unstoppable.

His father turned and looked.

Tom shuffled, feet clumsy in ratty slippers. He seemed to forget where he was—gazed dumbly at the thing in his hand.

"Give that to me," Curtis ordered, his voice ringing in his ears.

"Not hers to snoop," Tom mumbled, pushing the book into Curtis's outstretched hand.

"You scared Sage," Curtis said, his voice hard. "It's time for pills."

In the living room, his father slumped on the bone-colored satin couch, muttering about Frank and traitor family. Curtis surveyed him, the dark well of anger climbing the space between his bones.

"Here." He held out the sleeping tablets until his father offered his hand. Curtis let the chalky pills fall into his father's sweaty palm and watched as he swallowed all of them.

"No gun tonight," Curtis said.

Tom looked up. "My head hurts so much, Son."

"No gun." Tonight Tom wouldn't get the relief of teetering on the knife's edge, of holding that power.

For a moment, Curtis thought his father would refuse. Curtis watched for signs that he might have stepped too far out of line as his father's keeper, and that the normally tame bull was about to go on a deadly rampage.

In that moment, Curtis felt dangerous enough to risk it.

But then Tom deflated, eyes far away and desolate. "All right, Son." He reached sluggishly for the remote and turned on the television.

Curtis turned on his heel and headed for Sage's room, the whispers seething.

He felt larger as he climbed the stairs. He'd stepped outside his world and didn't recognize his place anymore. His chest throbbed and his bones hummed and he wasn't sure where he ended.

Who am I? He was who he'd always been, but right now he felt like more. He felt dangerous.

A muffled sob brought the walls close again, and his fingers dug hard into the notebook in his hand.

Sage.

His breath was shaky as delayed fear finally claimed him; his pace quickened.

He used to check on his sister at all hours, back when she had nightmares every night. Mom was dead and Dad was the moaning thing on the couch. Sage didn't take it well. He'd wake her from screaming fits and hold her trembling and furious five-year-old body against him till she calmed and could sleep again.

He knocked softly. "It's me."

Silence. He went in anyway.

Her room was like her—strange and wonderful and just on the endearing side of bizarre. The life-size papier-mâché, glitter-encrusted skeleton she'd constructed grinned back at him from a corner of the room, a runaway garden's worth of handmade flowers and leaves and vines trailing from it. She'd painted the largest wall with characters from the graphic novel she was writing: a ragtag team of five leaping from a wormhole, ready to kick ass and fight evil. Curtis didn't know a thing about art, but he knew what she could do was special.

Sage was on the bed, knees tight against her chest, jaw chipped from stone. The sight of it made Curtis want to tear something apart.

"He doesn't like us in Mom's old stuff," he said quietly.

A tear rolled down her cheek, and he twisted the book in his hands, the old leather creaking.

"It's for school," she said, a shudder barely held in.

"Yeah, it's just . . ."

"It's just *what?*" she exploded, a world's worth of fury focused on him. "What is it?"

"Sage—" He didn't know what to say. She was looking at him like she wanted to tear him to pieces. He put the journal on the bed, passed an uncertain hand through his hair. *I need to do something*, he thought. *I need to fix this.*

She grabbed the book and hurled it at the skeleton. "Get out!" she screamed. "Get out!"

He stared at his sister and didn't know what to do.

He left the room.

21

Curtis

In his dream, Curtis walks the halls and passageways of Gravenhearst. He can hear the Great House breathing all around him, stirring, settling, layers above and below, gateways locking and shifting, going on forever.

He is Jonah in the whale; he is Alice down the rabbit hole. Dark eyes keep watch from dark corners. Shadows ripple and grow.

He climbs a staircase that stretches into nothing but endless space. Whispers spread through the black like the breath of a thousand leaves. The staircase hangs in empty space, and at the last step there is only a wall, and on the wall there is only the mirror. Golden

vines and tentacles dislodge and shiver from the frame in a glimmering, undulating dance.

Curtis draws near as shadows flicker across the glass—faces and forms, there and gone. A young girl's face suddenly takes shape, mouth open in a silent plea. The whispers shriek in anger, and the girl's face pales with terror, stone-white against her dark hair, but she turns back to him, her mouth forming unspoken words.

The whispers screech like clashing metal and the grinding of gears, and Curtis feels the sound right down to his bones.

The little girl reaches toward him, the glass filling with female figures behind her, imploring him forward. The mirror grows larger and larger, bleeding molten gold, till it's as large as a doorway, and he hears the murmur of a voice on the other side. He presses his fingers to the glass, and it swings inward like a door.

Before him is a vast darkened space, the suggestion of shape coming only from large windows, their ghostly light crisscrossed by iron bars.

He walks farther into the space.

There is a figure in a narrow bed.

He comes closer.

Mila.

She wakes all at once, and her cat eyes widen, but she holds out her hand with a little sound like relief. He reaches toward her and feels the warmth of her skin on his, the pulse of her wrist under his touch. Brown sugar and almonds is her scent and he's drowning in her, his fingers caught in her hair, her rich voice murmuring low against the little hairs at his neck. His mouth finds hers, and he hears the choked cry that comes from his lips as if it came from another Curtis, a creature swimming in need and grief and want, and he thinks that if he keeps kissing her he might never find his way back to the Curtis he knows. And with his hands hard against her back and her body moving against his, he's not sure he cares.

"They are devouring me," she whispers.

He woke, gasping, the imprint of her fingers still pressed into his skin. Her words coursed through his mind, and the whispers pressed at his window, an incessant babble.

When he fell asleep again, he dreamed of Sage. She was running through Garrett House pursued by a monster with his father's face. Curtis raced after them, the hallway stretching out under him, thinning the space, turning the world to shreds just waiting to come apart. He screamed Sage's name and fell through emptiness, falling, falling, his stomach turning inside out, the ground getting closer. His father was a dark figure waiting down below, and when he looked up, he was not Curtis's father.

He was Curtis.

When Curtis woke for the second time—this time in the cold light of day—the first thing he did was check his father's room.

Tom slept the greedy sleep of the heavily drugged, limbs splayed, sheets tangled, a noisy rattle vibrating his throat.

Curtis closed the door and headed downstairs to the kitchen. The voices were rushing through his mind, filling his head with that shushing ocean sound that a thousand tiny rustling leaves make, and underneath it all, like a soft murmur, a voice like another language—not known, but half familiar. It had become the background to his life. He was almost used to it now and just that fact alone filled him with a quiet terror.

He spooned grounds into the coffeemaker, forcing his fingers not to shake.

Mila's face in the mirror, her voice, that dream, the feel of her—

His life was splitting in half: the too-real nightmare of the everyday and the impossible weight of things that *couldn't* be happening, but *were*.

The coffee was ready. He poured himself a cup and toasted waffles that he wouldn't eat.

He heard Sage's footsteps on the stairs and tried to read the expression on her face as she entered the kitchen. She didn't meet his eyes, and he could tell by the way she held her shoulders that she didn't want him to question her. She wanted everything to be normal and fine.

"Here." He placed a plate with two waffles before her.

She picked at one halfheartedly, and for a few minutes, there was just the sound of the tines of her fork on the plate, and the whispers in his head.

She propped her chin in one hand and looked up at him. "So, what are you doing today?"

"Huh?" he said. "Oh, ah, nothing much."

Smooth, he thought.

She gave him a look like she just couldn't believe he was this dumb. "Fine, don't tell me," she muttered, turning back to her mutilated breakfast.

"How'd you get home from school yesterday?" he asked in the most awkward transition in the history of conversations.

"You mean after you *forgot* me?" Sage said.

"Yeah, after that," Curtis said with a grimace.

"Grayson Deervine," she said with a slight smirk.

"Oh, not that little prick," Curtis groaned. "You don't have a thing for him do you? Because he totally two-timed . . ." His voice trailed off at the look growing on her face—a strange combination of anger and desolation. "What?" he said, a sick feeling churning in his stomach.

"You do know that I like *girls*, right?" she said, her brows arching in disbelief.

"Uh . . ." The eloquence of that response spoke to his obvious lack of knowledge. Her face twisted painfully.

"I don't even know why I try to talk to you," she said, angry tears forming in her eyes. "You're obviously not even listening."

"Wait, you've *told* me this? Other people know this?" he said, trying to wrap his brain around how he could have missed something of this magnitude, feeling incredibly stupid that he obviously had, feeling angry that other people knew more about his own sister than he did. And most of all, feeling like a complete and utter failure that he'd again reduced his sister to tears, and that every day he seemed to get further and further away from her no matter how hard he tried.

"Yes!" she shouted, standing up from the table with a violent shove of her chair.

He slammed his coffee cup down. "I'm sorry! Okay, Sage? I'm sorry! But I'm doing my goddamn best here, and it's not easy keeping everything on the rails all by myself!"

Her face went slack for a second, like he'd slapped her, and then she pushed past him. Curtis reached out to stop her, but the sound of a car on the driveway made him turn. He looked out the window in time to see Frank Garrett stepping out of his black Cadillac.

"Shit," Curtis said. He stood frozen for a moment, but Sage threw the front door open, so apparently a decision had been made and now Curtis just needed to get in front of the problem.

There was *always* a goddamn problem.

"Morning, Curtis," Frank said, tipping his head down and a bit to the side. It was a gesture that Curtis hated because it made Frank look reluctant and apologetic, when in fact he was neither.

"What do you want?" Curtis said harshly.

"Well, uh . . ." Frank trailed off and sunk his hands into his khaki trouser pockets. "I'm just a bit concerned about some things."

"Such as?"

"I think it might be time to consider making a change with your dad's situation."

"And what kind of change would that be?" Curtis crossed his arms.

Frank gave him an uncomfortable look, the silence stretching out between them. Finally: "He's getting worse."

Curtis stared at Frank, trying to find the lie. For as long as he could remember, something about his uncle made his guts squirm and his fists clench up. Dad's paranoia was extreme, but there was a seed of truth in that blind hatred—there had to be.

Frank sighed and looked about the yard, and Curtis was painfully aware of how run-down the place was. Sage shivered and rubbed her hands over her bare arms; there was something so terribly vulnerable about the gesture, and Curtis felt like a bigger failure than usual. How pathetic they must look—two desperate kids standing on the sagging porch of a rotting house, shouting at the world that they were fine.

The whispers scraped and pulled, and he repressed a shudder.

"I know how hard you try," Frank said. "You've done really good. Managed what shouldn't have to be managed. But you can't change some things." He shook his head. "Tom's just not *well*."

Curtis jammed his hands in his pockets. He knew Dad wasn't well. *Nothing* was well. Tears pulled at the back of his throat.

"Curtis, we're *family*."

"Yeah?" Curtis strode forward, the whispers suddenly scream-ing like a ravenous horde in his ears. "Where was *family* when Mom died? When Dad went completely off the rails? Where the hell was family loyalty then?"

Frank took a step back. "I know. Olivia and I were having prob-lems. I—I let you all down."

Curtis fought a sudden and totally unacceptable urge to cry. He looked at Sage. She shuffled her feet, then looked back at him, biting her lip.

She wants to go with him instead, Curtis thought with despair. *I'm less of a home than an uncle who's never given a shit.*

Frank stepped near again and put his hand on Curtis's fore-arm, very carefully. "You're doing your best. But maybe it's just too much."

Curtis would not cry. He would not.

Frank hesitated. Finally he gave a little grimace, one that Curtis recognized from the inside out—that moment of *fuck it*. "You're a lot like your dad. All this stress . . . it might not be good for you."

The atmosphere rang in Curtis's ears, the trees growing too sharp in his vision.

"That fight you had at school—it's not a good sign."

A wash of red fury colored Curtis's vision.

Kill him, Curtis, you could kill him.

You could wind your hands around his throat and squeeze till his eyes burst.

You could take his head and split it open like rotting fruit.

Curtis stumbled back a step, his breath racing in his ears.

Frank nodded regretfully and climbed into the Cadillac. He looked to Curtis through the open window.

"We're going to have to deal with this." He held Curtis's gaze for a long moment, then started the ignition.

Curtis watched the car pull away and slink down the drive, flashes of light glinting from its surface and glaring in his eyes. He crossed his arms over his chest, fingers digging into his own skin.

What was happening to him?

22

Mila

THE MIRROR MADE A SOUND LIKE SCRAPED METAL AND grinding teeth. A flash of light and then nothing.

The boy was gone; there was just her exhausted reflection staring back from the dusty pane. Her chest hurt and her mind was slipping, straining to catch hold of impossibilities.

"Don't go to Gravenhearst! You'll die!"

Yes, I've gathered that much myself, thank you.

"Do you know what happened there? Why's it cursed? Why's it in my head?"

That was a peculiar question. As horrifying as this place was, she didn't feel it *inside* her. Just the opposite—every moment she felt it gaping and shifting around her, like some kind of living puzzle box, enormous and hungry.

And there was no reason to trust *anything* she saw in one of its hateful mirrors.

But Wynn's voice, right before the boy appeared—she was *sure* she'd heard it. Was Wynn still with her? Did Wynn have something to do with the strange boy?

She thought of him sitting there on the edge of the bed, shoulders sagging, the line of his jaw tense and strained. He was all hard lines and sharp angles, like someone chipped him free from stone, but forgot to make him soft, forgot to give him hope. And his eyes—they'd been large and dark and louder than the rest of him. He'd stared at her, broken and desperate, as if he were at the brink of what he could stand and had given himself up for dead.

There was truth in that kind of pain.

She felt that hopeless truth inside her every time she thought of Wynn. What point was there in going on when everything she loved had been ripped away?

"Do you know what happened there?"

Yes.

No.

To a point.

Zahra had known. Known the instant they entered. Known enough to steal Deemus's mirror.

The thought pierced Mila like lightning.

The boy had Deemus's mirror—how else could he see inside Gravenhearst? How else could he know things he shouldn't? He'd looked as if he *recognized* her.

He'd looked as if he knew how all this ended.

She circled the room, her mind churning.

If the boy truly had the mirror, that meant he had a weapon. A piece in this game. Deemus had been frantic at the mirror's loss. A whole house of monstrous power, but there was something special about that glass.

And now—*somehow*—someone out there had what Deemus desired most.

That made that person powerful, even if he didn't know it.

She stared at the standing mirror that faced her bed—night after night her reflection stared back at her, forced to consume her own wretched failure. Deemus had put her here to teach her a lesson. To break her.

But the boy had broken *in*.

She grasped the mirror with a shout of rage and heaved. It toppled and crashed with an ear-splitting sound.

She was getting out of this room and killing that man if it was the last thing she did. She didn't give a damn what happened after that.

The door to her prison was barred from the other side. But the walls themselves, they were old boards; they held a chance.

She groaned as she lifted the heavy frame, scrabbling for the fragments of glass. There was a shard twice as long as her hand and she ran to the bed, stripped the pillowcase. She seized the piece of thick glass, winding fabric till she had a handle with a heavy knot at the top. She went to the roughest board on the interior wall and drove the blade into the wood.

The board chipped and split, and the floor shook beneath her.

She gasped and caught her balance, hacking again at the fracture. The floor shifted hard, and she fell, catching her hand in a spot of blood—not hers.

The wall was bleeding. This place was *alive*.

"I'm going to kill you!" she snarled, hand raised for another blow.

The world turned inside out—Mila slammed to the ground, retching and gagging, feeling like her bones had twisted in her meat. When she opened her eyes, her hand clutched nothing.

The shard was gone, the attic room completely changed.

Clutter, odds and ends, boxes and crates surrounded her. Furniture unused for decades stood sentinel like figures on a forgotten chessboard. It was the same room, but *not*.

And the wall wasn't bleeding.

She touched the unscarred wall. It was real. The room was real, but it felt different.

She felt different. A thing out of place.

Her skin tingled and the air closed in. The walls watched like they might crush her, like they waited on hinges, or hovered like a backdrop. Mila had the sudden knowledge that the stone and timbers of Gravenhearst were nothing but a façade for something darker and hulking, something that waited, shifting at its truest center.

It doesn't matter, she told herself, fighting pure terror. *Wynn is still here.*

Her breathing slowed; she carefully ordered her thoughts.

The room was different. That meant . . .

She went to the door, hand outstretched. Surely it couldn't be this easy.

Her fingers trembled on the handle, and the door creaked open under her touch.

A woman sat in a rocking chair, crying silent tears. Mila froze, but there was no reaction.

She approached, her neck pricking. The woman looked at her, but didn't see her. Mila passed a shaking hand through her, unnoticed.

I know you. The woman's dress was old-fashioned, something that might have been worn well over a century ago. And she'd seen it before—in one of the many portraits she'd passed in Gravenhearst's dark halls. *Sophia Deemus.*

This woman had been dead over a hundred years.

Mila shuddered, because now she understood.

This house contained every version of itself, like some winding mirrored hall looking backward and forward, endlessly repeating. She'd attacked the house, and it had swallowed her into itself, into its *past.*

She thought of all the paintings of mothers and daughters in the galleries and halls. She thought of that monstrous portrait room, trophies of ghostly faces.

They were all trapped here. Endlessly living out their paths through the house, their static moments in time.

Is this what happened to Wynn? she thought with panic. *Am I dead too?*

But, no. Deemus had chosen her. It made no sense to save her life just to take it now.

She walked past the woman and down a set of narrow stairs, her hand trailing the wall, her skin, her senses, everything so *alive*. There was a strange repulsion in the air, like her very essence was at odds with this awful non-space around her.

The house felt unreal, temporal.

She walked a long gallery and stared out the window. She was at the front of the house; the very drive she and Wynn had followed on their first arrival stretched out below her, the world beyond nothing but mist.

This house is a thing outside of time.

She felt her own solidness, and she felt the tremor of spirits all around her.

Mila smiled.

The house had made its first mistake. *You've shown your hand. You're a thing that's alive.*

Anything alive can be killed.

Mila could feel the house's exhaustion, like a horse that had foundered and lay shuddering in the grass. She'd forced it to defend itself, and now it was weakened, gasping for recovery.

Her path to the hidden library was quiet, but it gave her an uncanny sensation as though something enormous drew labored breaths around her. *"This is not an ordinary house, and I am not an ordinary man,"* Deemus had said. She'd sent the two of them hurtling to their certain deaths, and yet they'd both survived. The house had intervened, and something like that must take massive energy. This house was not invulnerable—not if she could force its hand like this.

She'd pierced the magician's curtain, and now she was going to strip away the secrets.

"Wynn, please help me," she whispered, the enormity of the library pressing down on her.

There was a sound like a stolen breath, and Mila turned, her eye falling on a book just a shade more vibrant than the others. She ran, her skin prickling with the feeling that she passed through the breath of a hundred stolen lives.

She opened the book and her pulse quickened. Handwritten—a journal. Diagrams and schematics and strange devices in faded ink.

I am getting closer—every day I feel it. I stand in the tower and hear the wind sing all around me, watch the stars dance in the heavens. They speak to me, they promise the knowledge of the heavens, but I cannot yet speak their language. But I know it is all around me—the breath of God, the language of the cosmos, the Music of the Spheres. All my long years on this earth, all the wonders I have seen—Gravenhearst shall be my masterpiece, my last work.

Mila turned to the inside cover—the name "Kepler Theodore Deemus" was written in ink. A shock went through her. That name was on the portrait outside her bedchambers—the man with the look of another world. *Could he be the one who built Gravenhearst?* She flipped forward: page after page of writing and strange technical drawings.

Her fingers paused.

An etching of a tall stone wall stretched between two towers. Kepler had drawn portions of the masonry as if they had been excavated to expose the interior of the wall itself. What she saw strained her mind—massive tubes that stretched through the wall from one tower to the next—one twisted like an elongated conch shell, another like a long thin trumpet, and the third a stretched oval.

It was labeled "Aural Architectures."

Mila gazed at the tubes, thinking of Zahra's face, her eyes so wide and panicked as she hissed, "*Don't speak!*"

Could devices like these be built into Gravenhearst? Could the walls themselves be listening?

Mila turned to the next page, her skin crawling. There was an enormous drawing, architectural in its scale. It showed Gravenhearst, layer upon layer, and underneath, the cellar. Dead-center was a device, rounded like an egg tipped on end. Countless tubes splayed out from the device, extending into the walls of Gravenhearst, a labyrinth of connections. There was a small sketch in pencil next to the formal schematics: an anatomical drawing of a heart, arteries branching off from its rounded form.

The night of the failed escape, Deemus had quoted her own words back at her; he'd known every detail right down to her plan to cut their hair and pass as boys. Mila had only spoken those words to Wynn in the privacy of their room.

Could Deemus hear everything that went on in Gravenhearst?

Mila's quiet words to Wynn in the darkness, their hopes of escape—it was all dust and ash in the face of Deemus sitting at the heart of Gravenhearst, stealing their words, devouring their future.

But the *mirror*, Mila thought, flipping through more pages with mounting alarm. Zahra had stolen a *mirror* from Deemus's room. The fury on his face as he'd demanded the officers return it to him—it was somehow the key, she *knew* it.

There was a sound like a child's gasp, and something flew through the air toward her. Mila bit back a scream.

An old book, its pages riffling as though blown by a strong wind. Then the pages stilled, held open by invisible hands.

Father's experiment went terribly wrong—his mad desire to funnel the energy of the heavens through Gravenhearst has wiped him from this earth, or perhaps absorbed him into the house itself. I cannot be sure. The man spent a lifetime in pursuit of madness, and all we have to show for it is a blighted astronomy tower and dwindling resources.

The house has a mind of its own, but I believe I can harness it. The energy of Gravenhearst can be changed. While father was obsessing about the stars, I was seeking real knowledge, the forbidden texts. My travels were fruitful and the library grows day by day.

A true spell contains something of the artist himself. I'm getting closer—I will compose a masterwork of my own.

The floor tremored and she cried out—the house was fighting back. She scanned the open pages, her heart a pickaxe against her ribs. *Read faster, faster!*

Then:

At last I defeat Father's lunacy—his sad, pointless benevolence. He thought to keep me away from magic, but I proved myself superior. Now I wrest his invention from its purpose. Gravenhearst is bent to a <u>new</u> will, bound to my male heirs, and the power of their desire. I have breached the 49th gate, beheld knowledge too great for lesser men. Blood-soaked glass is now the stopper in the bottle, the key to the everlasting alchemy of souls. I stand in the crucible of gateways, unstoppable, the true Master of Gravenhearst.

The room blurred, and Mila screamed, pain ripping through her. She dug her fingers into the book, but it shred from her grasp; her muscles and skin twisted and warped, and she thought she might die.

Everything stopped. She lay on the library floor gasping, the book gone from her hands.

"Nothing works as it should!"

Her blood froze at the sound of Andrew Deemus's voice above her, loud and angry.

"The power is still immense, Master. Your skill grows. I believe, in time, we can enspell another mirror."

Asher.

Mila looked up, just a fraction of a movement, and saw them on the iron catwalk above her.

"Time!" Deemus spat, advancing on Asher. "I am *blind* without the mirror—and you speak of *time*? The whole house is off balance. I can *feel* it! The spirits are restless, and someone is fighting me!"

"Yes, like something folding in upon itself. You must continue your spellwork—the most powerful spells are invented, not borrowed. You must make them your own."

Deemus turned with a curse and stalked toward the ladder that led to the main floor.

Mila slid back, trying to reach the cover of a nearby chair, trying to delay the inevitable.

Deemus saw her.

He stopped, his hand reaching for the railing, and Asher's eyes followed his master's expression of disbelief.

She ran for the corridor, the clanking sound of the men's feet on the iron ringing in her ears. She reached the switchbacking staircase—

A hand clamped on her arm and dragged her back.

23

Curtis

CURTIS DROPPED SAGE AT SCHOOL AND HEADED TOWARD MAIN Street, a desperate feeling clawing his ribs.

Things were spinning beyond his control. The voices were a constant chorus on the periphery of his mind, and he fought the urge to press his hands over his ears, to block the words that wanted to form from the chaos.

He'd wanted to kill Frank today.

So fix it, you pathetic fuck. He glared into the rearview mirror, his mind churning. *Get to work and fucking fix it.*

Last night he'd been so sure of what he'd seen in the gloom of the mirror—Mila, like a girl from a fairy tale, some mythical gorgeous image made flesh in his mind, brought forth by the sheer *wanting* of it—but in the harsh light of day, with asshole uncles and crazy fathers and voices in his head that would *not shut up*, he was moving toward less sure.

The Willowhaven fire station was a growing beacon on the horizon. The clues he'd found yesterday had finally penetrated his thick skull and he'd thought of a next step.

He pulled into the station parking lot with a sharp movement.

There would be answers here. There had to be.

Small towns were quicksand that never let go. Fire Marshall Evans of 1894 had worked the family profession, and you could bet the future generations did too. The whole damn town was like that.

One rotting incestuous echo of the past, burning that tread deeper and deeper, people living out predetermined lives.

He slammed his truck door and set his shoulders toward the Fire Hall.

He was going to get answers.

Inside, he ignored the glances of the firemen, rapping once on the door marked "Chief Evans." The Evans of 1894 had been there for the Gravenhearst fire, had mourned the loss of the Kenton girls in the newspaper clipping. That wasn't the kind of thing your ancestors forgot.

"In," a sandpaper voice said.

Curtis went.

Evans looked up from his desk, eyes narrowing. "Curtis." There was an edge to his voice. After Tom's frequent run-ins with emergency services, Curtis could hardly blame the man. "Hope everything's okay."

"Dad's fine." Curtis shoved his hands in his pockets, bracing himself. "I've got a question for you—something for school actually—history project."

Evans nodded and creaked back in his old leather chair.

"I was out riding the other day, and I think I found something."

Evans waited.

"The old site of Gravenhearst."

Evans nodded slowly. There were pictures all around the oak-paneled office, faded memories going back a hundred years. Curtis had the unnerving sensation that long-dead fire crews were watching him.

"And what makes you think that?"

There was one photo, a sepia portrait. The man wore a hundred fires etched into the lines around his eyes. "Well, my friend Avi, actually, he said—"

"Curtis," Evans cut him off. "What's this about?"

His heart stalled. "Your great-grandfather was there, wasn't he? He saw the fire?"

Evans looked up at the picture Curtis had noticed.

"Yes." He nodded slowly. "He was."

"Why doesn't anyone talk about it?" Curtis finally asked the crushing silence.

"Some chapters in history should stay closed."

"You don't believe in curses, do you?" Curtis said, the words out before he could stop them.

"I believe some fires are meant to happen."

"The Deemus men hurt women, didn't they?" Curtis kept his voice hard. "And no one stopped them."

"I'd say that fire means *someone* stopped them," Chief Evans said. "And that's all I'm going to say. Digging into that mess nearly ruined my great-grandpa's career. Some things should stay in the past."

Curtis stared at him a long moment, fists knotted, then left.

Back in the parking lot, the whispers seethed. *Some things* won't *stay in the past*, Curtis thought. And some people don't have the luxury of letting go.

He cursed and slammed his door.

If people wouldn't give him answers, he'd find them himself.

Queen's University was a half hour away—there had to be more details there. But he'd never be done in time for 3:05 pickup.

He sent Sage a text.

Want to spend the night at someone's house?

His phone rang.

"You trying to ditch me again?"

"Just got a call that there's a special-order part for the Beast I've gotta pick up in Kingston."

"Yeah, okay. Charlene's parents are out of town for the week, so I can hang there."

"Okay. I'll call later, make sure everything's cool."

"You mean check up on me to make sure we're not having drunken coke-crazed orgies?"

"Exactly."

"Later."

Curtis was four hours into completely fruitless research at the Queen's University library when he heard a voice that he really should have expected.

"And thus I see a mirage before me, a hallowed sight, a once-in-ten-years sight!" Avi stood, hands across his chest, mouth open in exaggerated delight. "Do I truly see Curtis Garrett, sloth, ruffian, his comely brow bent over a table of books on a Friday afternoon in this, the Stauffer Library lounge?"

"I will kick you over this railing," Curtis said, nodding toward the two-story drop to the atrium floor below.

"Ah me, yes," Avi said, throwing his lanky form down on the couch next to Curtis. "It is my Curtis after all." He propped his sneaker-clad feet onto the coffee table and turned his head dramatically toward Curtis. "Well, we know *I'm* here because of Friday AP research." His voice trailed off expectantly, waiting.

Curtis grimaced.

Avi sighed even more dramatically and leaned forward to search through the papers and periodicals that covered the table. "Economic holdings of Andrew Deemus." He squinted accusingly. Curtis crossed his arms and refused to answer. Avi made a gesture worthy of a magician and plunged his hand through the pile. "Oh, a real page-turner—*Charitable Donations to Willowhaven from the Years 1885–1895*." He looked at Curtis again, eyebrows disappearing under his floppy curls. "Dude, *I* am the one in the AP classes. Even *I* don't need to know this stuff."

Curtis sighed the sigh of a martyr and tossed him the photo of Mila.

"She lived at Gravenhearst. I want to know what happened to her in that house. I want to know why people thought it was cursed."

Avi stared at the picture, then back at Curtis.

"Dude, you finally fall in love and you're doing it *Terminator* style?" he crowed. "That's *awesome*. Now we just have to figure out how to send you back in time to protect her from evil cyborgs. Also, we should figure out how to make you not die in the last ten minutes of the movie. That's such a downer."

"Really, that's what you have to say?" Curtis asked, pitching a dirty candy wrapper at him.

Avi shrugged. "So I take it this is the result of all your mysteriousness yesterday?"

His tone was light, but Curtis could tell he was still annoyed by the rejection.

"I'm sorry about that. It was a weird day." He *was* sorry, and now that Avi had caught him, Curtis was strangely relieved for the company. He wished he could tell his friend what was really behind all this, that the wind was speaking to him, following him. That Mila was in his mirror and it all *meant something* and he had to figure out what.

But that sounded, you know, *crazy*.

Avi would hear one word of that hot mess and be carefully and lovingly booking him an appointment with Tom Garrett's psychiatrist.

Avi shrugged. "You will make it up to me with pizza."

"Yes, I will," Curtis replied.

"Okay, in honor of this newfound study-leaf you're turning over, I will assist while overlooking your various faults and deficiencies."

"How kind of you."

"I think so." Avi shuffled through the papers Curtis had collected, his academic eye scanning with frightening speed. "Okay, so the Deemus family paid for practically everything around here. They were the Rockefellers, basically."

"Yeah, I know," Curtis said, irritated. "I can read. But I don't care about that shit. I don't care that they owned half the land around here. I don't care that"—he picked up one of the photocopied pages and re-examined it—"Andrew Deemus paid for renovations to the Willowhaven Grand Hotel." He smacked the periodical back down on the table. "I want to know why whole families went missing."

"Oh, Curtis," Avi said, shaking his head sadly, "you are not a researcher." He ran his hand along the pages of the periodical. "These are breadcrumbs. Jumping-off points for further lines of inquiry." Curtis raised an eyebrow, unimpressed. "And then there's this guy," Avi said, tapping the top of the article. "Gerald Iveson, PhD. He wrote the article, so he must be fairly knowledgeable about Gravenhearst. And look, professor of economics right here at Queen's." Avi gave his ringlets a let's-get-down-to-business head-bob and typed something into his phone. He twirled a finger slowly through the air to indicate the line was ringing. Then he paused his finger mid-twirl.

"Office hours tomorrow between three and four thirty."

"So today all we have is the history of Gravenhearst economics," Curtis sighed.

"It would appear," Avi replied.

"All right," Curtis said, standing. "Pizza?"

"Pizza."

Avi examined the water-stained pamphlet of ghost stories as they waited for their pizza in the bustling Wooden Heads restaurant. It was filled with college kids and professors, and for a moment, it made Curtis want to wing the Parmesan shaker across the room into the backlit bar, because it reminded him that this was the life Avi would be disappearing into in less than a year. Leaving him behind.

Much to Avi's dismay, Curtis had given no thought to his own future. His future didn't exist. There was only moment-to-moment survival. There was the finish line of The Big Eighteen. There was Legal Guardian of Sage. The day Sage left Willowhaven for her own future was the day he might start to give some consideration to his.

If he even had one.

"So you stole this from a library," Avi said.

"Yeah."

Avi shook his head, ringlets bobbing, his lips pressed together in displeasure.

"What?" Curtis said.

"You *stole* this from a *library*," Avi repeated, as if this was a really terrible thing.

Curtis shrugged his shoulders. Avi gave up. He examined the pamphlet again. Curtis let his eye wander over the igloo-shaped red-brick pizza oven that dominated the open kitchen.

"And those other books?" Avi was staring at the spines of *The Mystery of Alchemy* and *Mirror Magic Through the Ages*.

"You were the one who said the place was haunted."

Avi leaned back in his chair and plucked at his shirt. The brown graphic tee assured his fellow café diners *I aim to misbehave*. "Yeah, sure. I'm just not sure why you care so much."

"Well, I'm thinking of a new career plan. Ghost hunter. Sage can be the camera woman, and you can be the assistant who trips over everything and screams a lot."

"I resent that," Avi said.

"No, you don't."

"No, I don't. It's completely true."

He paused as the waitress delivered their Volcano pizza with extra cheese.

"Look, I just think it's weird," Curtis said. "The newspapers report the fact of the fire, and then there's that business with the horses, and then nothing. No talk about what caused it? The biggest house in the countryside burns to the ground with everyone inside and that only merits two articles? Does that seem right?"

"Things burned down a lot in the old days, Curtis. They didn't have flame-retardant mattresses."

"It's like they're hiding something."

"*They* who?" Avi wiped pizza sauce from his chin.

"The whole town. It's like they'd rather just forget." Curtis stared down at Mila's photograph. "I think she knew something."

"They are devouring me."

No. That was just a dream. A nightmare.

Mostly. Curtis thought about the better part of that dream. The part where he'd pressed Mila against him, fed on her lips, and gotten swept away in the feeling that he could lose himself in her because she was just like him.

Was there such a thing as feeling that connected to another human being? Was he allowed to have something like that?

He ate in silence for a while and tried not to watch the couple at the next table holding hands. They looked I've-never-had-any-problems-in-my-whole-life happy, and it pissed Curtis off. He dropped his slice of pizza and wondered if he could get away with ordering a beer. Most people took one look at his height and shoulders and assumed he was way past eighteen.

He felt Avi's eyes on him. Curtis rolled his own in return. "Out with it."

Avi's eyes went wide with mock innocence. He spread his elegant hands in an exaggerated gesture. "Nothing, man. I mean, you usually go out with the same girl for a week, two tops, and now suddenly you're obsessed with some hot dead girl from the Victorian age. I'm just having trouble connecting the dots."

Avi was looking at him expectantly, and Curtis was reminded of fourth grade when he first met Avi. By that age, Curtis had already come to expect that kids his age wouldn't want to play with him. It was like people could smell Dad's crazy on him. Sage had always been somehow immune to this. Maybe because she looked so much like their mom; maybe because he looked so much like their dad. Whatever the reason, Curtis had made peace with it by the fourth grade and was content to simply be the kid that people mostly didn't challenge. A fifth-grade bully tried once, but Curtis dealt him such a swift and savage beatdown that few tried it again. Curtis learned the power of a dramatic statement that day.

But Avi had been new in town that year, and even though Curtis was sure Avi had heard the other kids' whispers, Avi sat in the top level of the schoolyard play structure and offered Curtis one of his die-cast cars. Curtis had been so taken aback by this display of automotive goodwill that he stood frozen for a moment, hunched over between the monkey bars and the big yellow tube, Avi staring up at him expectantly. *What are you waiting for? Come be my friend!*

This was the look Avi had now. His poet's eyes large and quizzical, his head half-cocked his dark eyebrows drawn together.

Curtis wanted to tell him the truth. But . . .

He couldn't.

Something deflated inside Avi, and it hurt Curtis to see it. It made him feel like an asshole.

Avi took another huge mouthful of pizza and shook his head. "Are you ever going to trust anyone?"

"Probably not."

"That's harsh, dude," Avi said.

Curtis looked away. Avi's disappointment was like a weight strong enough to pull him deep underwater. For a moment, Curtis could actually feel it, as if his shitty-friend status was an anchor around his foot, dragging him beneath dark waters, farther from Avi, farther from a world where he had any place. "I gotta check on Sage," he said, pulling out his phone.

"Convenient," Avi said, nodding in an unimpressed way.

They both threw some bills on the table and headed out as Curtis dialed.

Sage answered the phone laughing.

"You good?" Curtis asked. He could barely hear her over the sound of teenage girls singing at the top of their lungs to loud music.

"Awesome," she called above the noise.

"No orgies."

"Not yet."

"Well, call me if one starts."

"So you can come and ruin it?"

"Yep."

"Will do."

It was one of those cool fall evenings that brought university towns like Kingston to life. Curtis took it all in for a moment. The people all bright and jostling and full of smug, expectant things—course syllabi, philosophical debates, a *future*. These people were going to go out and change the world. Curtis was just trying to survive it.

But Sage belonged somewhere like this.

A group of artsy college kids laughed over drinks in an outdoor patio across the street, and Curtis could see her there, making friends with other little wonderfully pretentious weirdos, leading her league of admiring followers, establishing some sort of avant-garde art consortium.

But potential like that had to be taken care of. He had to get her through this nightmare unscathed, so she could have that life.

"I think there's an art store at the end of this street," Curtis said. And because Avi was such a good friend, Curtis knew he didn't have to explain what he could possibly want with an art store. Five minutes later, Curtis had bought a foot-long tin of colored pencils that had no business costing that much. Sage had a set one-third that size that she'd worn down to tiny nubs, and a mini shrine in her bedroom built around the tin.

Curtis and Avi headed back to the truck, the sky over Kingston turning gold and purple as the sun began to set. Sailing boats were docking in the harbor and, far in the distance, the old military fort kept watch over the horizon.

Curtis climbed into the truck, a bitter loneliness rising inside him. "Frank stopped by this morning," he said as he started the engine. The whispers picked up in intensity, humming with a stronger rhythm as if just the mention of Frank was enough to jolt them into high gear. Curtis struggled not to react.

"Came to bring a homemade pie and declarations of his undying love, I assume?"

"Yeah, that and threaten to call social services."

Avi's face darkened. "What?"

"Well, not in so many words. Bunch of bullshit about Dad being too big a burden for us."

Avi was very silent.

"I think it's just about the house," Curtis said quickly. "He's always wanted it."

"He's the oldest, right?"

"Yeah, he should have inherited, but there was a falling-out with Grandpa. The old man bypassed Frank and left the house and lumber business to Dad instead. But Dad's not really in any condition to run a company, so Frank contested the will. They awarded him the family business, but Dad got the house. And Frank has to pay him a percentage of the company profits. It's kind of fucked up, I guess."

They drove in silence.

"Curtis—" Avi began.

Curtis's phone rang. He answered, feeling like he'd just escaped hearing something he really didn't want to hear. "Yeah?"

"Curtis?"

"Yeah, who's this?"

"Angela, down at Duke's Bar?"

"Okay . . ." Curtis felt his stomach clench.

"You better get down here right now. Your dad is here. And so is Frank."

"I'll be there in five."

Curtis floored the gas pedal, the voices screaming in his head. "Shit," he said. "SHIT."

"What?" Avi demanded, clearly unnerved by Curtis's reaction.

"Dad and Frank are at the bar."

"Oh, shit."

24

Curtis

CURTIS'S STOMACH WAS A BUBBLING PIT AS THEY JERKED TO a stop in front of the bar. He jumped out of the truck and heard his father bellowing.

He wrenched the door open and his heart dropped out.

His father was standing in the center of the dark-red-lit room, overturned tables and chairs all around him. People were standing in clusters at the edges of the dingy space, some laughing, some putting the pool table and slot machines more firmly between them and the crazy guy. Angela was behind the bar, her tough-as-nails face down-lit by the little hanging lights along the bar, and she gave Curtis this soft pitying look that made him want to throw up.

"I know what you all want!" his father yelled, shaking a bar stool in the air with one fist. His face was red and flushed and there were little droplets of spit at the corners of his mouth. "You're all in on it!"

"DAD." Curtis moved in, but then something stopped him. Frank was sitting at the bar, his hands pressed a little too hard against the counter, his eyes wide. The man was afraid.

Curtis reached out for his father's arm and got a quick backhand to the face. He felt cartilage crunch and tasted blood in the back of his throat. His father turned and looked at him as if surprised to see him there.

"I've got proof now, Son," Tom said excitedly. "He said it right here in front of all these witnesses." Tom waved his hand to indicate Frank and the crowd of people.

The VLT in the corner was blinking its red lights in time with the '70s rock, and Curtis thought it was just too cruel that his world was about to come apart while a cheap-ass jukebox screamed "Highway to Hell." Someone took a picture with their phone and Curtis turned, ready to smash the thing, but then he heard the sound he dreaded more than anything.

Sirens.

Red and blue lights strobed through the windows and Curtis turned in a near-panic, knowing what came next.

"I—I just want to *help*," Frank said.

A sound came from Tom's throat, like a blood-drunk warrior rallying his raiding party, and as the two police officers came through the door, he charged Frank like a mad bull.

"Highway to hell . . ."

The brothers were the same height and build, but Tom slammed into Frank with an impact that sent Curtis's uncle flying backward into the wall. He hit with a *thump* and the sound of cracking paneling, and then Tom was on top of him, bellowing at the top of his lungs, hands around Frank's throat.

"DAD, NO!" Curtis yelled, sprinting forward. He grabbed the metal napkin holder off the nearest table and slammed it into the back of his father's skull. Tom didn't even react. The cops were there, trying to pull Tom off of Frank. Tom let go of his brother's throat long enough to send one cop reeling with a wild punch, then turned back to his prize. Curtis leapt on his father, his arm around Tom's neck in a choke hold, squeezing with all he had. *Please, God*, he thought. His father stood and slammed backward, and Curtis felt a burst of agony as his lower back smashed into the side of the bar.

"Nobody's gonna slow me down . . ."

Curtis held on and his father started to wobble under the choke hold. Then the other cop's baton flashed and Tom fell.

Curtis pulled his arms free from his dad's deadweight and fell back on the ground, gasping for breath.

"Nobody's gonna mess me around . . ."

The cops were trying to cuff Tom, but he was struggling again, bellowing these awful sounds like a deranged animal being burned alive. A cop pressed a stun gun to Tom's back and let loose a three-second burst. Tom's head dropped to the ground, and he finally lay still.

Curtis realized Avi was trying to help him up. Avi's face was white, his eyes wide with a kind of sympathetic horror. He'd heard stories, but had never seen.

First time for everything.

"Hiiighwaaay to hell, I'm on the hiiighwaaay to hell . . ."

The paramedics were securing Tom to a gurney, wheeling him away.

"Where are you taking him?" Curtis asked the officer, his mouth dry.

"Willowhaven General for observation. We'll need you to come down to the station, answer some questions."

"I think I might have gotten his meds wrong this morning," Curtis said in a rush. "I—I was distracted. This wasn't his fault."

"Hiiighwaaay to hell, hiiighwaaay to hell . . ."

Officer Brown sighed, giving Curtis the once-over. "He's going to have to spend forty-eight hours under observation at the hospital. Just how it has to be."

"This can't continue," Frank babbled as a medic swabbed at a cut on his head. "It's not safe for him, for these people . . ."

"This is your fault, you dumb bastard!" Curtis yelled, rage splitting his chest like a volcano. Avi's arms locked around him as he started toward Frank to finish what his father started.

"I just want him to get the help he needs!"

"All right, that's enough, sir," an officer said to Frank as Avi towed Curtis away.

Curtis could feel the walls closing in on him, the dark of that black well rising up, towering over him. Everyone was staring and Curtis wanted to give them something to stare at, wanted to take someone's face and beat it till it couldn't stare at him anymore.

"Cool it, man," Avi hissed.

Curtis jerked his arm out of Avi's grasp and pushed his way through the crowd.

"And I'm goin' do-own, aaall the waaay," Bon Scott screeched from the jukebox.

Curtis punched the door open and stepped out into the night to see the ambulance pulling away. More people were gathering to watch the fun.

Curtis put eyes on his truck, focused all his discipline on not reacting to the comments he was hearing, the laughter. A second Garrett could not be arrested tonight.

Inside the truck, he stared at the red dash lights and tried to tell himself that the world was not caving in. He could feel Avi's awkwardness beside him, his very normal, very sheltered friend trying to think of something to say.

But there was nothing to say. Things go wrong. Things that can't be put back together.

"I need to get drunk," Curtis said. "Who's having a party tonight?"

They pulled up the drive to Mercy Redmond's; and even before they'd reached the white-and-green-trimmed farmhouse, it was clear that the party was indeed here tonight. Curtis felt the thumping bass in his chest from outside in the yard. A crowd was clustered around a bonfire in the side yard, and Jennifer Mayhew was already puking in the bushes alongside the house.

Good.

"Curtis," Avi said nervously, "are you sure this is what you want to do right now?"

Curtis didn't answer. Hell yes, this was what he wanted to do. People let their demons out to play when they drank, and right now ,his *fuck it* demon was rattling the cage. It was going to kick the cage door down and set fire to the world. And Curtis was going to laugh and watch it all burn.

The front door was open, the hall littered with jackets and a couple of passed-out partiers. Frat-boy cologne, sweat, and prom-princess perfume mixed with the smell of old farmhouse. Curtis shoved past anyone who got too close to him as he made a beeline for the kitchen and the keg. The music was loud enough that it almost drowned out the jumble of whispers in his head. His nose was throbbing, probably broken, and there was blood down the front of his grey T-shirt. This attracted some glances, but the look on his face stopped any questions dead in their tracks. Sanjit Patel handed him a full cup, and Curtis downed it in one long gulp. He held it out for a refill. Sanjit complied without comment and glanced at Avi.

"You want one?" he asked.

"Yeah, sure," Avi said, watching Curtis drain the second drink as fast as the first.

Curtis spotted a bottle of vodka and grasped it around the neck with one fist. He nodded to Avi and they headed out the back door for the bonfire.

"Hey, that's Aaron's vodka," Sanjit called after them.

Curtis turned and stared at him. "It's mine now."

Sanjit decided it wasn't worth it, and Curtis headed out into the yard, taking deep swigs. Avi sipped his beer with a worried expression.

"Curtis, give me your keys."

"What?"

"Your keys, right now."

"Yeah, whatever," Curtis said, tossing the keys on the ground between them. He took another long pull off the bottle as Avi pocketed the keys.

The night smelled of pine trees and wood smoke, and the sky was a wash of blue deepening to ink-dark navy. The lacy silhouettes of trees stood black against the indigo, and just a sliver of champagne moon hung overhead. As Curtis tipped his bottle skyward, stars cut points of darkness from the sky and pinpricks of light pushed through, growing brighter as the darkness deepened. The vodka burned his throat and he relished the sensation—like maybe it would scorch the weakness inside and leave him charred and hollow. Just burn the voices right out of him.

Curtis spotted Mary Vandenberg in between the leaping flames of the bonfire. She was dancing with some of her clan and a couple of football players. He saw the moment she noticed him, and her face changed from mildly bored to all-circuits-are-go; she tossed her blonde waves and brushed against Jock Number One while giving Curtis a look that said, "*You like what you see?*"

Tonight, Curtis liked it.

He held the vodka bottle up, and she sauntered over as if half the fun of dancing with guys was leaving them wanting more. Her rejects groaned with disappointment and tried to call her back, but she ignored them, running her fingers along Curtis's as she took the bottle. She drank a shot, then put a hand on his chest. Sparks flew up from the bonfire, leaving little fire trails across Curtis's vision. The embers popped and hissed, and the air was full of smoke and spice and Mary's skin.

His head was pleasantly swimming, and he liked the feel of her fingers on him. It was simple and warm and didn't require any thinking. Her hands slid over the waistband of his jeans, low on his hips, and his breath caught when her fingers grazed skin. Her lips curved upward at his body's response and she took him by the hand, leading him back to the house. There were some catcalls as they headed up the stairs, and a moment where he registered Avi, leaning against a wall by himself, watching them glumly, but Curtis couldn't care. The whole world had spun past his control, and he was tired of fighting it. His *fuck it* demon howled in approval.

She led him to an empty bedroom and he sat on the bed in the dark, watching as Mary peeled off her top and let it drop to the floor. She was wearing a black satin bra, everything about her pure perfection. She straddled him, and he let his hands go where they wanted. His brain was on autopilot; there was only this moment, right now. He let the uncomplicated feeling of *want* swallow him whole.

Mary pulled his shirt over his head and tossed it to the side, and Curtis groaned at the feel of her skin on his. She stopped, her fingers in his hair, her gorgeously soft breasts pressed against his chest. She looked down at him, really *looked* at him. Her green-flecked eyes softened, grew concerned. "Hey," she said, her voice low, "did your dad really get taken away tonight?"

Curtis blinked as if he'd just been doused in ice water. "What?"

"Jeanine texted me, said she saw the whole thing. It—" She paused as if she wasn't sure how to say the next bit. She ran a gentle finger over the line of his cheekbone, her breath hitching, teeth biting self-consciously at her bottom lip for just a moment. "It must have been awful for you."

Curtis felt the fantasy crashing down on him. He had to get away from her.

This was not something he could handle right now. This was Mary. Hard, cruel, tough as nails, don't-give-a-shit Mary Vandenberg. She was not supposed to care. He was here with her because this meant nothing to either of them. And now she'd ruined it.

He turned away from her, trying to stand, trying to escape the flood of black that wanted to swamp him, hold him under, slam him against the walls until he was broken and bleeding and senseless with the horror of everything. The room spun as he grabbed frantically for his shirt.

"Curtis! What the hell?" Mary said, falling forward on the bed as he disentangled himself.

"Screw you!" she yelled as he escaped the room, the bottle firmly in hand once more. He heard pain in her voice, and his demon thrashed against the cage, howled blood-drunk on pain that wasn't his, pain that could match his. The whole world was pain and guts and horror, and Curtis wanted to see it all. He wanted to shred the façade and let the world feast on the entrails.

The stairs were a blur; people's faces were a blur. He heard Avi's voice calling his name, and he almost fell, knocked into some people and laughed. He fed at the bottle while the sounds and smells and crush of bodies spun around him, and then Avi was pulling him through the crowd toward the door, and he caught a breath that reminded him there was more to the world than just that screaming, spinning house.

They were out in the dark with the cool air rushing over them, and Curtis was on the ground, damp grass against his skin. The earth was pressing up against him, and his body was heavy and weightless all at once. Avi had taken the bottle away and was sitting beside him quietly. The bonfire leapt and burned in the distance, and the people standing around it were silhouettes in black paper. They were scraps that could go up with a single spark. The stars reeled overhead, dipping and swirling in the endless field of black above him.

And the whispers were everywhere. They were so loud the whole world must have heard them. The stars were speaking to him—speaking the language of the heavens—and Curtis could almost understand.

"Avi," Curtis said, reaching out for his friend like Avi could keep him from drowning. "Mila's trying to tell me something. I saw her yesterday, in the mirror."

The stars were so bright, he could touch them if he just lifted his hands. "I think I can save her."

And with those words, he was gone.

25

Mila

"HOW DID YOU GET IN HERE?" DEEMUS ASKED, HIS EYES HARD, lips pressed into a thin slash.

Mila stared at him, heart pounding, trying to think of what to say. Was there a point in lying? Did it matter if he knew what the house had done? He shook her, and her thoughts rattled, strategies breaking and scattering in her mind.

"I don't know," she gasped, trying to hide her anger. He was enraged, and she'd tested him to the breaking point already.

Make him believe he's broken you—take his guard down.

"I don't know," she moaned, forcing tears to build, calling up emotions she'd been burying for longer than she knew. "I don't know what's happening," she cried, letting her voice hit a high note. She felt tears slide down her cheeks and let her knees go soft. Deemus grabbed her, holding her up, and she let her head loll, her eyes flutter.

She heard Deemus hiss air through his teeth. "Get her back to bed," he snapped at Asher. "Her chambers," he added, his voice relenting just slightly. Deemus's hands were exchanged for Asher's, and she let the manservant steer her with an iron grip up the stairs and back to the black passageway. She forced herself to lean on him as though she hadn't the strength to go on, and he pushed her quickly through a door and out into a hallway she'd never seen before. She could sense he was trying to disorient her further, and she let herself be pliable in his grip, praying that her still-bruised body was enough to convince them she was too weak to be a threat.

When they arrived at her room, Asher led her to the bed and pressed her down by the shoulders. She kept her face weak and foggy, but noted that he seemed less sleek than the morning her mother had disappeared. But still not as worn and rumpled as he'd appeared when they first arrived.

She'd been struck with revulsion upon first sight of him, and she tried now to discern what was behind this sensation he gave her, as though he weren't quite real, as if he might change before her eyes into something else.

"What. Did. You. See?" Asher said, each word drawn out and spaced like a threat. He took her chin and examined her like a specimen under a microscope.

"I don't know," she whispered. "I was so frightened. Everything changed—the house changed, and I didn't know where I was!"

He stared down at her for a long moment, then released her chin.

He left the room.

Mila lay back on the bed with a gasp of relief. She looked up into the grey canopy and her body felt like a great weight. She'd made a show of weakness for them, but now as the adrenaline subsided, she realized she had nothing left.

The pillow was soft, the bedcovers so heavy and smooth. She twisted her legs up to her chest and pulled the linens around her. She'd done enough for one day.

She'd survived.

It would have to be enough.

She couldn't keep her eyes open. Sunlight streamed through the tall windows, but she closed her eyes and turned her face to the wall.

I've done enough.

She slept.

26

Curtis

CURTIS WOKE TO A POUNDING HEADACHE.

It took him a moment to realize he was in his own bed.

That confused him.

He rolled with a groan and his feet found the floor. He lurched toward the hallway. Bathroom. He needed a bathroom.

When he saw himself in the mirror, he knew he must have partied hard. His eyes were bloodshot with purple circles beneath, and his shirt was streaked with blood and other substances he'd rather not think about. He could smell booze and puke, and he fought the urge to retch.

He rubbed a hand over his face, trying to dislodge sharp crusty bits from the corners of his eyes. His nose flared red-hot.

Yep, Dad broke it.

Wonderful.

His mouth was a scum-filled sewer. He spat in the sink and searched for mouthwash, finally settling for his toothbrush and some aggressive scrubbing.

Curtis dragged himself down the stairs, toward the kitchen and the smell of coffee.

"Morning, sunshine," Avi said.

Curtis groaned and fell into a chair.

"And did you enjoy oblivion?" Avi handed him a cup of black coffee.

"Don't make me hurt you," Curtis mumbled.

"And how are you going to do that when you can barely stand?" Avi said, pinging a spoon on the side of his coffee mug several times in quick succession, just to really rub it in.

"Screw off."

Avi sat.

Curtis glanced around. "You bring me home last night?"

Avi nodded. "Around three. I wanted to make sure you'd puked it all out before I put you in the truck. Vomit in small enclosed spaces is really not my thing."

"You got me up two flights of stairs?"

"Oh yeah. I may have dropped you a few times, but no real damage to speak of."

"Thanks, your concern is touching."

"I know."

They sat in silence drinking their coffee.

"So, ah . . . you were talking pretty crazy last night," Avi said finally.

"Oh yeah?" Curtis had a vague impression of stars and wet grass, but couldn't put his finger on what he might have said. *Crap.*

"Yeah, you were going on about your Victorian girlfriend."

"Oh?" Curtis kept his voice neutral.

"Yeah, you said you could save her."

"Vodka, man. You should try it sometime."

"Right."

He had to save her. It was insane, but he'd felt it the first moment he'd looked at her photograph, this sense that they both understood loss, understood *trapped*. She'd looked out from her portrait at him across a hundred years, and he recognized his own isolation in that desperate expression—that horrible feeling under his ribs of nowhere to turn, no one to help.

Someone had broken her down. "*He took my sister, and he took my mother,*" she'd said. She'd been fighting to protect her family, and some rich bastard had stolen them from her. He'd be damned if he was going to let her burn to death in that evil fucking house on top of it.

Save her, save himself. The two had become almost one thing in his mind. This invasion of whispers, it had driven him to her picture, and then she'd appeared in his mirror. It was all connected, and he had to untangle the threads. If he could see into the past, if he could *save* her . . . then it would all make sense again. Something good could come out of this madness, and maybe his mind would be his again.

"*Curtis.*"

Curtis jumped. Avi was staring at him with an uneasy look on his face.

"Earth to Curtis."

"I'm gonna take a shower."

"Okaaay."

The whispers mixed with the roar of the showerhead and Curtis pushed them to that space in the back of his brain that he'd come to know in the last few days, that place where the whispers were still there, but softer, like a stream bubbling quietly at the edge of his consciousness.

The mirror. Her image in the mirror didn't make sense. The connection of the copse to Gravenhearst was obvious now. But how did the mirror fit? The only connection between the copse and the mirror was him. Wasn't it?

Maybe that was the problem.

He'd seen her photo at the library and now he was imagining things. Seeing things that weren't there. Now, who did that sound like?

Shut up, he told himself.

He turned the water off.

What he needed to figure out was how he was going to get the information he needed today without giving away what he was really after.

He was still mulling this over when he heard the front door burst open and Sage holler his name.

He was flying down the stairs, hair dripping little water trails on his T-shirt, bare feet leaving wet prints in the faded carpet.

"WHAT'S WRONG?"

She was standing in the entrance, engulfed in borrowed pj bottoms and a sweatshirt too big for her.

"What's *wrong*?" she said, like the words might inspire her to rip his throat out. Avi was leaning in the kitchen doorway, a look on his face like he just couldn't bear to watch. Sage stalked forward. "Dad gets *arrested* and I have to hear about it from my friends?" She thrust her phone at him and he looked down at the screen full of concerned messages. All those people who cared enough about her to flood her phone with texts. Curtis didn't have to look at his phone to know that there wouldn't be any messages for him.

"I'm sorry," he said, his head pounding with the shrillness of her fury, with the shame of the realization—he completely forgot about her last night.

"I didn't even know what HAPPENED," she raged, her face red, eyes slick and smudged with day-old makeup. "I thought maybe you were dead, or—"

"I'm sorry," he said again, trying to grab her and hold her—hold her like he used to when she was little and frantic and he'd wrap his arms around her until she'd stop crying—but she shoved him with surprising strength and he stumbled backward.

"You couldn't even be bothered to tell me?" she shrieked. "You didn't think I had a right to know!"

"I wasn't . . . thinking," he said, trailing off helplessly. He looked past her to Avi. Avi shrugged his shoulders, and Curtis could tell from the look on his face that he'd really fucked this up good. It was that same kind of quiet disappointment Avi wore when Curtis wouldn't level with him in the restaurant.

"I got you something," Curtis said abruptly. He'd noticed it on the kitchen table while Avi was reviving him with coffee earlier. He pushed past her, past Avi, even as he saw Avi shaking his head: *No, not now Curtis.*

But it's all right, he thought. *This will show her.* He *was* thinking of her. He was always thinking of her—she was the only reason he'd lasted this long. He snatched the bag off the table and rushed back to Sage, holding the long flat shape out between them. It wavered there while she stared at it.

"What?" she asked.

He pulled the tin of colored pencils from the bag. She'd be happy when she saw what they were, he assured himself—that brand she loved so much. The one that that famous artist she was always going on about used.

She looked at the tin, then at him. "You think you can buy me off with art supplies? Are you crazy?"

He stared at her, and the room felt very large all of a sudden, the air too loud. Her words kicked a hole in his chest, and he stood stock-still with the unreality of it.

They didn't use that word on each other. *Ever.*

She seized the tin from him and ripped it open. She threw half the pencils at him. They hit his chest and clattered to the floor, spinning and rolling into the corners of the room, and he felt something slipping away from him, felt the futility of it all. He'd failed, and now she was discarding him. She grabbed another handful of pencils and threw them at him again. The last couple she broke in half with considerable effort. She dropped them on the floor at his feet and climbed the stairs, leaving Curtis and Avi in a room full of colored pencils. Curtis felt his vision blur, felt the room turn to nothing.

He walked slowly to the door and stepped out into the morning. The wet grass was cold on his bare feet, and his clothes were still damp against his skin. He walked and felt empty, felt nothing at all.

The shed was dark and smelled of engine oil and musty wood. He had a whole second dirt bike's worth in parts out here, spread across every surface, the empty bike frame in the center of it all like a skeleton on display at the natural history museum. He stood in the darkness for a moment, then his eyes took in the pieces before him. His hands did what he could not. They started to fix things. He knocked the wrist pin out of a burned piston and looked for a new one. It would be good to have a backup ready for the day he finally rode the Beast too hard and something gave out.

Something was always ready to give out.

"Curtis."

Avi was behind him.

"Yes, Avi?"

"Are you okay?"

"No."

There was the sound of a car coming up the drive. They both turned and looked out the door.

The black Cadillac.

Curtis felt oddly calm. Like something inside him had just broken forever. It seemed right that Frank should be there at that moment.

"Stay here," Avi ordered.

Curtis followed him, slowly, mechanically.

Frank stepped out of the vehicle, holding a large manila envelope. He glanced at Avi and frowned.

"This isn't a good time," Avi said.

Frank frowned more insistently and looked to Curtis. "Thought I should tell you in person."

There was silence, and Curtis couldn't find the energy to care what came next. It was all a slow-motion train wreck, anyway.

Frank shifted uncomfortably and clutched the envelope tighter. "You know I have to do this. He could have killed me."

"What part of 'not a good time' confused you?" Avi barked.

Frank looked at Avi like he was a particularly annoying gnat, then redirected to Curtis with a wince. "I'm beginning legal proceedings to have Tom permanently committed. It's better if you don't fight me on this." He extended the papers toward Curtis, but Avi stepped into the space between them. He snatched the envelope from Frank and let loose a streak of curse words, some in Yiddish, some in Hebrew, and some that Curtis didn't think Avi even knew. He capped it all off by launching a large glob of spit at Frank's shiny shoes. It landed with perfect accuracy.

"Get the hell out of here, you *hatichat harah*!"

For a moment, Curtis thought Frank would slap Avi, but then another car turned up the drive, a battered blue Civic. Frank cursed and got back in his Cadillac, revving so hard it leapt forward and tore two strips of grass as he circled across the yard and out past the approaching vehicle.

Matt and Deanna got out, looking wary. "I brought Sage's stuff back," Deanna said hesitantly, proffering the backpack for proof.

"Sage is inside," Curtis said mildly, taking the envelope from Avi. He looked down at himself. "I guess I should get dressed if we're going to make those office hours in Kingston."

"Are you serious?" Avi asked.

"Sage has her friends," Curtis said, nodding toward the house. The movement felt unreal somehow, as if he was doing it very slowly. He should probably have felt more upset, but he just couldn't seem to find the strength to manage it. Maybe this was what shock felt like. "She'll be fine now. She doesn't need me."

"But what about your dad?" Avi was looking at him, his eyes very wide, eyebrows reaching skyward.

"I can't do anything about any of that." *All I do is make things worse.*

"But you can research a house that doesn't exist anymore."

"Avi, please."

There must have been something in the way he said *please*, because Avi closed his eyes briefly and took a deep breath. Then he said, "Okay, man, whatever you want." But he said it in this tone of voice that seemed to say, *"Please don't go off the deep end."*

Curtis turned and headed for the house.

The deep end is where I live now.

27

Mila

MILA KNEW SHE WAS RUNNING OUT OF TIME.

The lawyers had been back, and they'd brought an armload of paperwork and a nervous-looking notary. The annulment had been approved. Mila watched this all as boldly as she dared. To her black amusement, she realized that Deemus had no interest in hiding his plan from her any longer. She was his, and the devil was only in the details, things to be worked out by men in suits who looked *at* her and *through* her but not into her eyes. Mila sensed it was only a perverse sense of propriety that was holding Deemus back from announcing their wedding the instant the annulment papers were signed and the ink blotted dry.

He still wants to be admired, she thought. Men from Kingston and Willowhaven came to see Deemus; deals were struck, generous sums of money given in the name of charity and philanthropy. He was a patron of the community, a man of taste and forward thinking.

He doted on her with his sleek self-satisfied smile, giving her jewelry and dresses. He'd even taken her out to the stables to see Diablo. Her black devil had whinnied joyously, and Deemus let her feed Diablo sugar from her palm. She'd wept despite herself, knowing that Deemus had devised it as both torture and reward for her compliance.

She was fully recovered now, and she played the role of biddable decoration with skill that would have warmed her mother's stony heart.

She did this because she was waiting.

She'd had time to think, to plan. It might all go horribly wrong, but it was the strongest tactic she could construct. It was likely she'd have only one chance more, maybe two if fortune was on her side.

But her life didn't seem to support such a greedy hope. Each day she walked the halls, choosing a different path, and each day the house returned her to the shadow gallery of statues and skeletal cloches. The mockery was evident. This is all you are: specimen, still life, here for the Master's pleasure.

And Wynn's portrait grew stronger. Mila talked to her every day, asking forgiveness, hoping for another moment like in the attic—for her sister's voice to comfort, to haunt.

Her mother's portrait was complete, as distinct and clear as all the other mournful faces that lined the walls of that Bluebeard's chamber. Mila had little hope that anything could reverse what Deemus had done to them. But the words she'd read in the library—the son's scorn of his father, his claim that he would do what his father could not—that was the key. That man's dark ambitions held the key to Andrew Deemus's power, and if she could destroy him with her last breath, she'd count herself done, if not exactly satisfied.

At night she dreamed of Wynn. And sometimes of a boy with sad eyes.

The boy from the mirror.

Sometimes she dreamed him in her bed, his breath soft on her neck, hands hungry on everything else. But mostly she dreamed him in the rain, his strange thin shirt clinging to the lines of his body, his eyes bleak and lost, hands reaching out for her. Those dreams were like cold water in a blistering drought, like night air after being shut away in a tomb. They were escape.

He was escape.

I'm going to save you, he'd tell her, his hands—blown knuckles and scarred fingers—so gentle on her skin.

You can't. I'm a devil. Can't be saved. Can only burn.

One night she woke with a cry, the feel of Wynn's hand still in hers. They'd been back in Kent, with Father, and the warm certainty of *home* had been so real she hadn't known it was a dream.

She fought to keep the memory, to slide between the words and images, but they shred away—skittish, breakable things.

Grief rose, dark-cloaked and dripping oblivion. She wanted to give in—wrap herself in pain and unmake the wretched creature that was Mila. She could touch the place inside that enormous grief, the place where everything was over, let it seep through, black and heavy, until there was nothing left of her.

An eerie sensation prickled her skin like a cold wave.

She pushed up, the room cold as winter frost around her. She pulled back the covers and her feet found the floor, picking her way through the black forest of furniture. The mirror between the windows was a sheet of clouded ice.

She put her hand to it, eyes searching the darkness.

Fingertips mirrored hers, swimming up from black waters. Then a hand. Then a whole form.

Wynn regarded her from the glass.

Mila couldn't move, couldn't blink. She felt moisture on her cheeks and realized she was crying.

"I'm sorry," she whispered, the words such small things for the enormity of what they meant.

Wynn's eyes were too pale, her hair ghostly filaments, but her lip drew back in annoyance and she banged her palms sharp against the mirror. "*Pay attention,*" the movement said.

Mila nodded, strangling down tears.

Wynn blew slowly on the mirror, its surface fogging with icy crystals. Mila beat back panic as the crystals erased her sister, but then a single fingertip drew down the glass. A message formed, slowly.

leave me

Mila stared in shock, trying to understand. The mirror cleared, and now Wynn's cheeks were sunken, her arms almost see-through. This was costing her. "Wynn, stop!"

Wynn snarled that proud empress snarl and banged her palms again. Tiny splinters erupted in the glass, dark circles blooming under Wynn's eyes like black roses. "All right!" Mila gasped. "All right, I'm listening."

Wynn nodded, and the mirror fogged again.

trust the boy

There was a sound like cracking ice, and the mirror splintered in half.

Wynn was gone.

28

Curtis

THE DRIVE TO KINGSTON WAS A QUIET ONE.

Avi didn't seem to know what to say, and that suited Curtis just fine because he *had* nothing to say. He was empty inside—except for the voices.

The voices filled his head, and he imagined that Mila was somewhere at the center of the noise. He pictured her in the copse, the wind rushing past her, whipping wheat-blonde hair around her beautiful face. He saw it in slow motion, like she was underwater, her strands of hair waving like pale seaweed, her eyes wide and powerful.

Nothing about Curtis felt powerful anymore. Not that *powerful* had ever been quite the way he saw himself, but up till now, he'd existed in a space of certainty. He knew what he had to do and he did it. It didn't matter how stressful or boring or, sometimes, how gut-wrenchingly painful. He just did it.

But it had all gone to hell. He wasn't just three moves behind; he was lying broken under the accelerant-soaked game board while people threw lit matches and laughed.

He didn't know what to do anymore.

So he was doing this.

Curtis took the exit for Kingston and soon they were passing the grey stone of the old military fort, then over the bridge that crossed Kingston Harbor. It was easy to imagine what the place looked like back when Gravenhearst was still standing. Old stone buildings of Kingston grey limestone held court along the streets, brass plaques proclaiming their historic credentials.

As they entered the tree-lined boulevards of Queen's University campus, Curtis wondered if Mila had ever walked these lanes, maybe planned to attend the university. What did she want for her future before she died in a fire at seventeen?

The thought hit him with an unpleasant twist. He didn't think of her as dead. Two days ago, she'd looked at him, *right at him*. That moment was more real to him than anything.

"Are you trapped too?" she'd asked.

Yes. God, yes.

An unpleasant drizzle of rain started as they headed up the street from the parking lot, and it made a soft pattering sound on his old leather jacket. Avi pulled up the collar of his corduroy and bobbed ringlets out of his eyes as he muttered at his phone, trying to enlarge the campus map.

"This is it," Avi said finally, indicating the large four-story on the corner. "Dunning Hall." It was a heavy building faced in buff limestone, and as they passed through the thick stone-clad side entrance, Curtis had the sensation of entering a bunker.

On the second floor, they found the shoebox-size office of one Gerald Iveson, PhD.

Avi knocked on the half-open door. "Professor Iveson?"

Mr. PhD turned from his paper-swamped desk and swept them both with a look that took immediate inventory of their various merits and deficiencies. Curtis was summarily assessed and dismissed, but Avi's indefinable pedigree of perfect grades and unquenchable ambition was recognized and given momentary leave to hazard a play for Iveson's *extremely valuable time.*

"You're not my students," the thin-lipped Iveson said in a clipped voice made of deadlines and derision. His left hand balanced a red pen that hovered like a deathblow above its latest ink-slashed victim.

"No, Sir," Avi said, breaching the threshold. The man's hackles smoothed almost imperceptibly at Avi's respectfully intoned *Sir*. "We're working on a research project for our AP class, and I'm afraid our school library is sadly lacking in material."

Iveson liked this. Academic scorn of second-rate resources fit him like a glove. The red pen lowered, a temporary reprieve. His eyes reassessed Curtis momentarily, and Curtis could tell he was being tolerated on the merits of Avi's impressiveness.

"Take a seat," Iveson said, capping his pen and indicating the two flimsy metal chairs facing his desk. The chairs had not been selected with an eye to a prolonged stay.

They sat.

"Where are you boys from?"

"I'm Avi, Sir, and this is Curtis. We're from Willowhaven."

Iveson's eyes narrowed, shark-like.

"There used to be an estate near our town, Gravenhearst, and we saw that you wrote a paper about—"

"I don't have time for your morbid curiosity," Iveson cut in, his voice cold, eyes returning to his pile of papers. The red pen was unsheathed once more. "If you want to waste your time with superstitious nonsense I suggest you try my *colleague*"—he said the word like it meant just the opposite—"Professor Bell. You'll find her with the other primitives in the Religious Studies department."

"Sir, I think you've got the wrong idea—" Avi said with Oscar-winning credibility.

"But you're just fascinated by eighteenth-century economics?"

"We wanted to make a case for a similar symbiotic relationship between Gravenhearst and our town as the one you propose between Kingston and Gr—"

"Well, that's highly commendable, but I regret that my office hours are for Queen's students who are *enrolled in my classes*. But best of luck with your research." Iveson put pen to paper and slit an entire paragraph's throat with a look of deep satisfaction.

Curtis stared at the man's profile as Avi got to his feet, the cheap chair scraping on the aged linoleum unpleasantly. The whispers in his head were not happy. "You wouldn't be trying to hide something, would you, *Sir*?" Curtis asked, investing the word with the same intonation that Iveson used on *colleague*.

"I beg your pardon?" Iveson said in a way that didn't beg anything at all.

"Curtis." Avi's hand on his arm stopped him.

They left.

Outside in the cold once more, Curtis swore. "Arrogant prick," he snarled, kicking the oversized stone doorway. Avi was already scrolling through pages on his phone.

"Don't freak, man," he said. "He gave us a lead, remember?"

You're running out of time, Curtis, a taunting voice whispered, drawn out like a sigh of wind. *No tiiime.*

Curtis turned and closed his eyes. Avi couldn't know he was hearing these voices. He couldn't lose this one ally.

He couldn't lose his only friend.

"Okay, Theological Hall," Avi said. "It's not far." There was nothing but the sound of rain and traffic, then: "Curtis?"

"Yeah," Curtis said faintly, still trying to bring himself under control.

"Let's track this woman down."

Curtis turned. Avi was looking at him the way you would a child on the verge of a tearful breakdown, as though one wrong word could shatter Curtis into pieces. Normally this treatment would irritate Curtis to no end, but right now it felt just about right. This sort of helpless panic was uncharted water, and Curtis was drowning in it. He gave Avi a halfhearted grimace that was meant to be a smile, but missed the mark spectacularly, and they turned and headed up the street.

The heart of University Avenue was like stepping back in time. Turn-of-the-century Romanesque buildings, grey-roofed and limestone-clad, lined the wide brick-paved lane. The leaves were turning colors and pooling like fallen bits of confetti in the rain-slicked streets. Curtis jammed his hands deep in his pockets. The weather had turned into a fine horizontal spray, and he hunched his shoulders up as if bracing for something inevitable.

They turned at a building with a soaring clock tower and headed down a path that led to a large stone building flanked with tall windows, arching dormers, and a central tower covered in flame-toned ivy. *Queen's Theological Hall* was seared in black into the wooden lintel of the large double doors.

Inside, Avi took a moment to consult his phone, then gestured toward the stairs. On the third floor, they passed closed office doors until they reached the very end. If Iveson's office was a shoebox of cluttered blandness, Bell's was a jewel box of carefully curated treasures. But Curtis was immediately distracted from the wall-to-wall installation of antique books and exotic curios by the sound of a metallic thumping. They rounded the corner of the L-shaped office to see a slim woman with sleek blonde hair in an epic battle with the bottom drawer of her file cabinet.

"Professor Bell?" Avi said, and she turned with a start. She stood, smoothing the hair out of her eyes, her cheeks red with exertion.

"Mrs. Vandenberg?" Curtis said, his tension dissolving in a moment of total confusion.

Mary's mother smiled slightly, looking from Avi and his lanky poet's frame to Curtis and his Beast-manhandling shoulders. She nodded at him.

"Perhaps you could help me?" she said, casting a glance back at the offending cabinet.

"Uh, yeah, sure," Curtis said, awkwardly moving forward to investigate.

"Thank you," she said, smoothing her fingers over the slim black skirt that hugged a figure as shapely as her daughter's. "And it's 'Professor' when I'm on campus," she said, settling back into her leather chair with a little smile. "I thought you knew I worked at the university, Curtis."

Curtis finally succeeded in yanking the file drawer open the rest of the way and he stood. "Uh, yeah, I did. Just didn't realize . . ." He trailed off, feeling stupid. He was suddenly very aware that he'd left Bell's daughter half-naked and cursing him in a dark bedroom last night. He looked to Avi for rescue.

Avi did not disappoint. "Well, it's lovely to meet you here like this, Professor. We're doing some research for an AP paper on the prominent families that influenced the development of Kingston and Willowhaven back in the nineteenth century, and we were told that you had some expertise regarding one family in particular." Avi hesitated for just a second, then continued. "The Deemus family. They had an estate called Gravenhearst, I believe?"

"Who put you up to this?" she asked quietly.

"No one!" Curtis said.

"Professor Iveson just said you might—" Avi began.

Professor Bell smiled a short, tight smile and picked up a pen. "I would have thought Iveson had better things to do than send students to harass me." She tipped the gold pen back and forth, her annoyance palpable. "Perhaps you should return to the professor and tell him I suggest he not concern himself with things too profound for a glorified accountant to comprehend. And if he thinks stunts like these are going to embarrass me—"

"We're not here to make fun of you!" Curtis shouted, slamming his palms on the front of her desk with enough force to make her computer monitor wobble. "I need answers! I need to know what happened in that house!"

Bell's lips parted, the pen frozen between her thumb and forefinger, the tip pointed skyward. Her eyes narrowed and she studied Curtis with a scrutiny that he could almost feel.

"Curtis," Avi muttered, hovering at his side. Curtis could feel that Avi was truly concerned, ready to prevent him from doing something stupid or violent or both. The whispers went still in his head, as if waiting with suspended breath, spellbound and agonized.

Her lips drew in for a moment, and she tapped the pen lightly against the folder in front of her. "I'm sorry, Curtis, but I think you should leave now."

"*Please*," Curtis said.

Her eyes narrowed again, like she couldn't make up her mind about something and found her own indecision vexing.

"I'm sorry," she said finally. "I can't help you."

"WHY?" Curtis bellowed, and it felt like the whispers screamed it with him.

"Okay," Avi said, grabbing him by the arm as Bell's expression flashed with anger, a mirror of the one her daughter had worn the night before.

"It's time to leave," she said, her voice cold.

"We're going," Avi said hastily. "I'm very sorry."

"I don't wish to call security," she said.

"That's not necessary," Avi said, dragging Curtis backward. His nails were curled into Curtis's arm and Curtis could feel everything that mattered to him slipping away. He was trying to snatch water with spread fingers and it was all running downhill, leaving him scrabbling desperately, hopelessly.

Bell's perfectly manicured hand hovered over the phone, and Curtis swallowed tears of rage as he surrendered to Avi's desperate jockeying. Avi prodded him out through the hallway and down the stairs, and it wasn't till they were out on the wet miserable lawn in front of the hall that Curtis finally let himself erupt.

"They're hiding something! Did you see that? They're both hiding something from me. There's something they don't want me to know!"

"Curtis, why is this so important to you?" Avi pled. "You're scaring me! You were scaring her! That's why she wouldn't talk to you, you're freaking people out!"

"No! That's not it!" The whispers were screaming in his head and he wanted to scream at Avi and shake him until he took that wide-eyed concerned-for-the-crazy-person look off his face. "Weren't you listening back there? She's scared of something!"

"Yeah, you!" Avi yelled.

Curtis turned and started walking. He had to get back in his truck and get out of there before he really *did* do something crazy. Before he ran back inside and put his hands around Bell's throat and *made* her tell him what she was hiding. Avi followed him, yelling, "Where are you going?"

"The truck!"

"That's not the way we came, Curtis," Avi yelled back, barely keeping up with Curtis's long strides.

"It's called a direct route, Avi! Some people don't need a freaking smartphone map to find their way around a two-block radius!"

"Screw you, man, that's a low blow. You wouldn't even *be* here if it weren't for me!"

"Yeah, and it's done me so much good!" Curtis snarled over his shoulder. Students on the path were giving them a wide berth. Two soaking wet guys screaming at each other while they speed-walked through Canada's most distinguished university campus. Yeah, that was totally normal.

"I thought you were *smart*, Avi. Can't you tell when someone's hiding something? The whole world isn't filled with a bunch of nice honest people just waiting to pat you on the head and help you on your way to success. Sometimes you've gotta get a little dirty! Sometimes you've gotta fight for what you need!"

"Yeah, and sometimes you've gotta stop fighting *everyone*! You're just looking for an excuse to flatten people these days, Curtis! You can't just unleash on the world because you're upset about your dad!"

"What the hell would you know about it?" Curtis rounded on Avi abruptly. "You and your perfect little life with your perfect mother and father and your perfect future with your perfect-pedigreed brain! What the hell would you know about being *upset* with the world?"

Avi's face paled, and his eyes reddened as if Curtis had struck him. "I'm sorry that life hasn't shit on me like it has on you," Avi said, his voice low, his breathing barely controlled. "I'm sorry that it's not fair. I can't do anything about that. But you are my *best friend* and I hate that things are so hard for you. I hate that I can't fix it. And I hate that you're obviously going through something right now, and you won't trust me enough to tell me what it is!"

Curtis turned and wrenched the truck door open, his muscles

clenching deep at the back of his throat. He jammed himself behind the wheel and slammed the door. Avi was pulling at the passenger-side door, but it was still locked. Avi pounded a fist on the window, his eyes angry and hurt all at once. Curtis gripped the steering wheel, wishing he could rip it out, throw it, throw away the feelings blistering inside him.

"CURTIS!"

He dropped his head against the steering wheel. After a moment, he hit the unlock button. He didn't move as Avi climbed in.

"Curtis," Avi finally said. "Have I ever given you a reason to think you can't trust me?"

"There doesn't have to be a reason." Curtis said the words so quietly that for a moment he wasn't sure if Avi had heard him. When he lifted his head, the look on Avi's face removed any doubt.

"I don't even know what to say to that," Avi said, and Curtis felt like there was a divide the size of the Grand Canyon between them. How could someone with a life like Avi's ever understand the constant feeling that the world was two seconds away from yanking the rug out from under you? No one, no matter how much you love them, is worth the risk of letting your guard down. Everyone screws up, and everyone you love has the power to gut you if you trust them with too much.

People make you vulnerable with their love.

Curtis started the truck and they drove with only the sound of traffic and the windshield wipers for company.

After ten minutes, Avi suddenly spoke.

"My cousin is a mountaineer."

The words were so bizarre that Curtis couldn't help but look over for the explanation. Avi had that look on his face, the I-know-something-you-don't look, but it was faded, a sad, tired version of the usual expression.

"I'm listening," Curtis said.

"The last time he visited, he made me go climbing with him, which, of course, was a disaster." Curtis nodded in agreement. That *would* be a disaster.

"But there's this piece of equipment," Avi continued. "A spring-loaded camming device—SLCD for short. You pull the trigger and the cams come together, and then you can place it in a crack in the rock. When you let go, the cams wedge in place, and you hook on to the other end with your rope. If you fall, the catastrophic pressure from your weight is converted to friction by the SLCD, and it puts all of that force into the surrounding rock. The harder you fall, the stronger the save, so to speak."

Curtis waited.

"They've got another name for the SLCD, I guess 'cause acronyms are a pain in the ass. You know what they call it?" Avi was staring at him, his eyes boring a hole in the side of Curtis's face. "They call it a *friend.* Your *friend* catches you when you fall."

Curtis drove for a few moments, processing.

"Just in case you didn't catch the implication," Avi added, "you're falling fast as fuck."

Curtis pulled the truck over to the side of the road. He got out, even though it was still raining, because somehow he couldn't have this conversation in an enclosed space. Everything felt too close and confining in this moment, and he really needed to feel the movement of the wind on his face.

He spoke quietly, Avi just behind him, waiting. "What I said last night about Mila—it wasn't the vodka." He turned and faced Avi. "I saw her, clear as I see you now, in the mirror in my mom's old room. And the place where Gravenhearst used to be—I hear something when I go there. It's like a voice climbed in my head when I first found that place, and now I hear it everywhere I go. So I have to find out why, and I have to find out what Mila is trying to tell me."

Avi's eyes were very wide. His hands floated up abruptly, covering his mouth with a sort of helpless motion. Then they lowered. "It's going to be okay," Avi said. "We're going to figure this out together."

Curtis felt as if everything were going a bit sideways. The words were right, but the tone behind them was all wrong. And then it was all going in slow motion because Curtis knew what came next. And he would have done anything to stop it, to take it back.

"We're going to get you some help, Curtis," Avi said, his face so sad. "You're going to be all right, you just need a little help." He moved forward.

Curtis shoved Avi so hard he went sprawling backward into the ditch. The next moment, Curtis had jumped in the passenger side of the truck, locked the door, and slid over. Avi was at the door, yelling, trying to get in.

Curtis turned the key and left Avi in the dust.

29

Mila

THE HOUSE SHIFTED, AND MILA GRITTED HER TEETH THROUGH the skin-searing pain. The knife was gone from her hand, lost to another time, but that didn't matter. Deemus's words in the library— *"The spirits are restless, someone is fighting me."*

My sister is fighting you, you bastard. And so am I.

The mirror had been more than just a way to watch them. It had been the cork in the bottle. Zahra had risked everything to steal it, and now Mila knew why. Somehow the loss of the mirror had changed things. Given them all a chance that had never been possible before.

"Trust the boy," Wynn had said.

Trust had long ago been relegated to the dusty trunk of obsolete ideas, along with other useless things like hope and happiness.

She was a devil, and this was the only thing left to her.

She put a hand on the gleaming wood paneling, trailing her fingertips along the corridor. This house had a breaking point, and she was going to find it.

She smiled. "I'm going to kill you."

30

Curtis

CURTIS CLIMBED THE STAIRS TO HIS MOTHER'S ROOM WITH A dead, cold hole in his chest.

So this is what it feels like to be totally alone.

He sat in the gloom, breathing in the dusty scent of dried roses, Mila's picture gripped tight in his hand. His head was full of whispers, and they filled the room with their susurrating babble, pooling in the corners, welling in the shadows. They spilled out into the hall, flooding the stairs, wrapping the whole house in the softly shushing tones of madness.

He was made of tears and the last thin shreds of stubbornness.

He realized he could let the tears come—just really let loose and go with it. No one would need to know. It seemed like the sort of thing a normal person would do when they'd just lost everything that mattered to them. But if he lost control now, he wouldn't recover. He could feel it. He'd be lost in the black and never find his way out.

He took a deep breath and lifted his hand, turning it palm-up, so the cupped photo faced him. It was just a picture, but it felt like the only thing anchoring him in the world. Mila gazed back at him, her feline eyes wary and haunted, like she was caught in the same moment as him, like she was alone in a hostile place that could take her down at any moment. When their eyes met in the mirror, he'd felt something. Recognition flashed across time between them, and in the instant their eyes met, it was like she saw something in him, and he saw something of himself in her.

I need to save her. I need to save something.

He stared into the old mirror, like he could summon her image through sheer force of will. Like the *wanting* of her would materialize her image, would bring him his sharp-eyed Victorian girl.

Please, I need you.

His own eyes stared back at him, and he could feel himself slipping, reality starting to crumble. He couldn't feel his breath, and his hands were dead things on his legs—he was fading into nothingness in the prison of his mind. He was a bad thing—not deserving—broken and wrong and—

The mirror flashed, and he lunged to his feet, nearly falling, the whispers screaming a chorus of elation.

The glass cleared, like a lens pulled into focus. Her profile was facing him, blonde hair disheveled and half hiding her face. And then she turned. Her lip and forehead bled, and there were deep bruises on her throat.

"Mila!" he yelled, instantly furious. He would kill whoever did that to her.

She didn't react to his voice, didn't seem to see him. She was looking at something just below his field of vision, as if she couldn't believe what she was seeing. Her mouth twisted in anger and she snatched something up, something large and heavy, it seemed, from the way her arms strained. She threw it with a shout that reverberated through the mirror, through the darkened room around him. She stumbled, and the mirror went out of focus.

"No!" he cried, but then it resolved and she was looking back at the space below her, her face twisted in anguish. Her hands flew up to cover her eyes, her fingers splayed, nails digging into her own skin.

A scream ripped from her throat, a scream like the world had ended, like nothing would ever be good again. It built into a wail, into a savage sound that seemed to pour from the mirror and fill the room he stood in.

"Mila!" he cried out.

She turned, her lips trembling, eyes wild. Recognition went through her.

"You," she whispered, and the color of her cheeks deepened.

He remembered the scent of her skin, the feel of her hair slipping through his fingers, that feeling like he was safe with her. That she wouldn't be afraid of him.

"I'm going to help you," he said, grasping the carved edges of the mirror, as if somehow he could find a fault line in the glass that separated them and force himself through into her world. As if he could make the dream into reality. "What happened to you? What should I do? What have they done to you?"

She stared back at him, like he was something lovely but impossible, something she wanted to believe in but couldn't afford to.

"Please! What should I do?" Curtis cried, slamming his palm against the wall. The mirror began to blur again. Mila was shaking her head, a decision forming on her features, and then the image was gone.

Curtis bolted from the room. Professor Bell knew something—she was hiding the truth from him, and he'd find it if it killed him. There had to be a clue somewhere in her office. There *had* to be.

Halfway down the stairs, he plowed into Sage.

Her face was white and she grabbed him by the arms with ferocious strength. "Avi called me. What are you *doing*?" she demanded, her eyes large and fearful.

"I have to go, Sage." Curtis pushed past her.

"CURTIS!" she screamed. "Please!"

He reached the door. He turned to face her.

"Curtis . . ." Her voice trailed off.

He took a deep breath and raised the picture. "I can see this girl in Mom's old mirror, and I have to help her. I know it doesn't make any sense, but I need you to believe me."

Her eyes filled with tears.

"Curtis, you're sick. You've gotta let me help you."

The words were a knife, and he could only survive by running wounded. He was out the door and she was chasing him across the lawn. He heaved the Beast out the shed door and kicked it to life. The headlight illuminated Sage in a blinding halo, and then he was gone.

31

Mila

SHE WAS IN THE CENTRAL STAIR, AND SHE RAN DOWN, DOWN, down, the walls spinning around her, the house fighting back.

The stairs expanded, thinning out in both directions; doors that should have been there weren't. The narrow slits for light were filling in. She stumbled and cried out, fingers scrabbling.

Creaking sounds, like iron scraping iron. The black became absolute and she clung to the inside wall, her breath crushing her chest.

She couldn't feel the stairs, only blank space.

Her breath was too loud, the black too endless.

She worked her hands into fists; the nails cutting her skin were points of pain keeping her conscious. *Just breathe.*

The black twisted and lurched. She screamed Wynn's name, a helpless sound she didn't recognize.

Screams filled the black.

The black was pulling back.

The screams resounded, but they weren't her own. She had lost her voice in the darkness. These were others, screaming and fighting, beating the void back, beating the *house* back.

Mila's fingers uncurled from bloodied claws and she scraped them over stone steps, shaking in a huddled ball.

Light like pinpricks grew and stretched—the slits in the stairwell returning.

Mila crawled forward, spilled herself down the treads as they re-formed and became stair-like again.

"Thank you," she whispered, tears streaking her skin.

She stumbled, her hand on the inner wall, and finally the door was where it should be.

She fell through, exhausted and gasping, against the corridor wall.

Her own pale face looked back at her in the row of mirrors, terrified and small.

She stared herself down with something like hatred. "You will go on." Her voice was a hoarse shadow. She forced herself upright, the house hard against her back, the wretched smallness of her face goading her on. "You will go on," she said again.

This time, her voice was stronger.

32

Curtis

CURTIS PITCHED THE BIKE AROUND A SHARP CORNER AND grinned as he barely pulled out of the turn. The Beast screamed in protest and Curtis pushed through the gears like they were all that stood between him and answers. Steel and springs and sprockets and fuel—he'd crush it, break it, bend it to his will, and make it perform miracles. He'd pull life out of death and leave everyone amazed.

Sage's words burned in his ears and he jerked the bike up into a savage wheelie, then slammed it back down, swallowing the blow of pavement standing up against steel.

He should have known he'd never get a fair chance—that no one, no matter *how close*, would believe him. Dad's illness was the shadow lurking beneath him, the monster he could never escape, and everyone had just been waiting for one to consume the other. Watching the dead man walking, counting down the days till he snapped.

I don't care anymore, he thought as he blasted through the dark alleyway, the whispers screeching in agreement. *I don't care.*

To hell with trusting people. He'd always known that was bullshit, anyway. Trust was an illusion that broke the moment you pressed it too hard. You had yourself and that was it.

He drew the bike up short, his breath heaving in his chest. He glanced down the dark length of the tree-lined street. All was quiet, and he nosed out into the fog-shrouded Queen's campus, trying to steady his heart, to bring his thoughts back down to reign. The bike wasn't street legal, but fortunately there'd been no cops around to make a bad day worse. But he had to be careful. Too much was on the line to get stupid and screw it all now.

He cut the engine and leaned the Beast against a large tree. The air was damp and thick with the day's rain and his hands were half numb with the cold. He jogged the short distance to Theological Hall, the headlights of the occasional passing car flooding the growing darkness behind him. The ivy that covered the building glowed bloodred in the halo of the old-fashioned streetlamps, and a movement of wind set the leaves and vines rattling against the stone.

The entrance was gloomy, but he heard the soft murmur of voices coming from the lecture hall at the center of the building. Night classes.

Good. No one would find his presence suspicious.

The third-floor hallway was deserted, all the doors closed, the offices dark. Bell's door was locked, but a few moments with his folding blade and he'd jimmied the cheap lock open. He closed the door behind him and turned on the small desk lamp.

Her bookshelves were full of religious texts—unsurprising, considering her profession—and he saw nothing that looked like it could possibly relate to Gravenhearst. A search of the large filing cabinet turned up even more nothing. Finally, the only thing left was her desk. The first few drawers were full of typical office clutter, but the bottom drawer was heavy with files. He went through each one, but they appeared to be syllabi for various classes.

Curtis stifled a groan, frustration mounting, but then he noticed that the width of the files didn't match the depth of the desk. He pulled the drawer out as far as it would go and reached behind the metal slider that held the files in place, feeling awkwardly in the darkness, his face pressed against the side of the desk. His fingers brushed something—a metal box—and he heard a rattle. He strained at the awkward angle, but finally got a grip on the thing and pulled it free.

Just an ordinary box, but the paper label read "Interviews."

Inside was a mini tape recorder and a handful of tiny cassette tapes, each labeled with a different name. There was one in the recorder, so he rewound it, then hit play. A voice that he recognized as Bell's came from the miniscule speakers, hollow and small.

Can you tell me what your grandmother told you about her grandfather?

Another voice came over the speaker: a thin gravelly voice, clearly an old woman's.

It was a terrible thing, and she didn't like to speak of it. But she told me once that her grandfather confessed some things to her when he was drunk.

<Bell> Yes?

<long pause>

He'd worked for Kepler Deemus, and said he'd been a great man. But his son . . . his son was different. After the terrible storm and Kepler's disappearance, Jacob Deemus came home, and great-great-grandfather didn't like his job so much anymore. But times were hard, and Deemus paid well, so . . .

<Bell> Yes, of course. It's very understandable.

Well, he spent all his time in the cellars, and he wouldn't allow anyone down there. One man said he'd overheard strange noises coming from one room in particular, the master speaking some terrible language, talking to the very devil himself. And then that servant went missing.

<long pause>

<Bell> But your ancestor saw something himself, firsthand, did he not?

Yes. Gran said he told her that Jacob Deemus knew things about people— impossible things. He said the man had done something terrible to his own mother and sisters, made a bargain. And when he was done, there was a man who'd never been there before, and Jacob Deemus knew all the world's secrets.

The tape clicked off.

"I had a feeling you'd be back."

Curtis jerked around, his pulse spiking.

Professor Bell stood in the doorway.

Curtis stood, his mouth very dry.

She crossed the room and held out her hand.

Curtis's fingers tightened on the recorder, his eyes flicking down to the box of tapes—*finally*, information about Gravenhearst. He needed it to save Mila, to save *himself*. His breath was very loud in his ears and he fought the urge to grab the box and run.

Professor Bell's narrowed eyes looked just like her daughter's, and as he stared at the woman, Curtis realized that he'd put himself completely at her mercy. One call to the cops and he was fucked.

He handed her the recorder.

She sat in her chair and gazed up at him, surveying him coolly.

Curtis cleared his throat. "Please, I need to know about Gravenhearst."

"Why?"

"Because I can hear it."

The truth was out before he could stop it, and Bell's eyes flickered. She uncrossed and crossed her legs again. Curtis could feel himself being reassessed.

"What do you hear?" she asked with an academic's needle-sharp curiosity, her eyes studying him without mercy.

Curtis struggled for a moment. He'd told her the truth and he sensed it was the only reason he was still in her office and not being chased by campus security. He so desperately needed her help. Oh, *goddamn*, he was already so screwed. He might as well risk a little more.

"Wind. I hear wind, even when there is none."

She took a deep breath and looked down, her expression pensive. When she finally spoke again, her voice was a little softer. "Curtis, I don't know if you remember this, but your mother and I were good friends."

Curtis swallowed hard.

"You and Mary used to play together, and your mother and I would sit on the porch and laugh that one day you two might decide to do more than fight over toys or throw sand at each other, and then we'd *really* be in trouble."

Curtis looked away. It was a dim memory, obscured to all but nothing in his mind, but it raised something hot and painful in his throat. It had the sting of truth.

"I'm not proud of how I reacted when your father became ill," Bell said. "I thought only of my daughter." She cleared her throat. "I was afraid that by being connected to *you*, she might someday be in the wrong place at the wrong time, that your father might frighten her or . . . *injure* her in the throes of his illness. I pulled back from your mother. I pulled Mary back from you." She gazed at him. "It wasn't fair to you. I'm sorry."

She looked away. "I failed my friend," she said quietly. "But perhaps I can help her son now." She turned back to him. "It must be very tempting to find meaning in this old story of Gravenhearst, to find a *reason* for what you're going through. But Curtis, I promise you, this is not a ghost story—it's a story as old and banal as the world itself. Powerful men taking what they want and society looking the other way out of fear, and greed, and apathy."

"If that's all it was, then why wouldn't you talk to me?" Curtis said, his throat too dry, panic flooding in his gut. "Why were you hiding this? Why wouldn't Iveson talk to me?"

"Because he's ashamed," Bell said. "His family got their start with Deemus gold. The Deemus men had their fingers in every pie in Kingston and Willowhaven, and people looked the other way while terrible things went on. A lot of girls went missing in Willowhaven, yet no one seemed to do much about it. Iveson's only interested in whitewashing Gravenhearst's history."

"So why would he send me to you?" Curtis demanded.

"He's trying to discredit my research—twist it into something trivial and ruin my reputation at the university. Sending ghost-hunting teenagers to my doorstep was his idea of a pointed jab."

"And you?" Curtis said, his heart still half-frozen in his chest. "Why've you got this stuff hidden in the back of a drawer?"

"It's not *hidden*, Curtis. It's in a drawer in a very small, overstuffed office."

Curtis looked away, feeling stupid. She had a point.

"The reason I *have* it in the first place, is that I'm interested in the *superstition* that sprang up around Gravenhearst," Bell said. "People either normalize or fetishize—Iveson writes about economic climates, and newspapers write about curses and black magic rituals. The facts of Gravenhearst encourage these fanciful tales precisely *because* what happened there was so horrific. People want a *reason* why such things were allowed to continue. But it's just ordinary crime, Curtis. There's no magic spell there, no curse—"

"No, you don't understand," Curtis cut her off, his blood boiling under his skin. "I was fine. I was fine until I stood where Gravenhearst stood. It knocked me off my feet!"

She studied him, her face frozen, and then her lips came together, uncertain.

"I knew *nothing* about that place when I went there," Curtis said. "That line Avi fed you about an AP paper? That's bullshit. I was just out for a ride on my bike and something *happened* to me. Something happened to me there and it's not a goddamn coincidence!"

She blinked once, her lips twisting in concern.

"It's not," he repeated, his voice shaky. "It can't be."

"Your father's illness hit quite suddenly, didn't it?" Bell said very gently.

"That's not what this is," Curtis said, his fists clenched at his sides.

"Are you hearing voices?" Bell said, standing, her hand reaching out, her face very calm. "Are you getting headaches?"

Kill her, Curtis, the whispers seethed.

Kill her! That bitch thinks she can talk to us like that?

"*SHUT UP!*" Curtis yelled. He slapped a tray of papers off her desk and she stepped back. "I'm not crazy. This place is haunted and it's talking to me! Mila Kenton is in my goddamn mirror, and I'm *not* imagining it!"

Bell's eyes widened and she reached toward him again. "You need to calm down, Curtis. You need to think about what you're saying."

Curtis turned for the door. This was a disaster. He'd done exactly what he knew he shouldn't—confide in someone yet again. And now . . .

"Curtis!"

He left her behind, stumbling out into the hall, his head reeling with the impossible depth of his stupidity. She'd call the police. She'd call the doctors. They'd take Sage, lock him up, mainline him with drugs.

He'd completely fucked his life in five minutes.

He barreled down the stairwell, out the door, running through the black and mist, the moaning shrieking tumult screaming inside his head. Fingers of steel split his skull and he almost dropped to his knees, fighting her words—*"Do you hear voices? Are you getting headaches?"*

He had to keep going, had to get away.

Mila was real. He *knew* she was real.

Sage's face, her eyes wide with horror, tears bright—*"Curtis, you've gotta let me help you!"*

He reached his bike, kicked the engine over with one brutal stamp, and threw himself out into the back streets of Kingston.

Fuck the world and everyone in it. They thought he was crazy? He'd show them goddamn crazy.

He was going back to the copse, and he was going to tear that fucking place apart.

33

Mila

THERE WAS A LITTLE BREATH LIKE A CHILD HOLDING IN A laugh, and a slip of white darted out from behind Mila's reflection. Dark hair flashed and slipped to the next mirror.

Wynn.

Mila chased her sister from mirror to mirror, down halls she'd never passed, through doors that were walls one moment, passages the next. Wynn's laughter trailed out, like they were back in the stables in Kent, playing tag among the stalls and sawdust. Mila passed through the spirits, their energy prickling over her skin. They were making a way for her, pushing her through the house.

The Deemus men had stolen their lives, but now something had changed—the balance was shifting. *I can do this.* Mila ran faster. *I can finish what Zahra started.*

A final burst of laughter from the end of the hall, and a door opened.

Mila slowed to catch her breath. The energy ahead was darker, and she fought a shudder.

Ghostly figures labored at the day's chores, making bread and roasting meat for people who'd probably been dead a hundred years. She moved through the room, her skin crawling as she passed the faded echoes that didn't see her. She again had the sensation she'd had the first time the house shifted—like her body was a thing out of place, alien in this ghastly aberration in which time folded back on itself and the past echoed like an infinity of mirrors.

She passed the length of the room and entered a dark hallway, her heart cold in her chest. A figure walked the dark corridor, and she knew instantly by the cut of his clothes and haughty bearing that he was a Deemus.

He carried a notebook in his hands, and she recognized it for the book that had flown across the library at her. Then he looked up, and her blood ran cold. She'd looked into those eyes many times. This was the man who had turned Gravenhearst into a monster, the man whose portrait was right outside her bedchamber: Jacob Deemus.

He crossed the hall and stopped before a door, removing a key from his pocket. He unlocked the door and she sped forward, pressing herself in after him, but he turned, about to shut the door, and she had no choice but to rush right through him.

Her whole body shuddered with the feeling of passing through his spectral form, like a cold vapor had sunk deep into her bones. She froze on the step, staring back at him with horror. He paused, his hand extended to lock the door, and shivered slightly, looking about him with an expression on his face like he was unnerved.

Mila held her breath.

His brow quirked for a moment, but then he turned back to the door and locked it. Mila let him pass her, then followed him down the stone steps.

The air was cold and dank, and she could smell must and damp stone.

They were going into the cellars and she felt a grim thrill of triumph. She'd seen the drawing next to that enormous schematic of the machine that pierced Gravenhearst. A simple anatomical rendering of a heart.

He didn't draw that there on a whim, she thought. *That machine is the heart of Gravenhearst.*

And I'm going to kill it.

34

Curtis

HE COULD FEEL WHEN HE WAS NEAR THE COPSE. THE WHISPERS shrieked in joy at his approach, and he felt something struggling deep inside him to get free and join the place.

He shifted the Beast into fourth and the engine screamed, the whispers screaming even louder. He drove straight into the copse, dodging saplings and bushes, barely keeping the bike vertical. Branches whipped his arms and face, cutting his skin as he raced back out into the field. He wanted to shred this place—rip up the earth and tear out its secrets. He threw the bike into a tight loop, carving deep ruts in the dirt, leaving his mark.

The copse had raked its claws through his life, and he was going to return the favor.

He took a hard turn on the outskirts of the field, about to make another suicide run for the heart of the copse, when his back tire slipped and the Beast went into a wobble. The movement threw him off his game, and he hit a sharp stone at the wrong angle. It was a measure of just how gone he was that he didn't even try to pull out of it. He just let go of the handlebars and let himself fall back. He hit the ground and skid several feet while the bike went speeding into a nearby willow bush, where it spun out and stalled.

He lay there for a moment, letting his tailbone throb and burn. A ghostly film of cloud slipped across the night sky, shredding under the moon's bright glow, and the whispers crested, swelling with the wind in the trees.

A silver glint on the ground caught his eye.

Curtis stood painfully. He had ripped up a wide swath of field, and now he saw that what sent him into the skid in the first place was a patch of earth that wasn't earth at all. It was wood.

Old, rotted wood.

Below.

The whispers shrieked and Curtis threw himself at the ground, frenzied.

Of course. Of *course* this is what he'd been meant to do. He was a fucking *idiot*. Trance-walking in basements, scratching *below* into stone, every bone in his body trying to tell him to come back to where it all began, back to where the whispers slipped beneath his skin.

Below, below, below!

Curtis started digging. In minutes, he'd cleared the dirt from several feet of boards. Bands of aged metal glinted dully in the moonlight, and he redoubled his efforts, tearing up grass by its roots, scraping the dirt with his fingernails as the whispers shrieked encouragement. He reached one edge of the boards and found more dirt, but dug farther until he hit stone. Finally the entire section was unearthed—wide enough to have once been a doorway.

An entrance to the earth had been boarded up, spikes driven deep into the surrounding layer of stone. It hit him with a chill—the stone foundations of Gravenhearst had lain just beneath the field all this time. It had all been waiting for him.

He stomped on the rotted boards; they squelched and splintered, but not enough to break. He grabbed a rock and drove the sharp end into the boards. His heart pounded, and his hands were so sweaty he could barely keep his grip. The board gave way and his fingertips smashed wood as the stone sunk into the plank. He jerked it free, his fingers bloody, and saw a hole the size of his fist down into complete darkness.

The whispers screamed with joy.

He picked another point on the boards and started pounding again. In minutes, he had four holes. He stamped at the space between them until the whole thing gave way with a terrific crack. The boards imploded, and he dropped to his knees, grabbing at the splintered remains, pulling until he'd cleared the entrance.

He could just make out several stone steps that disappeared into impenetrable black; the scent of old, dead air wafted up, prickling the inside of his nose. The whispers shrieked a chorus, filling his head, their rhythm matching his heartbeat, surpassing it, frantic and urgent. He had to get down there *right now*.

He stepped down, finding his footing on the crumbling and warped stones. Darkness swallowed him. The moonlight spilled only as far as the first three steps, and his eyes strained, trying to make out the edges of things. He fumbled for his phone, holding the bluish light up to the dank, rotten black—his other hand scraping the damp stone at his side. He couldn't tell how far the stairwell went, and the harder he tried to see, the more he felt he was sinking into a deep, black well.

He froze.

There was a flicker of something down in the dark.

He squinted, trying to shake the feeling that his eyes were playing tricks. But, no, there was a small, glowing light in the darkness ahead, and as he forced his foot to find ground, the light flared and dozens more sprang to life before him.

The whispers spread like echoes through an endless chamber, and he struggled with a feeling too strong for words.

The impossible lights flickered and slid over a thousand bottles, flasks, and jars, each glass cylinder labeled in a faded, fluid script. The bottles lined the shelves and the shelves filled the wall, reaching off into the darkness, going beyond his sight. A workbench of stone followed the contours of the room, cluttered with dust-encrusted metal boxes, jars carved of stone or cast in porcelain, bowls of wood or metal, strange tools and devices.

The whispers chattered and Curtis moved farther into the room, toward that first light. It was nothing more than a glass jar, as clean as if someone had polished it, and a single flame was inside. No candle, no wick, no oil. He touched the tip of his finger to the smooth glass. It was cool.

This is insane, he thought.

The ceiling arched high above him, vaulted stone supported by pillars. A round stone furnace sat at the center of the room, a cobweb-deformed bellows leaning against it. Another furnace filled an entire section of wall, and beyond that metal tools of all description hung from dusty pegs, filling the wall for at least thirty feet. More workbenches and shelves stretched out from him as he moved on, and glass objects that reminded him of chemistry sets, but in strange bulbous shapes, glittered in elaborate configurations held by metal screws and wires.

The farther he moved through the vast hall, the stronger the smell of smoke became, and he felt another wave of panic at the thought of Mila burning, at the image of her face in the mirror, desperate and screaming.

What had been happening to her?

He looked up at the stone ceiling above him. Encased entirely in stone, this level appeared to have survived the fire unscathed, but the smell of old, burned things was unmistakable. He came to the far wall and an immense wooden door. He tried the handle, but it didn't turn. He shoved his shoulder against the surface, but there was no give. The wood hadn't rotted, and it appeared to be the thickness of a fortress gate. He wasn't getting into it without an axe or chainsaw. He pressed his ear against the door and for a moment he could swear he heard a voice, clearer than the others, a whisper that had more form than all the other nattering breaths and intonations. He pulled back, his mouth dry.

"Good evening."

Curtis jerked around, nerves screaming.

A voice had come from the darkness at his back—a thin, crackling, *terrible* voice.

35

Mila

MILA FOLLOWED JACOB DEEMUS DOWN THE STONE STAIRWELL. It was dark, but there was softly glowing light far at the bottom. Her heart still pounded at his earlier reaction, but Wynn had brought her here, to this moment in time; she could only trust that something in this past echo would help her fight.

His image flickered, and she swallowed a sharp breath, reaching out for the wall. A feeling washed over her like the house might shift, but the moment passed and Jacob Deemus reached the cellar and stepped beyond her vision.

She hurried down after him.

It was a laboratory unlike any she'd seen before—part chemist's shop, part blacksmith's forge, and part madman's chamber.

Jacob Deemus wound his way past constructions of glass vials and apparatuses joined together like great beasts and stopped at the round furnace that sat in the middle of the space like a glowing coal.

Mila looked about quickly. The room was enormous, but she could see that it branched into smaller rooms to her left. Far opposite the stairwell was another wall of stone with doors the size and scale of a fortress gate.

That was where she needed to go.

A sound drew her attention and she looked back to Jacob Deemus. He was unscrewing a glass vial from one of the elaborate experiments that bubbled over the fire. Mila recalled the diagrams she'd seen in the secret library, the alchemist's texts with instructions for reducing elements and distilling them over flames.

She moved past him toward the massive doors, but her heart sank as she saw the keyhole in the iron knob. She tried it, but the handle didn't move.

She went back to Jacob Deemus. He was smiling at the small quantity of yellow powder that had collected in the vial. He set the vial into a small metal stand, and she saw that he'd set the key beside it.

Could she take something from right under his nose? He might not see her, but surely he'd notice a key being picked up right in front of him. Or would he? Maybe her effect on the physical objects of this Gravenhearst was spectral too? All she knew was that when the house threw her from this time, that key would no longer be there; she'd be trapped in the cellars, caught between two locked doors.

A terrible moan filled the air and Mila froze.

Jacob Deemus smiled and looked toward the sound. He walked past the furnace, languid and unhurried, toward the muffled cries. Mila seized the key and ran to the door, her skin prickling at the awful sound coming from the far side of the cavernous space. She jammed the key in the lock and the handle turned under her hand.

She stopped.

She had to know what Deemus was doing.

She ran after him, past tables and crates and cabinets and curiosities of all descriptions. He was just turning out of sight behind an enormous armoire, and the moaning was louder now.

He opened the armoire and bent down, and she saw that there was a trapdoor in the bottom. He opened it and the moaning went quiet, then a desperate cry took its place.

"Please, Master Deemus!"

Jacob Deemus stood and smiled down into the opening, and

Mila's skin crawled at the look of absolute pleasure he wore. The man enjoyed pain.

"I beg you, Master, I'll say nothing. I'll tell none what I heard! I heard nothing at all!"

Mila turned and walked back through the maze of clutter, her stomach twisting. This had already happened, and this poor man's fate wouldn't help her destroy Gravenhearst. She had to walk away.

She went to the door as the screaming renewed. When she pulled the door closed behind her, the terrible cries went silent. She swallowed tears and turned to take in the sight before her.

The room was smaller, but the ceiling much higher, and at its center sat the machine, gleaming like a polished brass kettle.

It was roughly egg-shaped, much taller than a large man, and from its rounded surface, hundreds of tubes of varying dimensions branched out like the quills of a porcupine, extending into the walls on either side of her and up into the ceiling high above. The room was nearly filled with the metal tubes, and as Mila listened, she thought she could hear a sound like wind whistling through an aperture, not just one tone but many—like the distant hum of airy notes, faint and high.

Had she finally found the heart of Gravenhearst?

There was a rounded metal door in the side of the machine. It gave with a slight tug of the inset handle, and the breathy symphonic tones gusted out and surrounded her, the faint sound like an untuned orchestra. She pulled the door shut quickly behind her, for fear that Jacob Deemus might hear.

The rounded compartment was lit with the softly glowing eternal lights, and the flickering glow cast moving shapes along the metal that entombed her. A large chair, like one might see at a barber's shop, rose before the console that filled the left side of the machine.

220

Levers and handles grew like a rampant crop from the surface of the console, and all around her the inner surface of the machine was pierced with miniscule holes, the evidence of the tubes that grew from its form out into Gravenhearst.

This is how he could hear us. Her mind spun with the strangeness of it.

She climbed up into the leather-padded chair and leaned forward, examining the large expanse of labeled levers. One said "Kitchens." She pulled it forward, but nothing changed. The machine was still filled with the breathy sound of dissonant harmonies, dipping and swirling like a faint chorus. She tried another lever, then another. Finally she reached for the tallest one, almost out of reach and the largest of all.

Wordless tones exploded in her brain—an assault of sound, high and shrilly resonant. She fell forward, sagging against the console, her hands plugging her ears, a feeling like blood pounding, pressure colliding. The sound gripped her like a vise, tightening, burrowing, ripping things apart. She tasted blood on her lips and reached desperately for the lever. It was too far. Her knees were going, stars bursting behind her eyes. Her insides were turning to liquid.

The world shook and revolved, and she tumbled to the floor, silence ringing in her ears. She gasped for breath, a drum march of throbbing pain slowly dissipating in her ears.

The house had shifted.

She struggled to her feet and pushed open the curved machine door to the other side of the room, nearly falling to the floor. She sagged against the machine, trying to catch her breath.

This side of the room was a mirror image to the other—a large wall of stone and a massive double door of wood stood beyond her.

She forced herself up and forward, her fingers trembling when they grasped the iron doorknob.

It wouldn't turn.

Panic surged through her. She'd set the key on the console ledge before the house shifted.

It wouldn't be there anymore.

She ran back through the machine to the other side, but those doors were locked too.

She was trapped.

Just her and the maddening heart of Gravenhearst.

She leaned her head against the door for a long moment, then turned and surveyed the machine grimly. "This is what you wanted," she said into the empty room. "You made it here. Now kill it."

But how did one destroy a massive metal sphere? And assuming one even could with the proper tools, so far each attempt to damage the house in any way had resulted in her being thrown through time. She'd hoped that once she saw the thing—saw behind the veil of Deemus's magic—she'd know what to do. But now she was trapped in a room of stone with no tools and no ideas, the weight of her own ignorance crushing her down.

Voices caught her ear and she turned with a quick gasp, backing away.

She was flat against the machine, and as her fingers touched the smooth metal, feeling for the door handle, she realized whose voice it was.

Andrew Deemus.

She'd been returned to her own time.

36

Mila

SHE YANKED THE DOOR TO THE MACHINE OPEN AND PULLED IT shut behind her, her heart galloping against her corset. She threw the next door open, then carefully eased it shut at the sound of the large wooden door creaking open on the other side of the machine.

Asher's voice was muffled as the door closed, and Mila pressed herself down against the curved underside of the device. There was little more than a foot of space beneath the lowest layer of metal tubes, and she slid herself down against the rough stone floor, squeezing herself as far underneath as she could.

"I do not think Gravenhearst would take her, Master. She is your choice, and the house bends to your will."

"Well, then where the devil is she?" Deemus snarled. "I'm losing control of the thing. The house is at a tipping point—I can feel it. The gates have been knocked wide!"

There was the sound of someone wrenching the machine door open, and their footsteps ascending. Mila could feel the vibrations along her side.

"You said with two offerings the house would be sated, the power strong again."

"I'm sorry, Master. I did not foresee the blow that losing the mirror would be. I believe a third offering would fully solidify your power, though."

"NO! I want her. I will have her."

Mila heard Deemus working the levers, and she tensed, fearing the shrill burrowing pain would return, but there was only Deemus systematically working through each lever, much as she had done.

The Master of Gravenhearst could work the machine without pain.

"There's nothing!" Deemus cursed. "Master of Gravenhearst, and my prize is lost in my own kingdom!"

"You must increase your studies, Sir. We must enspell another mirror."

"Do not tell me what I must do. I am *your* master, and I'm beginning to doubt your usefulness. For all your connection to this place, you can't even sense where she is. What damned good are you?"

The machine door banged open, and Mila heard them descend.

"I want every man searching for her—the grounds, the halls. You go back to the library and make sure she doesn't get in there."

Asher murmured his assent, and Mila heard the wooden door push open, then closed. A moment later, there was the scrape of the key.

She let loose a shaky breath and crawled free.

She had only one option—provoke another shift and hope to God it took her to a time where she wasn't trapped.

She went back into the machine and took hold of a lever. She pressed up, straining as hard as she could. She had to make Gravenhearst defend itself. She heaved her shoulder against the lever and it finally snapped. She moved on to the next one, but it was harder. She was tiring, her muscles trembling, teeth gritted with exertion.

The door flew open and there was a hand in her hair and her face slammed into the levers. She stumbled to the floor, her nose and cheekbone on fire, ears ringing.

Deemus stood over her, his face contorted with rage.

He hauled her up before she could recover. He hoisted her by the arms and slammed her against the concave wall of the machine. Her head smashed into the metal, and his fingers dug into her skin, and she cried out despite herself. She kicked him, but he dropped her, and then her air was gone, her whole body curving inward around the blow to her stomach. He seized her again, fingers ripping her hair, cracking her skull back against the wall.

"How are you doing this?" Deemus screamed. "How did you *get* here?"

Her teeth rattled and her brain shook and she could feel her thoughts slipping, her mind falling past that place where she had control, where her hate for him was stronger than her fear. She had no air, no strength, couldn't fight past the waves of pain rocking her body.

"You think you can harm this machine and I won't know?" Deemus yelled, his face inches from hers. "You think you can strike at my heart and I *won't know?*" His fingers closed around her throat, and she scrabbled desperately, her fingers like water, nerveless, boneless, useless flaps of skin against his twisting iron grip.

Wynn, she thought.

Her vision was going dark, the whole world spinning, voices screaming—so many women, Wynn's voice loudest of all.

The pressure disappeared and she fell back, air gasping into her lungs like fire. She gagged and coughed at the sensation of her windpipe expanding, like a plant struggling to re-form after being crushed under a boot. She tried to swallow and felt like she might choke on her own saliva, but then the feeling receded and she knew she wouldn't die; she would take another breath.

Deemus was gone.

"Wynn," she whispered as she struggled to sit up. She forced her eyes to focus and saw dark metal—the key on the edge of the console above her.

She was back in Jacob Deemus's time.

Mila struggled with a wave of tears that wanted to pound through her like a torrential flood, but she clawed herself upright and grabbed the key. She'd disappeared right in front of Deemus, and surely now he'd realize what was happening. She couldn't be here if the house sent her back again.

The door on the far side of the room opened under her trembling fingers, and as she took in the relatively small space, she knew she'd finally found the inner sanctum.

The walls were hung with banners bearing strange sigils and markings. A wooden table with elaborately carved legs stood in the center of the room, and as Mila approached, she saw that the legs were carved in the shape of women, bound and on their knees, their bowed heads bearing the weight of the tabletop.

She swallowed a breath that wanted to turn into a cry.

One whole wall of the room was lined with shelves laden with candles, jars of herbs, and other substances she couldn't name. On the wall to her right was an altar draped in a white cloth with black markings. A large, flat stone, round and marked with intricate engravings, sat at the center of the altar, candles at either end, and above it all hung another mirror of old, clouded glass in a heavy black frame.

The notebook lay open on the center table.

Lists of ingredients and hurriedly jotted notes filled page after page, but then she turned to a new page, this one written carefully, the title penned in an extravagant hand at the top: "To Know All Things."

The words froze her breath. Beneath them was a series of complex diagrams: instructions for the alchemical processes, schematics of the great listening machine, and precise drawings of an elaborate ritual. Many notes amended the instructions, as though the writer had been constantly refining and adapting the procedure.

She read on.

I shall surpass and complete the wasted masterpiece of an old fool. Father wished for the Music of the Spheres, the knowledge of the heavens, but he was too blind to see that the knowledge worth more than gold was right here on earth—the knowledge of the heart of man. I shall open the gates to knowledge and every man's secret shall be mine—I'll perform true alchemy and turn men's thoughts and secrets against them. For none can stand while I know the darkest corners of their souls.

Mila thought of the excruciating pain that had almost killed her in the machine, like something sharp and terrible burrowing into her brain, a force too great to withstand. Had Deemus truly devised a way to pluck men's secrets from their minds? The police constables and city officials had looked at Andrew Deemus nervously, and it had seemed more than just caution or obsequiousness in the face of a wealthy man—it had seemed like genuine *fear*.

Was this the true source of Deemus's power? Was this what her mother and sister and all those other women and girls had died for? So the men of Gravenhearst could rule the world through its secrets?

Her fists clenched and she nearly ripped the book in half, but she forced herself to focus. She turned the next page and caught her breath.

A sketch of a mirror—*the* mirror—in perfect detail bloomed before her eyes. The elaborate gold frame, tendrils curling like overgrown vines or the reaching tentacles of an octopus—the mirror Zahra had stolen.

"The 49th gate" was written in a dark hand and underlined several times. Hurried notes were scribbled next to it.

The 49th is key to everything—48 gates to understanding, but the last trumps them all.

Something flickered in Mila's mind, the book she had discovered that first day in the secret library—*Forty-Eight Angelic Keys* it had been called. A shudder ran down her spine as she recalled the words of the text: "for One is not to be opened."

"The Seal of Mastership" was written in thick lettering, and below it were diagrams of an altar and a sigil-carved stone. She glanced at the altar beside her—at the round, flat stone marked with strange carvings. These things were clearly integral to the rituals. Perhaps destroying them would weaken the house further?

She looked back to the journal. Underneath the ritual diagram was an elaborate drawing of an oak.

Jacob Deemus had drawn his family tree, himself at the center, his mother at one side, his five sisters at the other, and at the bottom of the tree, held by gnarled roots, was a sketch of the mirror.

Blood spilled down onto it.

One half of the tree shall feed it, and the other shall command it, and it will be a seal upon the House of Deemus, upon the House of Gravenhearst, and the Will of the Master shall endure forever.

Specific instructions on how to carry out the ritual were beneath, but Mila stopped reading when she saw the phrase "slit their throat over the glass."

This was how Jacob Deemus had taken control of his father's house. Murdered his mother and sisters and sealed it all with a mirror that controlled everything.

She flipped to the next page, panicked. "The Ritual of Absorption."

There was a list of ingredients, followed by a complex ritual that involved calling on specifically named spirits, precise gestures, and more of the same strange guttural language she'd seen detailed in the books in the secret library. Her eyes returned to one ingredient in particular: "lock of hair from the Offering."

Her vision blurred and she tried not to fall apart. She tried to be grateful as her mind processed the fact that *this* was what Deemus had done to her mother and Wynn. He had not dragged them screaming in terror down to this dungeon, had not tied them up upon this grotesque table, had not ended their lives at the point of a knife. Their presence in the ritual was not even called for—they'd simply been *absorbed*. Fuel for Gravenhearst.

The slowly crystallizing portraits made sense now—their images grew clearer as the house consumed them.

She gripped the edge of the table and her nails splintered. Deemus hadn't been lying when he'd said the process had already begun. He couldn't give Wynn back to her, because there was nothing to give. You couldn't press ash back into wood. Couldn't return smoke to solid form.

A wail broke from her throat.

She'd been hoping against hope, hiding the foolish dream even from herself, that maybe this awful thing could be undone. She should have known better. She *had* known better.

She swallowed tears and turned the page.

What she saw made her mouth go instantly dry.

"To Make a Servant."

She skipped over the ritual and read the note at the bottom.

And he shall be Gravenhearst made flesh; he shall be the servant of the bloodline. He shall wax and wane with the power of the Great House. He shall counsel the men of the line.

Asher.

His strange appearance upon their arrival, that feeling she'd had like he was hollow, too *disheveled*. Zahra had told her the house had sat empty for years. If the offerings were the fuel that kept the house powered, it must have been ravenous after so long without a Master. And then the morning her mother disappeared—Asher had been sleek and vibrant.

Of course he had—he'd just been fed.

A wave of nausea gripped her and she thought, *No, not yet, don't shift yet,* but the book remained before her and she gagged, realizing the sensation was just pure horror at the thought of that hollow man consuming her family, getting fat on their spirits. She retched on the floor, her stomach heaving, acid burning her throat. The wave of sick finally relented and she spat, trying to clear the awful taste, trying not to buckle under the weight of so many terrible revelations at once.

And the fall, she thought, a bitter laugh barking from her. *That's how we survived the fall.* Deemus had said Asher had special skills. Gravenhearst's ultimate servant had looked considerably weaker after she'd woken, so he must have used significant energy to heal Deemus. To heal her.

Using Wynn's spirit.

"I'm sorry!" she cried. "Wynn, I'm so sorry!"

There was only silence for answer.

She screamed and seized the large stone on the altar, hurling it across the room with all her strength. The world wavered and she gasped and the stone never hit ground. It was still there, safe on the altar. She grabbed it again, threw it harder, felt the whole world skip and shudder around her.

The stone was safe again.

She screamed, long and feral, that savage beast rising up in her chest like it would break her in half—tear her meat apart and emerge, blood-soaked and grief-starved, ready to die, ready to burn, ready to do whatever it took as long as she died with her enemies howling beneath her claws.

"Mila!" a voice cried out.

She turned, lips trembling, her whole body struck with the sound of his voice.

"You," she whispered.

The boy from her dreams was in the mirror above the altar, staring at her with those same loud, broken eyes. He came closer to the glass, limbs tense and straining.

"I'm going to help you," he said, grasping his side of the mirror as though he could force himself through to her. He stared at her like she was his last hope and he might break if he couldn't reach her. "What happened to you?" he demanded, his voice hoarse. "What should I do? What have they done to you?"

Who was this beautiful boy who looked at her like she was something precious, something worth risking everything for?

She was standing in the darkened stables, watching David reach for her father like he was his whole world, watching her father look to David like he was all he wanted. She was standing in the front yard of their home as her mother told them the place had been sold, that they were never coming back, and Mila was screaming at her mother that they couldn't leave because Father would come back for them, he wouldn't leave them like this. She was standing in the dark of Gravenhearst, staring out at the rain and knowing that no one would ever come back for her again.

She was alone, no one left on this cold, empty earth who loved her.

And this boy with the sharp jaw and hungry lips whom she'd kissed in her dreams was looking at her now, begging her to let him help her. To let him come to her.

"*Trust the boy*," Wynn had said.

I don't know how, she thought.

She couldn't let herself hope for one instant more because it would break her to pieces. *You want to come for me, and I know it can't be. You can't be real; none of this is real.* He was a dream in this perpetual nightmare, and she only wished that when she finally lay dying, the image of his face would be the last one she saw before her mind went dark and this awful life was through.

But she couldn't look at him now. She wasn't done yet.

"Please! What should I do?" he cried, striking his palms against the wall of his room. His image blurred, and she felt the room begin to shift.

Goodbye, she thought, refusing to cry, refusing to let hope and want break her before the end.

The room shook again, but the objects before her didn't change. The notebook lay open to the same page; the key was still on the table. The room shuddered and she grabbed the table edge.

She'd been so foolish—throwing the altar stone, losing her temper like that. It was a miracle that time hadn't shifted, leaving her trapped in this room like she'd been trapped in the machine room just scant minutes before.

She was losing her focus. Had to think.

The house shook, and she grabbed the key and ran.

"*The house is at a tipping point,*" Deemus had said. Every time the house shifted it was using energy. And the ghosts were fighting back, helping her—"*The gates have been knocked wide.*"

This monster was vulnerable. It was a spinning puzzle box of time upon times, and it was missing its keystone. It was alive, and it could only fight back for so long.

She could feel it trembling around her as she ran through the listening machine and out through the alchemy chamber—that awful foundering sensation she'd felt the first time she cut through its walls.

Maybe, if she pushed it far enough, she could break it forever.

37

Curtis

THE DANK, DARK BLACK OF GRAVENHEARST'S CELLARS WAS ALL Curtis could see.

The impossible flames danced like fireflies, but they shed no light on that dark corner of the room from where the voice had issued. Then one piece of darkness moved within the black and a single flame materialized, lighting only the ruined contours of a face. Curtis took a step backward, his heart machine-gunning, his knife already extended.

It was a man in a tattered Victorian suit—or what was left of him. He had rumpled hair the color of old dust, and skin like cracked oilpaper. It sunk inward, like there wasn't enough of him, as if his bones wore an ill-fitting suit of flesh.

"Offering," the figure croaked in a voice like dry branches scraped over stone.

"Who are you?" Curtis demanded. The thing had to be a ghost—no one could be alive down here, sealed away in the dark for over a hundred years. "Where is Mila?" he said, forcing his voice to be stronger. He wouldn't be afraid of this thing. He would face down Gravenhearst and save his Victorian girl and take his goddamn life back.

The man moved forward, his movements stilted and uneven, and Curtis's flesh crawled at the cracking and popping sounds that accompanied each step, like bones and joints about to snap, tendons splitting wide.

"*Offering*," the man said, his eyes wide black pits, mouth hanging open like a corpse's. The mouth moved again but no sound came out, and the thing reached for him, a single emaciated hand, finger bones straining, and then the impossible lights flickered and went black.

There was *nothing* but black.

Curtis fumbled for his phone, backing up, knife still extended, his breath too loud. He held his phone up and the bluish beam illuminated the man's face out of the black.

The thing was unmoving.

Curtis came closer.

He reached out toward the frozen specter, fighting the urge to run, beating down that rampaging feeling in his chest that he'd fallen down into madness or hell and that if he didn't get out *right now,* he'd be lost forever.

His finger brushed the outstretched hand, the skin like desiccated jerky, and he cried out as the whole thing crumbled beneath his touch. The whispers shrilled and shrieked like a flock of birds as the impossible man fell in upon himself, dust and bone and chunks of dry flesh tumbling into the darkness, and then the whispers screamed like scraped steel, like metal claws thrusting through his brain, and he cried out, the darkness tumbling down like an oblivion that had been waiting for him all along.

He stumbled for the stairs, gagging on the pain, barely able to hold his phone. The light juddered under his panicked strides, and he saw with a throb of despair that the jars containing those impossible flames were gone—as if they'd never existed—and as he struggled up the stairs and out into the night he tasted terror like he'd never known before.

It was all *too* impossible.

Talking skeletons and flames that burned from nothing and beautiful girls who appeared in mirrors . . .

Maybe he'd really gone mad.

Maybe he was lost for good.

He hit dirt and lay, chest heaving, head screaming with pain, the cold night closing in around him. He rolled over onto his back and a broken cry fell from his lips before he could stop it. He jammed his fist against his teeth.

I don't know what to do, he thought.

He fumbled with his phone, his finger hovering over Avi's number, the first in a very short list of contacts.

"Fuck!" he screamed, pushing up and pitching the phone across the field as hard as he could. He dug his hands into his scalp, wanting to rip out his broken insides. The futility of it all hit him and he stood, resigned, and trudged across the field to retrieve the phone, because what else was there to do?

He found it, gritty with dirt but otherwise unharmed, and stared at his notifications. About thirty texts and missed calls from Sage and Avi.

You're crazy, and they're going to lock you up, he thought bleakly. *Maybe they'll give you a room next to Dad.*

He stared up into the night sky, the moon a sharp sliver, the stars almost vibrating in the perfectly clear sky. *I want to fall into those stars and never come back*, Curtis thought. *I want to walk off into the trees and lose everything I ever was. Everything I'm cursed to be.*

Why can't I just be different than what I am?

There was no answer, only the whispers—insistent, inescapable.

He turned and walked back to the Beast, starting it with a hollow feeling in his chest, no joy left in the act, just a dull sense of inevitability.

He couldn't outrun the monster any longer, so why keep trying?

Garrett House was a black façade against the darkness, its eyes lit up like the yellow glow of a forge.

Curtis leaned the bike against the shed, running his hand gently along the gearshift. Would he ever get to ride the Beast again? The drugs would probably take his quickness, his instincts; he'd turn into nothing more than a shadow of himself.

He gripped the handlebar tight and imagined how the barrel of Dad's rifle would feel pressed against his chin—cool and smooth, a steady point in the universe.

Garrett House watched, hulking and impassive. Curtis stared back at it with hatred, this irrational feeling in his bones like the house was the symbol of everything that was wrong with his life.

We never should have come here.

They should have let Frank have the place. His mother should have packed them up and left this town in the dust when Dad got sick—they should have gathered up the tattered bits of their lives and escaped, left Dad behind.

Maybe she would have lived.

Maybe her love would have been stronger than the faulty synapses in his brain. He might have turned out right. He might have had a chance.

But there was no chance now. His broken life was waiting.

Curtis crossed the yard and felt cold trails of ice squeezing his breath, his footsteps an inevitable march toward living death.

Sage's scream cut the air, and he broke into a sprint.

He threw the door open, raced up the steps, the sound of her cries making murder spring up in his fists.

Up the second set of stairs, his footsteps pounding, her voice louder, a desperate "*PLEASE!*" that shattered his world. He tore down the hall toward his mother's room. He rounded the corner and saw his father shaking Sage like she was a rag doll. She clawed at him, and he shoved her down on the bed and went for her throat.

Rage made Curtis invincible. He seized his father by the back of the shirt and heaved, twisting his own weight, hurling Tom back into the dresser behind them. Tom's head hit the dresser and wood cracked, glass splintered. Curtis's father moaned in pain, stunned, but started to rise. Curtis stomped on the back of his knees and kicked him over onto his back.

"YOU STAY DOWN!"

He seized a broken shard of dresser mirror like a knife and pressed a knee against his father's neck.

"YOU'RE SICK!" he screamed, the jagged piece of glass just inches from his father's face. "YOU'RE SICK!"

He hurled the shard across the room, and then there was just his fist smashing his father's face over and over and over, the smack of bone on skin, cartilage crushing, blood on his knuckles wet and warm, the bright fire of his own skin splitting, bones bruising, no feeling now, just rage and fury and death and the man not even fighting him, just lying there with dead-looking eyes, taking his punishment, chin going slack, teeth knocking together with each blow. And then Curtis couldn't take it anymore—he screamed and pushed up, kicked his father as hard as he could, and turned back to Sage.

She was still trembling on the bed, eyes staring up at the ceiling, hands warding off the attacker who wasn't there anymore.

"I'm sorry," Curtis gasped, reaching toward her. She went to pieces all at once, crying like her body would break apart, the kind of crying she did when their mother died, only worse.

Curtis looked down at his father—unmoving, but his wheezing breath and stuttering chest were evidence that he lived—and Curtis knew he had to get them out of the house right away, or he would kill the man.

"We're going," he told her, pulling her up. Her knees buckled, and she fell against him, and he almost turned back and put that shard of glass through his father's throat. Her whole body was trembling, but when he tried to pick her up, she fought him, and he wanted to die, because in that moment, she didn't know not to be afraid of him, and all he could do was hold her shoulders, try to get her down the stairs without her falling.

"He got released early," she said, her voice far away, dazed. "I told him I didn't want to live with him anymore." Her legs wobbled again, and Curtis held her against him tightly, slung her arm over his shoulder, and tried not to throw up. His hand was throbbing, the cut from the glass slick and wet, knuckles twice their size and purplish-red, split skin leaking blood.

"Forget him, Sage," he said, his voice hard. "It's not your fault. We're done with him."

No more, Curtis thought. *No more tearing my life apart to keep you safe, you crazy old fuck. No more living in hell so you don't have to.*

The whispers screamed at him and he tried not to gag. He didn't know if it was from the pain in his head, the acid in his guts, or the feel of his father's face still beaten into his hands, but the night air was cold and leaving that house felt like the best decision he'd ever made. The whole thing could go up in flames for all he cared.

And take that broken misery of a man with it.

Sage was half sagging against him, so small, her head just up to his chest. They crossed the lawn—heading toward the bright glare of Diamond Mae's house—and Curtis felt like a speck of black in the endlessness of a dark sea. Mae's was the lighthouse, flashing bright in the distance; if he could only get them there—get them past the cold and the rocks and the depths that wanted to pull him under— then maybe, *just maybe*, everything would be okay.

Every window was ablaze, the light sparking through the trees, and Curtis yelled out, "MAE!"

His voice echoed across the yard, and he pushed through the mess of trees and plants, his voice cracking out again like a gunshot, hard and angry, and then Mae's door flew open and she looked at them, and Curtis saw that he didn't need to say a word—she'd read the horror in their eyes, and knew it was bad.

"Call the cops," Curtis said. "Dad attacked her."

Mae's face went still for a moment, and then she turned back into the house, and Curtis pulled Sage up the steps, locking the door behind them.

Curtis could hear Mae's voice speaking urgently into the phone, and he got Sage into the kitchen. He sat her down in one of Mae's ridiculous plush-velvet chairs, and then he heard Mae snap, "Just get the hell down here right now!" She slammed the phone back into the cradle. "Useless bag of shit," she muttered.

She turned back to them.

Curtis followed her eyes and studied Sage. He put out his hand, his fingers just settling on her tiny shoulder, and she jumped like he'd burned her.

"Don't touch me!" she screamed, her eyes like someone else's, like a person who didn't know him—as if someone older and half-dead were wearing his baby sister's face—and Curtis stumbled back and watched Mae wrap her arms around Sage, watched his sister cling to Mae and weep; her delicate fingers dug into Mae's skin.

She'll never be the same again.

The thought was despair and Curtis backed away, a feeling bubbling up inside him that he didn't know how to contain.

He threw the front door open and escaped out into the night, claws scraping through his brain.

You failed, Curtis, failed.

You don't belong here.

Come to Gravenhearst. Come home.

His hands were on the Beast and he was starting the engine, and before he pulled away, he looked back at Garrett House and saw his father's silhouette, a hulking black outline against the third-floor window.

Curtis pinned the throttle and sped out into the woods, heading for the only fate left to him.

38

Mila

GRAVENHEARST SHOOK, AND MILA RAN FASTER DOWN THE shadowed gallery.

Rooms. Endless rooms of fine furnishings and hulking mirrors, ghostly figures moving in starts and stops, the spectral echo of their voices cutting in and out like a shutter banging in the wind.

She had to get somewhere quiet and out of the way before the house changed back to the present—if she was caught, like before, it was all over. Deemus would never trust her again.

She turned a corner—wrong way—turned back and retraced her steps.

She rounded another corner and came face-to-face with a towering mirror, a sad-faced woman in green staring back at her from the glass. The woman's eyes went wide, lips screaming with a sudden vehemence, but no sound, and Mila ran. She sped down the hall, each mirror she passed turning to another reflection, another woman, their lips working in silent fury.

She pelted out through a moonlit gallery, and her stomach turned in horror as she realized she'd stumbled into the main drawing room. The dining room was just down the hall, and after that, the grand front entrance. She couldn't have picked a more likely place to be caught.

Her lungs were burning, her throat raw. Her dress was too hot, skirts too heavy, her tongue like a thick parched sponge. "Wynn," she begged as she dodged a table laden with silver curios, her knees almost buckling as she felt the nausea-inducing tremor, the shifting of things that would spell her doom. "Please!" she cried.

The house shuddered again, and Mila heard women's voices like a chorus of wails, high-pitched and long, and as her steps clattered against the checkerboard floor of the entrance, she felt the whole world shift, like a giant had picked up the house and rattled it in a fit of temper.

The wailing grew louder.

She bolted up the stairs, the red and gold walls a blur as she passed. She made the decision without thought, turning left at the landing, hurtling down the passage toward Deemus's bedchamber.

He wouldn't be there; he was looking for her. He wouldn't stop until he found her—and certainly wouldn't go to bed.

Please, Mila thought as the house quaked again, as the images

of screaming faces flickered and snapped in the mirrors as she passed.

She threw herself against the door, and it flung open under her weight. It was dark, and she crashed to the floor, burning her palms on the carpet, but then she was up again and scrambling for the back left corner, for the door she'd noticed the last time she was there.

Dear God, please be right, she thought.

She pushed the door open and almost cried with triumph at what she saw—Deemus's dressing room—a sumptuous chamber of gleaming mahogany shelves, drawers, and cabinets. She took in the details for an instant, then squeezed herself into a narrow space between the deepest wardrobe and the wall. She slid down until her thighs were pressed tight against her chest, and then let her head sag against her knees with a little whimper.

The house shifted.

It was dark and silent in the dressing room, only the faintest light filtering through the two tall windows that pierced the wall. Her own breath was loud in her ears, and she forced it still against her breastbone for a long moment—listening, *listening*, but she heard nothing—no movement outside the door.

She let herself breathe again and tried to think.

Could she be certain she was in her own time? There was really only one way to know for sure.

She struggled to her feet, legs unsteady, throat aching, and stepped carefully to the door. It eased open under her fingers with just the barest creak of hinges, and her breath caught again. The dark room was cut with stripes of moonlight pouring through the floor-to-ceiling windows. She followed the swath of ghostly light to the impressive desk, and beyond it to the empty blot of darkened wallpaper—the space where the golden mirror had been.

This was Andrew Deemus's Gravenhearst.

Her breath stuttered from her lungs, her skin tight against the boning of her corset. For once she was grateful for the thing—it felt like the only thing binding her together in this moment.

She had one chance to bring this house down, and if she failed, she'd be lost forever, and Gravenhearst would go on, ravenous and unending.

She went to the desk and retrieved a brass letter-opener, then went back to the dressing room and knelt in the space between the wall and wardrobe.

She had to be *certain* the house was strained to its limit before she launched her final attack.

She stabbed the wall with the letter-opener, the wood denting, then splintering under her blows. She kept going, her fist hot and sweaty around the handle, her arm aching with effort. Her stomach twisted and she felt the house tremor, but then it relented, and her blade sunk into wood again. She'd worn a deep gash in the paneling, and she gritted her teeth, increasing her attack. She'd passed the mahogany and breached the rough structure behind now, and she felt one feeble twist in her stomach just before she broke through to the hollow space behind the wall.

Mila stood slowly, her lips curving. That was it. The house had nothing left to fight her with.

She stood for a long moment, trembling, trying to work out her moves in advance. She couldn't hesitate, had to keep going until she'd done enough or simply couldn't do any more.

I am a devil, she thought as she tugged at the fastenings of her heavy overskirt. She ripped the stiff bodice down, the beaded edges scraping at her arms, and let the whole thing fall around her feet with a soft *shush*. She stepped free and worked the ribbon laces of the heeled silk slippers on her feet. She stripped the slippery stockings from her legs, her toes sinking deep into the thick fibers of the Oriental carpet. She loosened her stays for easy movement and deeper breath, retying the laces in a hurried knot.

She stared at herself in the mirror over Deemus's dressing table. Her hair was a tangle of falling coils and frayed edges, her face slashed with bruises and blood. She wore only her thin white chemise, soft and lace-trimmed just below the knees, the neckline square and adorned with more delicate trimmings of silk and lace. Her corset was armor, pressing her firm, holding her proud, the whale boning stiff strips down her chest and sides holding her up.

She pulled the slipped and tangled pins from her hair, re-pinning only the front strands so they were out of her eyes. The rest she let hang free.

She scrunched her toes and breathed deep, her hands knotting at her sides.

"I am a devil," she said to the darkness.

She turned and walked into Deemus's bedchamber.

She picked up a thick sheaf of paper from the desk, rolling it quickly into a tube in her hands. She went to the lamp that extended from the wall behind her and removed the smoke-tinged glass globe. The metal felt cool under her fingers as she turned the gas up, just enough to catch, and offered her own bundle of tinder. The flame licked at the pages, curling, turning black, the tongues of fire leaping and swaying.

She went back to the dressing room, the flame held before her, already hot against her skin as it reached for her. She opened cabinets and drawers and passed the flame over Deemus's suits and shirts, waistcoats and collars, backing away through the room before the ever-growing puddles of flame that caught and spread. She held the burning sheaf to her discarded stockings and smiled as they went up like magic, a snake of fire that consumed itself with a hiss and then turned a hungry tongue to her fallen dress.

She left the dressing room, her diminishing papers held only by the tips of her fingers, and strode toward the thick velvet drapes that fell in great swaths from the windows. She let the flaming chunk of paper fall against the puddled fabric and smiled to see it wick and spark hungrily. She caught hold of the other drape and passed it over the growing tongue of fire that licked and sighed, devouring the heavy dark of the room with bright, flickering heat.

There was a sound like *whooomfff*, and the flame leapt up the side of the drapes.

Her eyes went bright-blind and she stepped back, her face sweating with the heat of it. She backed away and watched the flames lick at the plaster ceiling, then billow out like rivers of molten flood.

She went back to the desk, not done yet. She wouldn't be done till she'd set every staring eye of this house ablaze with hungry light, until she'd watched flame curl and twist across every carpet, every painting, until she'd seen mirrors crack and windows shatter and beams fall and the whole world turn to hell.

She tasted smoke and bit back a cough as she searched through the desk drawer for what she knew should be there. Her hand closed over a blob of sealing wax, and she went to the door. The hallway was quiet, the gas flickering softly in the gloom. She heard a voice, but it was far away.

She darted out.

She ran the length of the passage, and for one moment, she thought of the portraits—of setting Deemus's trophy room ablaze— but she knew that drapes would catch quicker. She forced herself to run past, to reach her mother's room. The gas was on in the red room, and Mila fought a shudder of revulsion as she surveyed the last room to ever see her mother alive.

Once Mila had seen a cow slaughtered—witnessed the blood gush from its throat, the blade slit the belly wide. The butcher had pulled out the entrails, red and scarlet and sticky purplish-black, and Mila had fought back tears and bile at the sight. Now, as she stared at the mottled red carpet, the dark claret drapes, and the gleaming silk walls, she felt like she'd fallen inside that warm, stinking cavity—at any moment, the walls might shudder and throb with air and blood, the stink of flesh and fluids.

The glass on the lamp was hot, but she snatched it off anyway, holding the wick of the sealing wax to the flame till it caught. She held her hand in front of the flame and went to the farthest window, letting the stringy purple tassels that edged the drapes erupt in yellow flame. The leading edge caught like a line of running fire, and then bled into the thick of the curtain. Mila went to the next one, and then the next, and then the next. She cupped her hand around her flame and went to the door.

There was far-off shouting, the tramp of feet.

They'd found the first fire. She had to hurry.

She slipped out the door and dashed to her room. She lit the bed on fire, then the drapes, not staying to watch the flame lick up toward the bone-white moldings and elaborately trimmed ceiling. She turned and crossed the room, the long shadowed gallery of books and statues her next target. She wanted to stand before the spinning globe that had made Wynn laugh and watch it be consumed in a ball of fire.

She passed the sad minutiae of her old life: books and trinkets, her fine clothes, Wynn's sketchbooks strewn across a low table. The flames flickered in the silvery foil of the wallpaper, like eyes alight in a forest of reaching branches. And then she stopped short, staring into the mirror opposite the door.

Wynn stood in the glass, her hair like black silk against her white skin, her defiant eyes wide, lips open, moving. No sound, but Mila didn't need to hear a voice to know which word was on her sister's lips—she'd seen Wynn's mouth form that shape a thousand times.

Her name—*Mila*—and Wynn was *screaming* it.

The door behind her flew open, and she whirled as a fist came toward her.

39

Mila

THE FIRST THING SHE WAS AWARE OF WAS THE PAIN AT HER wrists, tight and cutting, her fingers already tingling from lack of circulation.

She drew a quick gasp of air, panicked at the sensation of being pulled spread-eagle, her back pressed hard against an unforgiving surface, her wrists stretched above her, her ankles spread wide below. She bit back a moan and forced her eyes to stay open, and what she saw made her wish she'd never woken up, for she was in the cellar, tied to that ghastly table. Deemus stood at the altar, his back to her.

The ropes were immovable.

"I've grown so tired of this," Deemus said without turning. He was leaning over something, and Mila could hear the quick flick of parchment.

"There comes a time when the horse, no matter how fine or how *much* potential, is simply not worth the trouble any longer."

He turned, striding to the wall of shelves, and snatched some ingredients. There was a large metal bowl on the altar and he returned to it quickly, clattering the items down and referring to the book before him.

"It was very clever, Mila," he said, his voice grim. "You are truly magnificent." He turned and placed the bowl beside her and glared down, his eyes cold, lips pressed in a thin line. "But not good enough." His fingers gripped her chin with savage pressure. "This house was baptized in fire and blood, and it may be burning right now, but it won't be when I'm through with you."

He slashed a knife blade over his own palm with a quick motion and she flinched, straining against the ropes as he knelt and made marks on the floor with his own blood.

"You go to hell!" she screamed at him.

He seized a piece of black chalk and began scribbling symbols on the table around her, and she fought her bonds with a feeling like she might go mad right here and now, might slip from her skin like that gutted cow and emerge blood-slicked and screaming, nothing more than pain and misery and endless vengeance.

But she couldn't. She could only snarl and strain and wish that she were a beast with claws, a thing too powerful to be contained.

Deemus was muttering behind her, harsh guttural sounds, making sharp motions with his hands, turning as though addressing the four corners of the room. The air was changing, charged—like sparks flowed through the air—and she could taste something bitter and acrid on her tongue. He picked up the knife, walking toward her, and she screamed Wynn's name, terror gusting out of her like an explosion in her chest, shredding her throat.

Screams filled the air, like a hundred voices raised all at once, and as Deemus looked about, his eyes wide with surprise, Wynn's spectral form leapt from the mirror behind him like a wild animal, sinking into him like a diver through water.

His face went tight with rictus, and Mila could see Wynn's form within him, glowing like the afterimage of a bright flash in the dark. Wynn took hold of his body and forced his hands toward the ropes, the movements stilted and jerky. The pressure released on one of Mila's ankles, and then the other. Deemus's face was a ghastly sneer, fighting for control, his whole body twitching with the effort, but

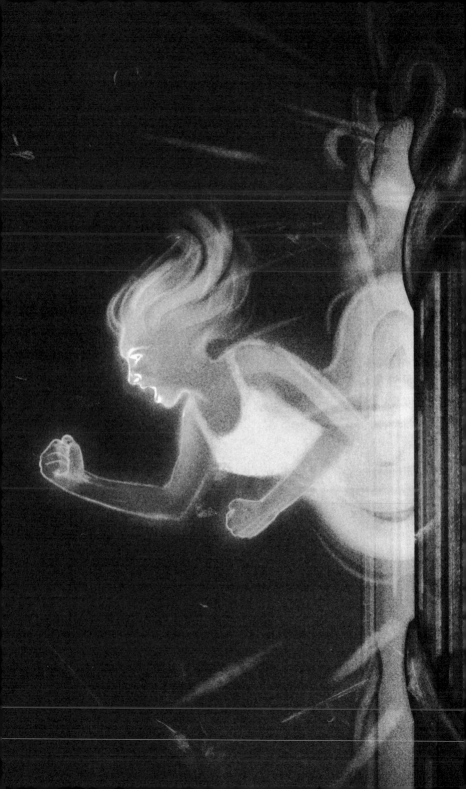

his legs moved, and then his hands reached for the remaining ropes. Mila's left wrist was free, and then her right.

She pushed off the table, kicking the ropes still tangled around her feet, clawing the loops off her wrists, and grasped the altar stone with a feeling like fire in her veins. She threw it with a feral scream, and Deemus's eyes went wide with horror. The stone hurtled through the air and cracked against the opposite wall, breaking in two with a sound that shook the room like an earthquake.

"GO!" Wynn screamed, her form fading, her light flickering. "GO NOW! GOOOO!"

The world heaved and twisted, and Mila doubled over with the force of it, and Deemus lurched toward her, his face a mask of murder—his body his own once more—and then everything went black.

40

Curtis

THE MOON WAS A SHARP SLIVER POINTING DOWN TO THE center of the copse, and Curtis left his bike where he'd dropped it three days earlier, the day his life had been changed forever—the moment his fate was sealed.

I've failed everyone, he thought, pressing his fingers against his eyes, trying to bite back the gasp of pain.

He turned with a little laugh of despair and walked into the copse, the whispers coursing and shrieking, the space behind his eyes twisting steel-bright like the whirring head of a drill.

It was always going to end like this, he thought. *My father's son.*

He'd tried to turn madness into a quest, tried to play the hero.

Tried to save a girl in a photograph who died a hundred years ago.

I'm insane.

How long, he wondered, till he became as bad as his father? Till he didn't look like himself anymore and everything that was *him* was obliterated beneath pain and voices and pills. How long till he was unmade by his own demons and hurt the people he loved?

A lightning stab of pain sliced his brain, and his knees buckled as the whispers screamed. He crawled through the copse, wave after wave of agony rippling through his head.

His face was stuck with tears and dirt, and he rolled onto his back in a silent scream as the pain crescendoed. The stars were knifepoints of silver hung high above him. The whispers screamed in a hurricane chorus.

The pain relented just a bit, a wave being sucked back down into the sea before it came crashing on the shore again. Curtis pulled his phone from his jeans pocket. It took all his concentration just to press the power button. His trembling finger hit Avi's contact, and he brought the phone to his ear with a little gasp.

Avi answered on the first ring.

"Curtis!" he said, his voice rife with panic and relief.

"Avi, I'm sorry," Curtis mumbled. "You were right. I'm sick."

"No, Curtis, I'm sorry. I've been a shit friend. I told you to trust me, and as soon as you did, I made you pay for it. Look man, if you say Victorian girl is haunting you, I believe you. We'll figure it out together. I've always wanted to be a ghost hunter."

"No, Avi, I've messed everything up. I have to keep Sage safe. I've gotta stop it before I get sick like him, before I hurt people."

"Curtis, man, what are you talking about? You're scaring me, dude."

"It's going to be okay, Avi."

"No, Curtis, don't be stupid. Don't you dare scare the shit out of me like this, man, don't you dare!"

"I'm really sorry, Avi."

He shut the phone off.

The pain wave rose again and the stars screamed. Curtis fished the folding knife out from his pocket. The blade sprung out like a crisp salute, silver in the moonlight. His father gave it to him for his tenth birthday.

He pressed the knifepoint against his own throat.

Something deep inside him gasped in grief—the hope snake slithering inside him that had *wanted* so badly. The blade point wavered just slightly.

He reached with his other hand and pulled the picture out for the last time.

"I wanted you to be real," he whispered, tears blurring his vision.

Mila said nothing, only stared back at him with eyes that burned his soul.

He pressed the knife, his hand trembling—felt it just break skin, draw blood on his neck.

The trees bent with the gale-force of the wind, and the stars and planets screamed all around him. Rain poured from the heavens, and thunder cracked like the sky was breaking. His mind flashed dead-white like the blast of a nuclear explosion. Everything went blank in his eyes, a mushroom cloud of destruction.

And then the pain receded to nothing, a shock wave being sucked back down to the source point. His ears rang with the sudden absence, and everything around him went perfectly still except for the rain.

Before him stood a girl.

Mila.

41

Mila

RAIN POURED DOWN ON HER, COLD ON HER BARE SKIN, HER chest shaking with the fire of rage and grim triumph, and she swayed unsteadily, Wynn's voice still echoing in her ears.

There was a boy on the ground before her.

He lay partly upright, a knife held to his own throat. His eyes were wide and grief-sick, and she almost gasped in relief when she realized that it was *him*—the beautiful boy from the mirror.

"Mila?" he said, his voice hoarse.

The blade was still at his throat, and she saw a dark drop of blood bead and wash pink down his skin in the rain. He seemed to realize what he was doing and dropped the knife, his eyes blinking as though he weren't sure where he was.

She went to her knees next to him. He reached out tentatively, just barely brushing her arm with his fingers. His eyes widened, and he looked up at her like he wanted to believe she was real but wasn't quite sure he could.

"You're the boy from the mirror," Mila said, her mind racing, trying to get her bearings. Had he just escaped too? Where had he come from?

"Curtis," he said. His eyes flicked to the knife he'd dropped in the grass and then back to her, and she could tell he was processing the scene from her perspective. He seemed embarrassed.

"How do you know my name?" she asked, because it was suddenly all she could think to say.

He opened his mouth, then closed it again. He reached out, something in his hand. Their fingers brushed as she took it, and his eyes wavered with that same desperately hopeful look, his jaw tight, whole body braced as though expecting her to disappear at any moment.

The intensity of his need was more than she knew how to handle, so she stood and stepped away a few paces, looking down at the thing he had given her.

It was a photograph.

Her own face looked out at her, and for a moment, she was back in the garden that terrible night of the wedding. "*For the papers, Miss,*" the man had said to her, stealing her image without her permission, immortalizing a moment when she'd felt utterly, *terribly* alone.

"How did you get this?" she asked, turning back to him.

"The library," he said with a helpless little sound, as if the situation were so surreal he was about to slip into laughter. His fingers plucked at his dark shirt. It was pasted to his chest with the rain, and heat rose on her cheeks as she remembered the way his body had felt against hers in her dreams.

I dreamed you here, she thought. *I dreamed you in the rain with tears in your eyes.*

The dreamlike memory and the sharp, solid reality of him was almost more than she could accommodate. Suddenly all she could think of was the feel of his breath against her neck in those flesh-drunk dreams, the sounds he had made as they fed on each other. It was too strange a memory to fit in this moment, so she shoved it down, wresting control of her thoughts.

"Where am I?" she asked, her voice tight.

"Gravenhearst. What's left of it. Or not left of it, I guess," Curtis stammered. "It burned over a hundred years ago."

"Ha." The laugh burst out of her like a gunshot. She pitched forward, reeling under the weight of the sudden knowledge, the absolute triumph.

She'd done it.

She'd destroyed Gravenhearst.

Curtis reached for her as she fell, his hands uncertain on her arms.

"Did anyone get out?" she asked, her breath trembling at the back of her throat, her whole body vibrating with the desperation of the question.

"No," Curtis said, his voice soft, his face so close to hers. She could feel his breath on her skin, and she sagged forward with utter relief. She caught the unnamable scent of him and gripped her fingers in his skin and laughed, everything about her mad and bold and absolute.

"I killed you, you bastard!" she yelled. She scrambled up and spun around, her arms thrown wide, screaming up at the sky. "I killed you!"

"*You* set the fire?"

She looked down at Curtis. The expression on his face was somewhere between bewilderment and disbelief.

"I—" He broke off, then started again, his expression sheepish. "I was trying to save you from it."

She went to her knees and seized him by the back of the neck, kissing his lips the way she'd kissed him in her dreams. He gasped against her, but then his hands slid up her back, hard, and he returned her kiss like he might die if he didn't.

It was better than the dream, her whole body rushing with the feel of him, a frantic pulse in her chest like she couldn't get close enough, needed to feel their skin pressed together. Her head felt like she'd had too much strong wine, and she thought she could get used to the delicious feeling, used to the sounds that her lips coaxed from his throat.

"So it's true!"

She gasped and pulled away, heart pounding at the strange female voice. A figure was emerging from the edge of the trees, making its way toward them through the soft pattering of rain.

The woman was pointing a pistol at them.

42

Curtis

CURTIS STEPPED FORWARD, PUSHING MILA BEHIND HIM, HIS mind racing. Professor Bell's face was grim, cold. She didn't look like Mary's mother, like his mom's old friend, or even the dispassionate professor of earlier that day—she looked like someone ready to kill.

For a moment, there was no air, just that look on her face and everything inside him frozen in fear. Then:

Get it the fuck together.

Cover in the forest, but not enough in the copse, the trees too thin, too spread apart. The bare field in between even worse. Nowhere to go, no play to make. He forced Mila back, hand tight around her wrist, body between her and the gun. Get some space, some breathing room. *Figure out what the hell is happening.*

Bell was twenty feet away now—getting closer. She took in Mila and her whole face changed.

"How did you do that?" she said, looking back to him, her voice sharp as splintered glass.

"Do *what*?" Curtis demanded, furious with how terrified he was— with how much he realized he *didn't* want to die after all.

"Her." Bell pointed to Mila. "She should be burning in Gravenhearst a hundred years ago."

"What the fuck are you talking about?" Curtis said, stalling for time. Could he rush her? Was she a good shot? And why the hell was she pointing a goddamn gun at him?

"I've seen the archives, Curtis, I know *exactly* who she is. And I know she doesn't belong here. How did you do it?"

"What *do you want*?" Curtis screamed.

"I want Gravenhearst!"

Curtis stared at her in shock.

"So take it," he said, finally. "It's a fucking boarded-up basement."

Bell laughed, a brittle sound. "I think we *both* know it's more than that." She stared at him like she'd flay him alive to unearth his thoughts. "It's been talking to you."

"You're crazy," Curtis said. But she wasn't—and apparently *he* wasn't either. Mila was here, she was *real*—Bell could see her.

"Did it tell you *how* to bring her forward?" Bell asked, advancing on him, pistol steady. "Or did you just *feel* how to do it? Was it instinct?"

"I—" Curtis started to say, shaking his head.

"I will kill her right now, Curtis," she cut him off sharply, adjusting her aim. Curtis tightened his grip on Mila, something desperate building inside him. He could still hear Sage's cries reverberating in his ears, feel the hot gush of his father's face breaking under his knuckles, and the whispers were screaming at him, screaming and screaming and screaming—

"I didn't do anything!" His words knifed through the air. "I tried to *kill* myself! I came up here to fucking kill myself because I'm god-damn crazy . . . and then the whole world went nuclear and she was here!" The words felt dangerous out in the open, *finally* said aloud for someone to hear.

He'd wanted to kill himself.

Bell's face changed, things clicking in place.

"A sacrifice," she said. Her eyes raked over him, then settled on his neck.

He could still feel the sting of the cut—just a small pierce of the knife, but he knew there was blood there. Her words jarred something loose in his mind. The skeleton man in the basement—"*Offering*," it had croaked at him like a desperate plea.

Offering.

"And then the storm, and then her?" Bell said, like the truth of it was more important than anything, like the entire fate of the world hung on his answer.

"Yes," he whispered.

"You made yourself a sacrifice," she said quietly. "You didn't even know . . ." She trailed off, unease on her features. Then her expression shifted and she was hard stone again. "Where's the mirror?"

"In my mom's old room," Curtis said, his stomach twisting. He had to get them out of here. Had to think of something.

A flash of curiosity quirked Bell's features, and her eyes shifted to Mila. "Did you know?"

"Know what?" Mila asked, her voice furious.

"That the Persian servant girl was Andrew Deemus's daughter?"

Curtis looked back at Mila. Her face was frozen, like she finally understood something monumental.

"The Deemus line didn't end in the fire," Bell said, and Curtis looked back to her.

Her eyes bored through him.

"It ends with you."

43

Curtis

THE WORDS RANG IN HIS MIND, RAKING BLOODY FURROWS through his life. The whispers screamed confirmation, and Curtis felt the world tipping over, like everything he'd ever known was realigning.

Mom's old mirror—Andrew Deemus's mirror. His mother a Deemus. *He* was a Deemus.

I could hear the house because it's mine, he thought, the whispers shrieking confirmation.

A feeling built in his chest, something large and powerful, and for a moment, he felt immense, like the universe trembled beneath him—the earth, the trees, the stars, *Gravenhearst.* He felt it like an inevitable chain, strong and unbreakable, stretching back centuries, and he thought he could wind it around Bell's neck and pull till he heard a *snap.*

A flash of something caught his eye, and he pulled himself from the hypnotic moment with terrifying effort. There were lights in the distance, coming through the edge of the forest like reaching fingers.

Bell's eyes flicked to the movement.

Curtis lunged for her. She looked back at him, panicked. For a split second, she aimed the gun at him, then turned it back toward Mila.

She needs me alive, Curtis thought.

"RUN!" he yelled as he slammed into Bell, grabbing her by the gun arm and snapping it back as they crashed to the ground. The gun went flying and Curtis raised his fist, knuckles ready for the feel of her blood.

"Now that's enough, Curtis!"

The shouted voice was a knife to the gut. Frank.

For one brief, idiotic moment Curtis hoped that maybe, just *maybe*, his uncle was there to help him.

Yeah, nice guess, moron.

Frank had a rifle, and another man was backing him up with a shotgun. Both wore headlamps. Frank's companion was none other than Darron Vandenberg—the professor's husband, Mary's father, and the owner of the rapidly fading Willowhaven Grand Hotel. He looked at Curtis with the stony gaze you turn on things that are already dead.

Curtis almost laughed, and thought that Avi would appreciate the irony if Curtis lived to tell him about it. "*I don't care about this shit,*" Curtis had complained in the Queen's campus library. "*I don't care that Andrew Deemus paid for renovations to the Willowhaven Grand Hotel.*" Avi had shook his head and told Curtis that the boring facts were breadcrumbs.

It seemed so clear all at once, like a faded silent film shuddering through his mind. The town of Willowhaven was a desiccated corpse trying to breathe, its shriveled heart still gasping out a silent rhythm beneath the crumbling bones of the town it had once been, waiting for the touch that would bring everything back to life.

Waiting for him to revive Gravenhearst.

Curtis looked back for Mila, hoping against hope that she'd made it to the other side of the clearing. For a moment, he thought she had, and he felt a reckless satisfaction. He would face three guns if she was safe—he'd tear them apart. These people thought they were tough? They were *nothing* compared to the nightmare life he dealt with every damn day.

But then he saw Mila—she'd fallen in the tall grass, frozen in the glare of the men's headlamps.

I never get good news, Curtis thought, something wild and accepting building inside him.

Professor Bell had retrieved her pistol, and she waved the gun at him, the implication clear. He sighed and rose to his feet, backing slowly toward Mila, his eyes never leaving the gun. Mila cried out, and he turned, barely catching her out of her stumble. She whimpered and leaned on him, clearly favoring her left ankle.

"You sure about this, Abigail?" Frank said.

Curtis bared his teeth, furious. He'd known Frank was an ass, but this was next-level assholery, truly magnificent heights of *I have the worst fucking family in the entire universe*.

"I should have run you over and buried you in the backyard," Curtis snarled. Frank looked nervous and edged closer to Bell.

"You're really sure my brother married a *Deemus*?" Frank said.

Bell looked back to Curtis, her eyes passing over him in slow evaluation. "I looked it up after he left tonight. Corrine Garrett, great-granddaughter of Zahra Amahdi." She shook her head. "Corrine told me once that she had Iranian heritage. But I never considered . . ."

"Well, who's she?" Frank said, pointing at Mila like he was pained. Curtis tightened his grip on Mila. "You never said anything about a girl. Where'd she come from?"

"*She* is the girl who burned the place down," Mila snarled.

"She changes nothing," Bell said, but she didn't look pleased.

"Look, Abby." Frank tilted his head, eyes darting to Curtis and away again. "Maybe we don't have to do this. If he's the Master, maybe he could change things. He could make the house stop sucking the town dry—break the link."

"Frank, have you dedicated an entire career to studying the mysteries of Gravenhearst?"

Frank shuffled his feet.

"Spent a lifetime learning spellcraft, or perhaps the last fifteen years delving into the soul-stealing dangers of blood magic?"

Frank looked away.

"No? Then *shut up*."

Mila shivered against Curtis. He could still feel the cut on his neck, the sting of the knife piercing his skin. Her photograph in his hands, a whispered desire—*I wanted you to be real.*

And then Mila brought through time. *Blood magic.*

Bell made a sound of frustration. "The Master does not simply order the house to play *nice*. The very *nature* of the beast must be changed, wrenched from one path to another. It took Jacob Deemus sacrificing five sisters and his mother to turn Gravenhearst into the monster it is today. You want to march your niece up here so Curtis can feed her to Gravenhearst? And then what?"

Frank cursed and looked away.

"He is the most powerful sacrifice the house will ever see—the last male Deemus. With his life, I can end it all."

Frank rubbed a hand over his face. "It's just . . ."

"Don't you understand?" Bell yelled. "There's hardly a family in Willowhaven that didn't make a deal with a Deemus—we're all tied to the House's fate!"

Curtis felt panic rush through him. Looking at Darron Vandenberg, he could see an echo, a phantom memory that wasn't his—a name signed in blood, a deal struck. A family line forever linked with the gaping stone beneath them.

He gagged, hunger overwhelming him, this awful feeling like he wanted to taste the man's blood, wanted to *take his due.*

This isn't me, Curtis thought. *It's the house. Not me.*

Frank licked his lips, looking from Abigail to Darron.

"Look," Bell said, "he's been getting more unstable by the day. If he disappears tonight, no one will be overly surprised. Sage never has to know anything."

"We have to think of our daughter," Darron said. "We can't be at the mercy of this thing anymore."

Frank ran a hand through his hair, refusing to meet Curtis's stare. "It's just—"

"It's him or us," Bell yelled. "And if I have to shoot you myself and deal with him after, I will."

Frank's hands tightened on the rifle, and Curtis could finally see the true coward in him. Frank was relieved to have his hand forced. This way he could tell himself he'd never had a choice.

"I know this is distasteful," the professor said more quietly, "but there's no way around it. You can't unmake a deal with the devil, and you certainly can't outrun it."

Curtis shuddered, that same strange feeling coursing through him, like the weight of many lives was pressing down on him, like he could feel the ground beneath his feet shift and groan.

He felt Mila's eyes on him, razor-sharp intelligence weighing everything he was and ever would be. The world was growing larger, the roots of every tree, the blood of each ancestral line calling out to him, and he didn't *want* it—didn't want this fucking nightmare that had risen up from the grave to split his life apart.

"We have one chance while the house is still weak," Bell said.

"You may be a spineless coward, but I will *not* live in the shadow of this curse a moment longer. We sacrifice a Deemus and Gravenhearst changes ownership tonight." She turned to her husband. "You brought it all?"

He nodded.

Bell looked to Curtis and motioned to the gaping black maw of Gravenhearst.

"After you."

44

Mila

THEY WENT DOWN INTO THE FETID DARKNESS, SHE AND THE boy named Curtis. The woman came behind them, the two men following after. The strange lights they wore on their heads cut wavering swaths from the darkness, sending stripes of yellow light over the stone steps and close walls.

This place cannot have me, Mila thought, her blood running cold. Not now. Not after everything.

It smelled different—fouler. She could almost feel the place exulting as she sank down into the dark. Just when she thought she'd escaped, just when it had all been over.

It's still alive, she thought, repressing a shudder. *But it won't have me. It won't have Curtis either.*

She wasn't thrilled to learn he was a Deemus, and for a moment, she'd almost shoved him away. But then he'd looked at her with those sad dark eyes, and she knew she'd never have anything to fear from this boy who held her, muscles tense and coiled, ready to turn his body into a weapon or a shield.

He was more than the Deemus blood that ran in his veins.

But he's a little on the slow side, she thought. She manufactured a pained whimper as she put weight on her "injured" ankle. She just hoped he'd catch up. He seemed very protective—she was 90 percent sure she could count on those instincts to kick in when she made her next move.

She shrieked and let herself fall forward, and Curtis grabbed her—*thank God*—his hands firm on her arms, her name breathing from his lips. She let out a pitiful whimper and clung to him, reaching deep for some tears just to really sell the act. The woman shone her light on them, and Mila blinked, momentarily blinded, but she didn't need to see—just needed to slip Curtis's knife into his right trouser pocket while the woman was distracted.

Curtis's breath caught, and she felt his whole body tense as she passed off the blade. The woman lowered the light and nodded for them to keep going, pistol still pointed at Mila. Mila thought of the metal tools that had hung on the wall down below—or, at least, they had in her time—and her fingers clenched as she imagined smashing the woman's face.

Curtis kept his arm around her, his other hand bracing her right arm in a show of helping her down the stairs. Their faces were mere inches apart. Mila gave him a meaningful look, and he nodded once, just barely.

Thank God, Mila thought. *He's clever after all.*

"Left," she whispered, so close and quiet that she was almost breathing into his hair.

He nodded, squeezing her hand once, then shifted to palm the knife. Mila kept her body pressed close to his, blocking his movement from view.

She felt him tense, knew he was ready.

He turned back to Abigail Bell, his arm flashing out, knife blade aimed for her foot on the stair above. Mila ran as the woman's scream pierced the air, high and agonized, the men erupting into confusion above her. Mila was already down the last few steps and around the corner, racing into the black toward that wall of tools.

She fumbled in the dark and felt dusty metal. A thin bluish light came up behind her, and she seized two long metal calipers, ready to swing; but it was only Curtis, a strange light in his hands. She grabbed his hand, dragging him away from the stairwell, back to the only place she thought perhaps they had a chance to regroup and survive.

There was a *bang-hiss*, and the sound of rock splintering—and then the woman's voice screaming out, "WE NEED HIM ALIVE!"

Mila yanked Curtis around a corner and nearly fell, tripping over something, but he held her up, and she pulled him onward, praying she could find it, praying she'd not misremembered. Praying it hadn't been moved or altered in the intervening years.

Curtis's thin light danced jerkily under their frantic pace, barely lighting the way, bouncing off equipment and pillars and the nightmare swaths of cobwebs, but then she saw the hulking shape of a wardrobe, and it *had* to be the right one. *Please, God*, let it be the one.

She threw the door open and shoved Curtis inside, the scent of rotting wood filling her nostrils. She pulled the door closed behind her and shoved him up against the inner wall, kneeling, her hands trembling. "Light," she hissed. The bluish light found her hands, illuminated what she was looking for—the old metal latch.

She jammed it back hard, scraping her fingers, the gritty feel of rust under her nails, and she pulled up the trapdoor, cringing at the creak of old metal and wood.

An older, mustier smell filled the cabinet, but Mila gasped in relief at the sight of the ladder. She started down. Curtis followed her.

"Close it," she said, and heard him obey. The echoing cries from above became muffled.

"Where did you stab her?" Mila asked as Curtis climbed off the ladder, turning the strange light on again and holding it between them.

"Her foot," he said with grim satisfaction. "Nailed it right to the ground. Wanted to keep them bottlenecked behind her and give us a head start."

He scrubbed a hand over his face and looked around, shining the light about the small square prison of stone. There was a pile of bones in the corner, and Mila wondered if it was the remains of the man she'd heard begging Jacob Deemus for mercy or someone else, some other poor soul who'd incurred the wrath of the line of Deemus.

No, she thought. *I will* not *die in this house.*

"Is there another way out of here?" Curtis asked, his breath coming in little gasps.

"No."

"Shit," he said, "we don't have much time. That place is an inch thick with dust—it won't take them long to find our trail. We can't just stay down here. We're sitting ducks." He started climbing back up, but Mila grabbed him, her fingers tight on his shirt.

"Curtis," she said urgently, "you have to listen to me. If you're really a Deemus, you have power in this house. You can make things happen."

He stepped down and turned to her, his face twisting with unease.

"You want me to channel the evil house?" he said.

"I want not to die."

"Yeah," he said quietly. "That would be good . . . But I don't know what I'm doing, Mila. I'm not some fucking sorcerer."

"But you're the Master!" Mila hissed. "It's *your* h—"

"I know!" He turned away and raked a hand through his hair. "I know." His voice was a little softer, his eyes dark with frustration. He let out a deep breath. "Okay . . . I was down here before and there were these lights. They were burning by themselves and there was this—guy—hardly anything of him left. I thought I was going crazy. He turned to dust right in front of me."

Mila's blood ran cold. *Asher.*

"He turned to dust? He's dead? For sure?"

"I don't know, he looked like he was mostly dead already," Curtis said, exasperation tingeing his voice.

"He's your servant, Curtis," Mila said, her skin crawling at the thought. "He's part of the house. He must have been living off the last shreds of what he'd consumed, just waiting down here." But if he was dead, if he'd crumbled away to nothing, maybe there was no power left in the house after all. Maybe Curtis couldn't do anything to stop them. "Did he *say* anything?"

"'Offering,'" Curtis said, his face strained.

A voice from above made Curtis jump and then he turned back to her, his words a desperate whisper. "Mila, there's three guns out there, and I need to get my hands on one of them or we're gonna die, evil magic house or not. Frank's a hunter, and he *will* find us."

He shoved the light into her hands and started up the ladder, and Mila nearly cried out in frustration. "What are you going to do?"

He stopped and looked back at her, his lips twitching into a slightly unsettling smile. "I'm going to wait for one of them to open the wardrobe. And then I'm going to knock their *fucking* heads off." He disappeared up the trapdoor and Mila nodded.

It was a start.

45

Curtis

CURTIS PRESSED HIMSELF AGAINST THE INSIDE OF THE armoire. He heard Professor Bell's voice loud and clear. She didn't sound close, but she was *very* angry.

"What do you mean? You HAVE to open it!"

Curtis heard a male voice reply, but he couldn't make out the words over the chorus of furious whispers swirling through his brain.

A slow shuffling sounded directly on the other side of the armoire. His heart kicked up, and for a moment, it was all he could hear—his heart and the whispers raging together, screaming louder than the whole world.

The shuffling quickened, then stopped. A beam of light leaked through the cracks in the wood, picking out the outline of the door.

The door flew open and Curtis heard the quick sound of a weapon being drawn up and aimed. But it was a deep armoire, and the guy wasn't expecting anyone to be pressed right into the front corner.

The headlamp cut through the darkness, and the shotgun barrel lowered as the man noticed the open trapdoor and moved forward to investigate. Curtis hoisted the caliper in a vicious one-handed upswing that caught the man directly in the jaw. There was the crack of his jaw breaking, and the man's knees buckled. Curtis grabbed the shotgun from nerveless fingers and moved back as the unconscious body fell at his feet with a soft *thump*.

No movement.

He shut the headlamp off and removed it, his brain noting that he'd just performed brute-force facial reconstruction on Mary Vandenberg's father.

He tried to feel something, some sense of remorse that he'd done this to her father, but all he felt was cold anger. His breath was loud in his ears and he could *feel* Gravenhearst, feel the cellars spreading out around him, ravenous and waiting, things smiling in the black, thick and hungry, the whole place breathing in the dark. His heartbeat was enormous again, echoing all around him.

He was the warm flesh-beat of Gravenhearst.

"Stand back," he whispered as he dumped Darron's deadweight into the hatch. There was a *thump* like raw meat hitting stone and then he heard the *swish* of iron slicing air and the *thwack* of metal on flesh. Mila's calipers.

"He's already out," he hissed. "Just watch him."

He heard one more *thwack*, and then silence.

He ran his fingers over the gun and his heart sank. He switched the headlamp on again, just long enough to confirm his suspicions. Vandenberg had brought a freaking antique two-barrel shotgun to the evening's festivities. That meant he only had *two damn shots.*

Thanks a lot, you pretentious asshole.

"Mila, stay here," he whispered down into the darkness. "Make sure that guy stays unconscious. No matter what happens, you stay out of sight."

A hand reached up out of the trapdoor and grabbed him by the wrist.

"No," she said flatly.

"They need me alive," Curtis whispered furiously as she climbed up and crouched beside him, her hand still clamped on his wrist. "If they can't catch me, they can't do whatever the hell it is they're planning. But if they get you, I'm done. I'll—I'll give them whatever they want."

Her breath quickened in the darkness, and she leaned a little closer to him, a hand settling on his chest. For a moment, he could feel something stronger than the whispers rattling the cage of his mind, felt only her hand warm over his heart, the faint heat of her breath against his cheek.

Her lips pressed his, and his whole body melted toward her.

She kissed the breath from him, her hand twisted in his shirt, then pulled back and said, "I know this place better than you do." She rose and slipped from the armoire.

"Shit!" Curtis hissed, grabbing for the shotgun and the remains of his brainpower, the whispers flooding back twice as riotous.

He maneuvered himself next to her, both of them crouching low and moving silently through the maze of decaying artifacts and cob-webbed pillars. The flash of a headlamp swept through the darkness, and Mila yanked him down hard.

His heart sped at the footsteps; Curtis stifled his breath, dust as thick as hoarfrost tickling his nose, the sharp scent of moldering fabric settling in the back of his throat.

The glare of the searching headlamp went over and past them, and Curtis peered around their cover as Frank disappeared into the black.

Curtis dashed out, the whispers shrieking a war cry.

Kill him Curtis kill him kill him killlll

Kill him dead bury his bones deep never worry again, never worry never fear just take his blood scatter it wide—

A light flashed from behind and Curtis swung around, the glare blinding him.

He fired, the blast like firecrackers rocketing against the close stone walls.

Feet pounded behind him and Curtis turned, gun drawn up to fire again. A headlamp flashed his vision useless, and then there was the dark shape of a rifle butt speeding toward him.

Pain exploded.

He fell back, the shotgun flying from his hands. His body smacked stone and his ears rang, the black of the room and the black of his mind a sticky mire. A fallen headlamp was the only thing he could force his eyes to recognize, as he clawed back from the brink of unconsciousness. He saw a streak of white, Mila's skirt flashing past, and he realized she was going for his fallen shotgun. She fired, but Frank dodged, return shot going wide in response.

The smooth scrape of the rifle bolt being pulled back—Frank reloading.

Curtis threw himself in a desperate tackle, taking Frank out at the knees. They crashed to the floor, Frank grunting in pain, but then came another flash of light, the sound of running steps echoing in the dark.

"ENOUGH!" Bell yelled.

Curtis heard the click of her pistol cocking as if from a great distance. His ears rang, the whole black world spinning around him, the whispers a mad mob screaming at him from all sides.

"Get him up," she ordered.

Frank hauled Curtis to his feet, and waves of pain broke through Curtis's head, almost sending him down again. He staggered, and Frank held him harder, meaty fingers digging into his arm.

"Where's my husband?" Professor Bell demanded, her voice like ice.

"Go to hell." Curtis spat a wad of blood at her feet.

She pistol-whipped him, and his knees buckled; only Frank's grip held him up.

"Where is he?" she said again.

"I shot him," Mila said with a laugh.

Curtis's blood ran cold, everything in him sinking as Bell turned to Mila.

"You didn't," she breathed.

"Then where is he?" Mila asked, reckless fire lighting her eyes.

Curtis wanted to tell her: *No, don't do this—don't take the heat for me. I've been a walking dead man since the day I was born.* Deemus blood mixed with Garrett blood and it all came due today. But the whispers were rushing through him, distortions scraping the raw parts that were supposed to think, supposed to be *him*.

There was a long silence as Bell stared at Mila, and Mila stared back, wild-eyed and unflinching.

"Take them to the altar."

Frank shoved Curtis forward. The whispers screamed while his vision tried to adjust, still half-blurred and slowed down, a pulse like fire radiating from the back of his skull. Curtis wanted to tell the whispers to shut the fuck up, since they were clearly useless, and his head hurt too damn much for their noise right now.

Master of Gravenhearst, but none of it did any damn good because he didn't know what to do—had *never* known what to do with his life except barely scrape by.

The cellar was about what you'd expect from a murderous psycho ready to work dark magic and steal your evil house. Red pillar candles flared at even points circling the space, and at the center of it all, a workbench had been cleared and covered with dark cloth, a round stone at its center—white with strange markings.

Mila's face went pale, her eyes frozen on the stone.

Bell limped in after them, wincing with each step, and as she entered the circle of candlelight, Curtis saw she was leaving a trail of blood blots behind her. Her right foot was a mess of blood seeping up through the single stab wound that went all the way through her boot. He'd gotten her *good*.

"Looks like that hurts," he said with a short laugh. It probably wasn't smart to piss off the woman who was going to kill him, but no one had ever accused him of being an intellectual.

He was *angry*.

Yes, angry. His *fuck it* demon was rattling the bars of the cage, screaming that it wouldn't go quietly. It would break its claws leaving bloody trenches dug into stone and flesh and bone; it would set itself on fire to scald its enemies.

Bell hobbled forward, breathing hard. "That's a paper cut compared to what you're going to feel." She shoved a filthy rag in Curtis's mouth and tied another tight around his face with a vicious *snap*. She did the same to Mila as Frank maneuvered Curtis into a circle drawn in black chalk.

Grabbing her knife off the altar, Bell seized Curtis's right hand, and he hissed as her nails bit the deep gash on his palm. She hesitated, staring at the raw wound for a moment; it had clotted and puffed out like an angry red boil, and it throbbed like fire. Holding broken glass to your father's throat didn't come for free.

She slashed the knife across his hand.

It hurt more than Curtis expected. He gritted his teeth and tugged his mind away, away from the hot blood slipping down his palm, wetting his fingers, away from the flesh memory of being ready to slit his father's throat while his sister gasped like a dying fish. Away from the frantic bird-thrum of his heart as his whole body screamed that he was going to die, Mila was going to die, Sage would be alone—

FOCUS! he ordered himself. This couldn't be it. He had to do something. Mila said he had power—evil house power—and if he could just *think*—

Bell caught his blood in the bowl, then ran the blade across her own hand. The image of her blood flowing like a thick stream against the textured silver of the bowl was almost hypnotic—like he could feel the moment his blood mixed with hers and the awful things it symbolized.

Bell moved to her own chalk circle, drawn in white, and stood in its center. She plunged the knife in the blood, then ran the blade in a line across the floor from his circle to hers, muttering under her breath.

He could *feel* it—feel things shifting inside him as she worked the ritual. Stealing his life, stealing his future, stealing his *power*.

Something wrenched like his organs were being pulled inside out, and he screamed against the gag.

Focus, Curtis, his mind cried. *Focus*. He fought the trembling that gripped his body, the feeling that he was being unmade from his core, his basest fibers untwining, turning his flesh to unraveled shreds.

Mila.

He pulled his eyes to hers, the movement as weighty as heaving concrete. Frank held her, but she strained against him, eyes wide and locked on Curtis.

It was her eyes that had done him in to begin with. He'd turned that photograph over and they'd burned him like fire. He'd wanted to know the girl who could look at him with such eyes, sear his soul through a photograph.

Focus, Curtis, his mind begged.

"*Offering*," Curtis recalled with an effort that almost finished him. The not-dead man had reached out to him like a dry tree branch swaying in the wind. "*Offering*," he'd whispered.

Bell's voice rose louder, and Curtis felt the house scream in his head. Pain split his body, like sinew flayed from bone, skin peeled from meat. Thousands of voices were screaming, the darkness rising, sounds like stone cracking and metal grinding. Gravenhearst was being torn from his body, leaving him shredded and slit, broken and empty.

Maybe I'm nothing, Curtis thought. Maybe all he'd ever been was darkness pressed into marrow, rotting corruption propping up the paper walls of his soul. He'd never had anything good to give anyone, and now he knew why.

Curtis couldn't move—his body wasn't his anymore. Abigail Bell's voice rose in a chant that swept the room.

His chest was hollow; icy darkness was carving him out, unmaking him. Tears slipped down his cheeks, the only thing he could feel anymore, and he saw them mirrored in Mila's eyes as she screamed against her gag and fought like a devil.

His vision blurred; there was only dark.

And then a growling sound far off in the distance.

It was familiar, like a second skin, but he couldn't remember why.

The world was gone, he'd finally fallen down that black well for good. The light was gone and he was alone in the dark. They'd cover him over and forget he'd ever existed.

There came the sound of metal smashing stone, gears and an engine and moving parts screaming wide open. Curtis's eyes struggled open as the knowledge hit home like a splash of cold water. He knew that sound.

Steel and fuming engine careened down the stairs—his dirt bike, the riderless Beast.

46

Curtis

THE BIKE ANNOUNCED ITS PRESENCE LIKE AN AIR-RAID SIREN followed by a Luftwaffe strike.

First there was the high, buzzing-chainsaw sound of the motor screaming as it careened down the steps. Then a wobble, the sound of handlebars scraping stone, zigzag-colliding into the walls. The impact kicked the bike into another gear, and the chainsaw was more like a dentist's drill crossed with an airplane motor. And then the sheer weight of the bike—and all its unleashed momentum as it propelled itself down the stairs—came into full effect and the bike flipped end over end, the motor still grinding like a hell-demon. The bike skipped the bottom step and barreled into a massive alchemical apparatus. The contraption exploded like a glass grenade as the bike went whipping onto the floor, finally flat on its side. But the throttle stuck and now the bike was chasing its own tail like a possessed spinning yo-yo.

It all happened so fast that the event gave the general impression of the world coming to an abrupt and very noisy end.

But Curtis's world started turning again, because Professor Bell's concentration was not immune to spectacular bike wrecks. The cold slipped from Curtis's body like plunging frostbitten fingers into warm water; his whole body burned, but he could move again. He kicked the professor in the hip and sent her flying face-first from her magic circle. Ripping the gag from his mouth, he caught a brief impression of Avi (*Avi? Really?*) charging down the stairs like freaking Braveheart, and then Frank stopped fighting Mila and tackled Curtis.

His breath was gone, and Frank was strangling him, this awful look on his face like an apology, like he was begging Curtis to understand, and Curtis punched and flailed, pressure building in his throat, rising like a flood tide sweeping up his head, like water drowning him, everything foggy, going dark. Then a scream, and Mila cracked the butt of a rifle over Frank's head. His grip loosened, and air flowed back into Curtis's lungs. He threw Frank off with a yell of rage and grabbed the rifle from Mila.

Frank stared up at him, his eyes foggy, hands raised.

For a moment, all Curtis could feel was the lust for killing. He'd been swimming in blood his entire life, and now was the moment to bring everyone low, to bathe the stones of Gravenhearst in gore until they were finally sated. The whispers screamed, and he wanted to smash Frank into the flagstones of Gravenhearst until he was nothing but a red stain in his memory. He wanted to tear the walls down and bury them all in black. He wanted blood on his fingers, gore in his hair. He wanted *death.*

He felt the house stir around him, felt Gravenhearst stretch and shift. He could feel the immense scope of the house through time and space, the spectral forms of the towering chambers, the snaking halls no longer there, stairs that lead to nowhere, passages without end. And within, a presence, dark and waiting, hungry and coiled. The darkness rose up in his chest, boiling like a gathering storm, filling the corners of his mind.

I am Gravenhearst.

He felt the next words before he heard them, turned in anticipation, his body responding before the professor could even speak, as if her voice came from a thousand miles away. She had Avi and was dragging him by the hair toward the white circle, the pistol jammed in his cheek.

"Drop the gun or I blow his head off!"

"Take her," he told the darkness.

A sound like thunder echoed through the chamber, and Bell's body went rigid, her mouth popping open with a sound of terror as Avi scrambled away. Her limbs shook like a marionette, head lolled over her chest. Then her head rolled up like it had been swung on a ball joint, and a smile like a death-mask's grin leered from her frozen features.

Thunder shook the room once more and a jagged fissure ran down her face, like splitting under an axe's blow.

There was the *crack* of stone breaking and the whole floor shook as a fault line split the floor, starting in the black circle where Curtis had stood. It ruptured the line of their mingled blood and cracked through the circle of white. As it reached her bloody foot, the crack in her face spread down through her abdomen, her chest blossoming blood, the color spreading through her white shirt, thinning out from the bright center.

Frank ran for the stairs, but Curtis seized him by the back of his shirt and whipped him face-first into the nearest pillar; he fell and didn't move.

Curtis stared at his uncle's fallen body and felt a sensation as if something heavy and thick was being sucked from the room. Energy substantial as smoke was drawing back into the crevices of Gravenhearst.

He turned back to Bell.

She was gone—all traces of her blood draining into a thin fault line in the stone.

He felt the house preen, slink back, and settle into itself, glutted with satisfaction.

Curtis looked to Mila, his heart pounding. She was staring at him, eyes wide.

A voice echoed darkly in the recesses of his mind. A voice made of smoke and black and claws and hunger. His breath caught, and he reached out for Mila.

I don't want this, he thought with profound terror.

Her hands on his chest were warm and steady, holding him up, holding him in one piece.

This isn't me, he told the dark.

He felt the voice recede and slip back into the darkness, the whispers swirling quietly, settled, but not gone.

He drew a ragged breath and let his fingers relax on Mila's skin. His heart found its own rhythm again. Mila nodded, her eyes wide, hands steady against him. He felt like she understood what he'd just turned away from.

"Soooo . . . that was new," Avi said.

Curtis turned, trying to sort out too many thoughts at once. "How did you know I was here?" he asked finally, having thought of nothing better.

Avi gave him a look that said he was kind of stupid. "Dude, you're obsessed with this place. Of course you're here." His eyes shifted to Frank's unconscious form. "I see Frank finally lived up to highest expectations."

Curtis nodded grimly and passed the rifle to Avi. "We'll put him with Mr. Vandenberg."

"Mary's *dad*?" Avi said with disbelief.

"Yeah," Curtis said, nodding grimly.

"Jesus."

"Yeah," Curtis agreed. He seized Frank by one arm and Mila grabbed the other. They began dragging and Avi followed. When they reached the armoire, Curtis put his foot on Frank's neck as Mila released the catch on the trapdoor. A frantic scream echoed up from the pitch-dark beneath. Mr. Vandenberg.

"Shut up," Curtis ordered. He looked down at Frank. He could just press his foot a little harder. He could press till he heard a snap.

He felt the darkness stir, felt its claws flex.

No.

"You're done," Curtis said, taking his foot off Frank's neck. He pushed him down. There was a thud, and Curtis felt something release in his chest. "You're fucking done."

Mila snapped the hatch closed, and a panicked scream rose up as she slid the bolt in place.

"Relax!" Avi yelled. "The police are coming. They'll find you." He looked to Curtis. "I called the cops," he said with pride.

Curtis clapped a tired hand on Avi's arm in a well-done sort of gesture, then walked slowly back to the first chamber, his breath stuck in his throat. He could still feel the house, the phantom shell of Gravenhearst all around him, but it seemed quiet, like an animal temporarily appeased. He swallowed hard and tried not to think about the implications of such a thing.

"Curtis," Avi said. "What the fuck is going on down here?"

"I'm Master of an evil house."

Avi stared at him, eyebrows raised. "Clearly," he said.

Curtis sighed. "It's a long story. I'll fill you in on everything, but . . . let's just get out of here."

They came out of the ground to find the rain had stopped. The stars were like shards of ice flung over a field of black.

They'd survived, but Curtis could feel Gravenhearst tucked into the spaces between his bones like little slivers of darkness. A chill that wouldn't leave.

Mila was watching him, her eyes grave.

He saw the wet, red fissure split Abigail Bell's face, felt Gravenhearst swallow her whole. "*Take her,*" he'd said.

I did that.

"It's all right," Mila said. "We're out now."

For the first time, Avi seemed to fully take in Mila's presence. He turned to Curtis and pointed at Mila questioningly. Curtis held out the photograph. Avi took it and stared, then held it at arm's length next to Mila's face. He compared the two while Mila stood, hand on hip and one eyebrow raised.

"Holy shit," Avi said.

"Say you're sorry," said Curtis.

"Dude . . ." Avi said, his eyes wide and blinking. "But, hey!" he exclaimed with sudden enthusiasm. "You did it—and you didn't die at the end of the movie! Much better than *Terminator* one."

"Avi."

"Actually, technically *she's* kind of the badass time-traveling dude—nice trope reversal."

"Avi."

"Yes, Curtis?"

"Thank you."

Avi blinked as if he hadn't quite heard the words right. His lip tugged upward, and he ducked his head like he didn't know what to do with himself. "You're my best friend."

Curtis locked his arms around Avi, trying not to think how near he'd come to never seeing him again.

"Just don't scare me like that again, okay?" Avi said, his grip tightening around Curtis.

Curtis hugged his friend; when they broke apart Curtis laughed softly.

"What?" Avi asked.

"You really saved us."

Avi smiled. "I told you I would."

47

Curtis

THE COLD NIGHT AIR WAS FULL OF RUMBLING QUAD MOTORS and the scent of rain-laden dirt as Curtis, Avi, and the officers made their way out of the woods. Curtis felt unreal, an imaginary thing flying back toward the real world.

In a fairy tale, he'd won—saved the girl, fought the traitorous uncle, slain the evil sorceress.

But the truth was dirtier.

Heroes in fairy tales didn't have the spirit of an evil house inside them. They didn't have fathers locked up in the mental hospital. And they didn't send their Victorian girl to hide in the freezing forest because the cops were coming and her existence in this century couldn't be explained.

Curtis wondered if life would always be like this—some terrible compromise between the unthinkable and the necessary.

The whispers hadn't been signs of him slipping into his father's illness. But was the truth any better?

A truncated version of the event—Curtis had been followed to the copse by three individuals with guns, assaulted, and then a strange demonic ritual had been attempted. This account was clearly supported by the scene beneath; a spell book in Bell's writing, red candles and chalk-drawn sigils, and a bowl containing traces of Curtis's and Abigail Bell's blood.

No one could deny she'd been up to something unspeakable.

All three adults had brought guns registered in their names, and even now, purple bruises formed around Curtis's throat, a clear match for his uncle's grip.

It seemed logical that Abigail Bell had taken the chance to escape when Avi's interruption ruined the ritual.

Officer Matthews briefly pressed Curtis, saying that Frank had said something about a girl, but Avi gave Matthews his best blank stare and Curtis shook his head as a medic bound his hand. Avi made a comment that Satan-worshipping freaks would apparently lie about anything. Matthews moved on.

A helicopter had come for the two suspects; Darron Vandenberg was brought out on a stretcher, Frank in handcuffs. He'd stared at Curtis, pure hatred distorting his features. Curtis wondered if he'd made a mistake not feeding Frank to Gravenhearst after all.

The Beast had been retrieved from the cellar, miraculously in working order, and Officer Matthews looked only too relieved to order the scene cleared. Evidence had been collected and photographs taken, and the cold and sheer *wrongness* of the place was heavy in the air. *No one wants to know about this place*, Curtis thought.

Now the Beast's headlight cut a ghostly swath as Curtis rode through the trees, pointed for home.

He'd left as one creature, returned as another.

A Deemus. Inheritor of a legacy far worse than Tom Garrett's. The whispers pooled and trickled through his mind, and there was stark despair in the realization they might never leave.

He passed Garrett House and the cop car that sat in the driveway. Pulling into Diamond Mae's yard, he killed the engine and leaned the bike against a tree. The beacon of Mae's floodlights cast white fingers of light across the black trees.

Across the yard, the door to Garrett House banged open, and

Police Chief Neufeld yelled for him. Curtis ignored the man and climbed the porch steps to Mae's.

The house was quiet, the low light soft over the multicolored Persian carpets and twinkling treasures that lined the hall and spilled into the kitchen. The long hallway stretched before him, and he saw Sage, alone in the darkened living room. She was sitting in an old leather club chair, her tiny legs plucked up against her chest, eyes far away. A floorboard creaked under his step, and she looked up.

Curtis felt too much rise inside him.

He'd almost left her tonight. First by his own hand, then by someone else's.

How could I have done that to her? he wondered, shame clenching the back of his throat.

She let out a soft sound and ran to him, and he sagged against her with a rough gasp he couldn't hold in any longer.

"I'm sorry," he whispered. She gripped him tight with her fierce little fingers, holding him closer, and he buried his face against her shoulder.

The front door opened, and Chief Neufeld called out his name.

Curtis turned, heart riding the lining of his throat, but Mae stepped out of the kitchen as though she'd been waiting for this moment, her blue-black robes flashing out around her like settling wings. She said something Curtis couldn't make out, and Neufeld came back at her, louder. Mae cut him off again, and this time Curtis heard her perfectly.

"They live with *me* now!" she spat, her chin raised sharp.

"Fine!" Neufeld yelled. "But I want them both in my office tomorrow morning for questions. We've got a bloody Satanist on the loose, for Chrissakes! I need answers."

"Get the fuck out of my house, Jimbo," Mae replied in a tone of voice that was suddenly remarkably agreeable. "You'll get your goddamn interrogation. Don't blow a nut."

Avi edged through the front door, followed by Officer Matthews.

"You be there too," Neufeld said, pointing at Avi. "Eight A.M." Curtis caught a glimpse of Avi saluting Neufeld in a manner that managed to say "screw you" while agreeing to the terms.

"Out!" Mae ordered, her shoulders hunching up, a disgruntled crow.

Neufeld went.

"You can stay," Mae said to Avi. Avi looked pleased, like he'd been given a particular seal of approval.

Matthews nodded a silent acknowledgment to Curtis that wasn't exactly friendly, then looked over at Avi. "Son, I really should be taking you home to your parents."

"No one home. They're both on call at the hospital."

Matthews sighed. "All right. I'll see you all tomorrow at the station."

He left.

Curtis stood. "I have to go back out there."

"Good Lord, boy," Mae said, "I'm going to tie you to a damn chair if you do any more running away into the goddamn forest."

"It's not like that," Curtis said quickly.

"It's really not," Avi agreed. "Although, you do run away a lot." He glanced at Curtis. "What? You *do*!" He looked back to Mae. "There's someone he's gotta bring back." Then to Sage: "It's okay. He's really *not* crazy. I promise."

Curtis glanced at Sage. She had a look of dull acceptance on her face, like she'd expected this moment.

"I'll come back," Curtis said. "I promise."

Sage rolled her eyes but motioned him to go.

Curtis looked to Avi, who nodded and said, "I'll hold the fort down."

"Boy, you won't hold down *nothing* in my house," Mae snapped.

"Ah, I mean I'll make myself available to be of assistance. If you say so."

"Better," Mae said.

48

Mila

MILA SAT ON A FALLEN TREE, HER THIN CHEMISE DAMP against her skin, legs pulled tight against her chest like a shield. It was cold, and the forest felt endless.

I've been swallowed by sharp teeth and old bones.

Wings fluttered in the dark and Mila fought a shiver. The jacket Curtis had armed her with creaked, the leather stiff against the cold, but the lining was still warm, and it smelled of him.

"Leave me," Wynn had said. *"Trust the boy."*

She'd known. Somehow, Wynn had known.

Short months ago, they'd left their home behind, sailed for a new country.

And now? Every bit of the world she'd ever known or understood was long gone, buried under the weight of a hundred years. The life she'd never even gotten to live was old and dead, a lost moment trapped in a crumbling photograph. All that time and distance—it meant nothing to everyone else, but it was as vast as the sky above her, an immense and drowning thing.

I survived, she thought fiercely.

But for what?

She pressed her face into the jacket collar with a gasp and strangled the sob that plucked the back of her throat. It was like losing Wynn all over again, the crushing grief rising around her, making her small and indefensible in the cold night. She wrestled for control of her body, breathing in the jacket's scent—*in and out, in and out*—forcing her body to obey.

Thin willows clacked in the chill breeze, dancing like white bones in the gleam of moonlight.

"*I'll come back for you*," Curtis had said.

No one comes back.

She'd lost them all—everyone who ever mattered to her.

Mila clenched her fists. The world was full of monsters, and she had to be stronger than all of them. She had to think, had to be ready, had to find her own way out of the darkness. She'd left too much of herself in Gravenhearst—she hardly knew what was left anymore.

An owl cried somewhere in the black, and Mila fought the maelstrom of despair. It beat against her walls, pressing the broken parts of her that trembled, wearing away her resolve.

You'll always be mine, Gravenhearst taunted.

Mila shuddered. A voice made of smoke and metal and cloaked in whispers scraped through her mind, resounded in her bones. She could feel Gravenhearst breathing, like a great beast buried in the earth, jaws snapping, lungs like bellows billowing heat and ash. *It's awake*, she thought with a thrill of terror. *It's awake.*

A sound caught her ears and her heart snapped against her ribs.

There was a high sort of whine that rose and fell, gaining intensity on the cold night air.

Her fingers tightened on the knife.

The sound was so loud, getting closer, now a growling cacophony. She stood to her feet, gathering the tatters of her strength. She would kill. She would *kill* before she died alone in these woods.

The noise cut abruptly.

Her breath stilled.

"MILA!"

There was the sound of branches breaking, a figure moving through the woods. Fear gripped her white-hot and insensible. Andrew Deemus had followed her through time, through death; he'd never let her go. The knife trembled in her fist, and she bit her lip till she tasted blood.

"MILA, IT'S CURTIS!"

The figure was close now. Too close.

"Mila," the figure said, voice cautious, eyes wide. He stretched his hand out.

"Curtis?" she said, her breath hot in her throat, voice tight and strained.

"It's me. You're safe," Curtis said.

"I thought—" She was shivering and she didn't know if it was from cold or fear. It made her angry, because she was a devil who'd set the monster on fire and now she was breaking, her strength dissolving in the dark chill of the forest.

Curtis ducked under a low-hanging willow branch and reached out for her, so careful. The knife fell from her grasp, and he took one quick step and folded her in his arms.

Her resolve splintered and she forgot how to care. She stifled silent sobs against the curve of his shoulder, fingers dug tight between his ribs.

"I'm sorry," he murmured into her hair. "I'm so sorry."

She shuddered uncontrollably, and Gravenhearst stretched and preened, reaching out like a sea of dark roots beneath the forest.

"I can feel it," Mila whispered. "I can *feel* it."

"I know. But we're leaving," Curtis said. "This place can go fuck itself."

"It won't stop." Mila's guts twisted around her bones.

"Yes, it will," Curtis said. "*You hear that, you piece of shit?*" he yelled in the direction of the clearing. "That's the last blood you ever get!" He seized her arm, marched them forward. "This place can starve." He winced, like something sharp had shot through his ears. "This whole fucking town can starve and die, for all I care." He pushed a path through the willows, his grip on her arm unrelenting.

Mila stumbled and tried not to cry out, vertigo washing over her. This place would never let her go. She'd been pressed through its marrow, changed forever. The dark would rise up, teeth clacking, jaws stinking, and drag her back down to Gravenhearst.

They broke through the trees and Mila realized she was gasping. Curtis was holding her up and she was raking claw-marks in his skin.

"It's over," he said, propelling her toward the machine that vaguely resembled a bicycle.

She looked back at the black wound in the ground. There was nothing there, but the stench of smoke and blood filled her senses.

You're free, she told herself like a desperate plea. *Andrew Deemus is dead. You beat him.*

She tried to believe this. Tried to believe she hadn't left a piece of herself in that cellar.

Curtis climbed atop the silver and black contraption. A mechanical growl broke through the night air as he stamped down on part of the machine, and she jumped, the sound a gunshot assault on her ears. He motioned for her to get on, and she forced herself to move.

"It's like a really fast horse!" he called over the noise. She nodded, numb to new fears, and climbed behind him, tucking her skirt up free of the wheels. Diablo's joyous whinny cut like a lash through her memory. *He's dead too*, she thought.

She locked her arms around Curtis's waist and they shot forward, her gut clenching like she was being pulled inside out. She gritted her teeth and pressed her face to his back, lost herself in the hard rattle of the engine.

The boy from the mirror took her into the trees.

The pink house was swimming in the brightest lights Mila had ever seen.

Curtis cut the engine and quiet flashed out around them. A door swung open and she saw a skinny silhouette.

"They're here!" a boy's voice called, looking back into the house.

Avi, she thought. She saw his wild jumble of curls as they got closer and the look of stark relief that spread across his face.

She stopped, panic rising inside her. *What am I doing here?*

Curtis put a gentle hand on her arm.

"It's okay," he said.

No, it's not, she thought. *How can I be here? How can I be alive?*

She followed him up the steps, holding tight to his sleeve.

"I prepped them," Avi said to Curtis, holding the door open. "So now they think *I'm* crazy."

Curtis snorted.

Mila caught the scent of something savory and her stomach tightened, caught by a sudden wave of memory—the kitchen in her old home in Kent. Agnes, their cook, teaching Wynn to make meat pies.

She was in a narrow front hall, warmth flooding around her. Colors and lights from a thousand unnamable things fought for space in her mind; she could feel eyes on her and she looked down, fighting for control. Vibrantly hued Oriental carpets glowed up at her from the floor.

The door closed behind them, and she jumped. Curtis placed a careful hand on her waist, and she leaned closer to him, suddenly aware that her bare feet burned like cold fire.

Curtis led her into a large kitchen.

A girl was perched on a teal velvet chair, knees propped against the edge of a table. Her hair was dark and short—an odd configuration of angles—but her delicate features had a mix of defiance and innocence that struck at Mila's heart. There was a stubbornness in the set of the girl's lip that could have belonged to Wynn if she'd lived to be a few years older.

Mila slammed the thought down and forced her attention to the other waiting figure, a strange woman in dark robes.

She stood in the center of the room, chin tipped high. Her lined face placed her at least in the range of sixty. Kohl-rimmed eyes narrowed and a hand went to her hip, voluminous folds of blue-black fabric shifting on her arm with a *shush*.

Fortune-teller, Mila thought. They'd seen one once, at a fair her father took her to. "*Don't tell your mother*," he'd said.

Red lips pursed, and sharp eyes swept Mila with a look that was long and deliberate.

"The picture!" Avi said, his voice startling Mila. He reached toward her, then stopped. "Ah . . . may I?" he said, hands hovering over the heavy jacket she still wore.

Mila nodded.

He took the leather edge between his thumb and forefinger, pulling it far from her chest before reaching carefully into the inner pocket. He turned back to the woman, but she was uninterested, her eyes still scrutinizing Mila. Avi stood flustered for a second, then rushed over to the girl at the table and thrust the photograph at her.

The fortune-teller moved forward, one age-veined hand cocked artfully beside her. She shifted the edge of Curtis's jacket and carefully inspected Mila's bloodstained clothing, thin, ring-bedazzled fingers passing over the elaborate lace of the petticoat, the hard edge of the corset.

"All right," she said with a satisfied nod.

"All right?" Curtis said, shock evident.

"Boy, for forty years, I designed the best costumes the Toronto Dance and Theatre Company has ever seen. You think I can't recognize nineteenth-century needlework when I see it? And not more than a few months aged." The woman snorted. "You can't buy lace like that for love or money. 'Time-traveling maiden' is more believable than anyone putting that outfit together in this cultural wasteland of a town."

Mila tried to scrape together some kind of reaction to this assessment, but found she had nothing.

"Besides," the woman said, her tone dark, "growing up in this town, I heard things. Knew damn well not to go near that place to begin with."

Curtis shifted awkwardly beside her. "Um, okay," he said finally.

"Can you sew?" the woman asked, eyes narrowed.

"Not well," Mila said faintly. Maybe the woman would make her leave now.

"Hmmm, pity." Clearly disappointed. "So, I suppose no one's going to come looking for you, then—it's just you?"

The words stopped her breath—awful, *terrible* words. It took a moment to reply.

"Just me."

Silence.

"All right then," the woman said with a definitive nod. "I'm Mae. Welcome."

"Thank you," Mila said, her voice unsteady.

The girl got up from her chair abruptly and left the room, pushing past Curtis like a nimble cat. A moment later, she was back, something bright and garish clutched in one hand.

"Your feet look really cold," she said with a nervous smile, fine eyebrows raised uncertainly as her hand wavered toward Mila.

Stockings. The realization was like all her insides coming undone at once. Mila huffed a sound between a laugh and a cry and reached for Curtis to steady herself.

"I'm Sage," the girl said.

Mila nodded and took the stockings. Striped in rainbow hues and something that resembled silver thread, they were hideous, *wonderful* things. Soft and warm, a piece of impossible magic.

Her hands were shaking.

Curtis steered her toward a chair, and she grasped it gratefully, the polished cameo back just like the ones that had sat in her own dining room back home. She sat and pulled the stockings on, shorter than she was used to, and strangely elastic.

"Thank you," she whispered, unable to arm herself enough to look up yet. She did not want to look at them and cry.

"I made tea!" Avi announced with enthusiasm.

"Maybe she doesn't want tea," Sage said.

"She's freezing and she's British. Of course she wants tea," Avi said.

"Give me the damn tea," Mila ordered, finally looking up. There. Her voice was her own again.

Mae set a teacup in front of her, lips curved in approval. "Spirit."

49

Curtis

WHEN CURTIS WOKE, IT WAS STILL DARK.

Light from the muted television flickered over Sage and Avi, both fast asleep in the blanket nest on the bedroom floor.

No Mila.

He pushed up and discovered the bed behind him empty too.

I didn't dream her, he thought, panicking. *I didn't.*

"I'm here," a soft voice called.

Through the open window, he saw the girl from the photograph perched on the veranda rooftop.

He came closer, the scent of cold pine and forest loam drifting on the breeze, the stars sharp points in the square of night sky; for a moment, he thought he was dreaming, the reality of her being there was so strange, so wonderful.

Do I really get this chance? Do I get to be happy?

The whispers sang on the night air, telling him terrible, *powerful* things.

He could feel names and spells and gestures like secrets written under his skin; he thought he could stand in those woods now, and walk right into the air, a magician, a dark king. The halls and rooms of Gravenhearst called to him—*bring us back, bring us back, bring us back!*

He struggled for breath and focused on Mila. She was watching him carefully, catlike eyes narrowed and wary.

"You feel it, don't you," she said.

For a moment, he couldn't speak.

Yes, the whispers said, *yes. So many things in the dark!*

Things with hunger and claws; things never sated.

He knew what they wanted.

"I need to show you something," he said finally.

Mila was still for a moment, then nodded.

Garrett House was cold and dark, like it had already given up hope of future occupants. *I can't believe we stayed here so long*, Curtis thought. *This was always a place to keep the dead.*

His mother's room was a shattered memory. Moonlight spilled through the windows, shards of broken glass catching the cold light like jagged stars. Half the dresser mirror still hung in the frame and it reflected only Curtis, his image distorted and splintered. Something about it made him angry—he was so tired of feeling cut down the middle. *No more*, he thought.

"What happened here?" Mila asked quietly.

Curtis walked across the fractured moonlight, shards crunching under his feet, and retrieved the fallen wedding picture from the floor.

"My father tried to hurt Sage. I stopped him. Now he's been taken away."

He sat on the edge of the bed and Mila sat next to him, her long fingers settling carefully around his cut and swollen knuckles, grazing the edge of the bandage that covered his cut palm. "I'm sorry," she said.

Curtis looked up at the opposite wall, Mila's reflection in the golden-framed mirror sending a chill down his spine.

"I was sitting here, just like this, when I saw you."

Mila's eyes met his in the mirror, her gaze unflinching. "Why did it show me to you?"

That moment felt like a lifetime ago—pure need and desperation, the crushing sense that he'd die if he had to be strong and cold as stone for a second longer.

"I didn't want to be alone," he said finally, tears clenching the back of his throat.

Her eyes flared like his answer had done something to her, and she tipped her head toward him with a little sound. He dragged her closer, her fingers clutching at him.

I've never wanted anything this badly, he thought, gasping into her hair.

The mirror was a burnished doorway above them, its gold frame a twisting knot of vines and tentacles.

Mila steadied her breath and pulled slowly from his arms. She stood and stared the awful thing down.

Curtis stood, too, their reflections an eerie portrait in the glass. "It's part of Gravenhearst," he said, passing a hand over the mirror. "The house wants it back." His fingers brushed aged gilding and fossil-dry crevices; the whispers surged and his heart roared in his ears. Smoke bit his throat and heat seared his bones.

Bring it back, bring it back, bring it back!

He ripped the thing from the wall.

For a moment, the world teetered on a knife edge, the halls and towers of Gravenhearst spilling out in his mind as he held the mirror aloft.

He hurled it from him like a burning coal.

It tumbled to the floor like time sped up and slowed down all at once, the whispers screaming and screaming, Curtis falling too— falling forever through the maelstrom of whispers, the darkness rising around him in a chorus of desperate screams.

The mirror hit the floorboards and cracked, the sound like a gunshot blast of heart-struck ice. The glass split down the middle, a fissure that gaped like an open maw.

Silence rang in his ears, absolutely deafening.

The whispers were gone.

"Now it's done," he said.

I won't *be a Deemus.*

Mila ground the heel of her slipper on a jagged half and it splintered with a *crack.*

They left his father's house. Above them the sky was a mottled cloudbank of black and navy, the horizon streaked sherbet pink and electric blue—dawn coming fast.

The quiet in Curtis's mind bordered on sacred. He could feel *everything,* every bit of him that had been taken up by those maddening whispers. *Yes,* he thought, holding Mila's hand tighter. *Yes, I can do this.*

It was cold. The almost-November chill was finally setting in, winter on its way with a vengeance. Mila tucked herself against him with a shiver, and he wrapped both arms around her.

The girl in the photograph. She was really here, and they had both survived.

"My Victorian girl," he murmured.

"Do *not* call me that," she said, tipping her chin back, eyes narrowing.

He thought a moment.

"Monster slayer."

"Better," she said. A hint of a smile tugged her lips, and she kissed him very softly.

Oh, yes, he thought. *I can do this.*

A cold breeze swept past them, and Mila shivered again.

"We should go inside," he said, rubbing a hand over her bare arm. Mae's windows were flashing gold as dawn crept over the horizon, and his chest had that inside-out feeling that came with sunrise.

Mila squeezed his hand. "No," she said. "I want to see it. I want to see the sun."

Curtis nodded. "Okay."

Another breeze swept the trees and a sweet note sang through the air, a bird's call repeated again and again—the world coming to life. The sky was spilling honeyed light across the yard, turning Mila's hair to gold.

The door creaked behind him, and Curtis turned.

Sage gave him a look that said, *What the hell are you doing up this early?* But then her eyes went to Mila. His sister sat on the porch step and patted the boards next to her, a knowing look in her eye.

Curtis went and sat.

"You really like her," Sage said.

Curtis cleared his throat.

Sage chuckled and leaned against him, her little bird-boned shoulder sharp against his arm.

They sat silently together and watched Mila watch the sun rise.

Acknowledgments

AN ENTIRE WORLD GOES INTO A BOOK, AND AS SUCH, A WORLD
of thanks:

First, to my parents: Dad, your practical accountant genes somehow managed to produce a stuffed-animal-obsessed girl who built
fairy houses in the backyard and had zero aptitude for math. Sorry
about that. Thanks for paying for university anyway.

Mom—for endless trips to the library, repeated readings of *Lisa
and the Grompet*, evening performances of the Chronicles of Narnia,
and for generally turning a small child into a voracious reader and
lover of the arts, thank you, thank you, thank you.

To my editor, Anne Heltzel, and the entire Amulet team—for making an aspiring writer into a published author, my eternal thanks.
You have truly changed my life.

Sam Wolfe Connelly—a writer wrangles words, but artists are
another creature entirely, making worlds out of brushstrokes and,
obviously, sorcery. Thank you for making your own wondrous magic
out of my words.

This book has lived several lives, and different people have been
instrumental in each. Thanks to Lisa Maxwell, Kira Blue, Anne
Persons, Lana Popovich, and Pru Holcombe for assorted proddings,
encouragement, and invaluable insights.

My gratitude to Merrill Wyatt, Tom Hoover, and Kristin Ciccarelli
for book swaps, mutual fangirling, and sanity-saving talks.

My fabulous Furies, Kate Boorman, Nikki Vogel, and Natasha

Deen, for friendship, wisdom, and—most importantly—prosecco. For Elflaaannnd!!!

To my agent and sublimely inappropriate friend, Heather Flaherty—my love for the things that can be admitted in public, and even more so for the things that can't.

And finally, to Jon, for sharing your story with me, for the years of love and support—this book doesn't exist without you.